In Memory of Charles

D. ERSKINE MUIR

With an introduction by Curtis Evans

 Moonstone Press

This edition published in 2021 by Moonstone Press
www.moonstonepress.co.uk

Introduction © 2021 Curtis Evans

Originally published in 1941 by John Murray, London

In Memory of Charles © 1941 The Estate of D. Erskine Muir

The right of Dorothy Erskine Muir to be identified as author of this work has
been asserted in accordance with the Copyright, Designs and Patents Act 1988

ISBN 978-1-899000-44-9
eISBN 978-1-899000-45-6

A CIP catalogue record for this book is available from the British Library

Text designed and typeset by Tetragon, London
Cover illustration by Jason Anscomb
Printed and bound by CPI Group (UK) Ltd, Croydon, CRO 4YY

Contents

Dorothy Erskine Muir published her third and final detective novel, *In Memory of Charles*, in 1941, seven years after the appearance of her previous mystery, *Five to Five*, which had followed hard on the heels of her first essay in the genre, *In Muffled Night*. The period between 1934 and 1941 was emphatically no holiday for the author, however. During that time Muir kept tremendously busy, as a widowed mother (her husband Thomas Muir having died in 1932) raising an adolescent son and daughter, tutoring college students in history (Muir had achieved a first at Somerville College, Oxford, although, this feat having occurred during the Edwardian era, she was not allowed to receive the degree which her work had rightfully earned her) and publishing the well-received historical studies *Machiavelli and His Times* (1936) and *Prussian Eagle* (1940), as well as biographies of Oliver Cromwell and Queen Elizabeth in Blackie and Son's Great Lives for Young Readers series. When she did finally return to the crime-fiction genre with *In Memory of Charles*, she again based her novel on an actual murder case, stating in a prefatory note: "This is a true story. This murder really happened, in the way described, and it was solved in the way described, but not in this country." Unfortunately, I have not been able to determine the actual murder case on which the novel is based (perhaps some of its new readers will know). Still, evaluated simply as a crime story without specific historical context, *In Memory of Charles* is quite a good one.

The novel tells the story of an overbearing and querulous individual ironically named Charles Courtley, a millionaire and "something in the City" who has bought a country estate in East Anglia and is determined to retire there, over the objections of his attractive, much younger and much discontented wife, Anne, who does not want to be marooned, as she sees it, in rural desuetude. The odious Charles spends the first third of the novel virtually begging to be murdered by someone. When he is found shot dead in Fosse Wood, there is certainly no shortage of suspects in the crime. Investigating the murder this time around is young Inspector Simon Sturt of Scotland Yard, an East Anglian native himself and "one of the new type of police" with the "benefit of a modern training" and awareness of the "psychology of crime". As the "son of a Chief Constable of a country district", Sturt from childhood had been "specially interested in that strange undertone of crime which sometimes shows itself flowing beneath the surface of the most peaceful-looking rural life"; and he finds a strange case indeed in the matter of the murder of Charles Courtley.

Truly Charles Courtley was a loathsome interloper in the country, despised by his family, neighbours and even the lesser folk of the rural district; and the admirable Sturt in his diligent investigation faces a wall of obfuscation on every side. Certainly, Dorothy Erskine Muir had devised memorably tyrannical males in her previous novels, but Charles Courtley takes the cake. Readers can judge for themselves how much of a feminist subtext is present in the novel. Certainly Muir had to overcome sexist discrimination in her own life, and her eldest sister, social worker, feminist and pacifist Mary Sheepshanks, a fascinating individual in her own right, conscientiously devoted a long lifetime to battling it. One's only regret upon finishing *In Memory of Charles* is that there were no additional detective novels from the author's hand to follow it.

CURTIS EVANS
Germantown, TN
28 September 2021

In Memory of Charles

This is a true story. This murder really happened, in the way described, and it was solved in the way described, but not in this country.

All the characters are imaginary, and people and places have no connection with real people and places.

CHARACTERS IN THIS BOOK

CHARLES COURTLEY, millionaire.

His wife, ANNE.

His daughter, PAMELA. Aged twenty.

His daughter, PRUDENCE. Aged thirteen.

His mother-in-law, MRS. MITCHAM.

His secretary, FREDDY WADHAM.

His guest, DICK ARNOLD.

His gamekeeper, SMITHSON.

His estate agent, PETER SYLVESTER.

HUGH BARCLAY, artist.

INSPECTOR SIMON STURT, C.I.D.

SERGEANT GROVES.

DR. WILLIAMS.

MARY GAME, barmaid.

MRS. GWYN, proprietress of the inn, the "Broken Bough."

OLD WALTER.

EVELYN WOODARD, hairdresser.

JOHN STEDMAN, clerk.

Chapter I

CHARLES SHOWS HIS TEMPER

C harles was in a vile temper, and Anne was catching the full benefit of it. Anne was his wife, and she regretted that fact. She sat beside him in the great Rolls Royce, swirling towards their beautiful home, but even while they speeded along the country road she reflected bitterly that money did not outweigh a bad temper, in the matrimonial scales.

She glanced at her husband, and her eyes travelled over his thin, rather distinguished face. She noted his cold, highly-intelligent grey eyes, his thick thatch of grey hair, and her gaze came to rest on the mouth which to her was now the key-note of his character. Large, thick-lipped, coarse and resolute. Perhaps that mouth ought always to have warned her?

At that point his voice, with a disagreeable ring in it, broke across her reflections.

"I am not going to discuss this any more, Anne. You can make up your mind to that. I'm too old to change my ways now. I don't intend to start a flat in town. So say no more about it."

"You're very unreasonable," she retorted, as coolly as her own rising indignation allowed. "I don't suggest you should use the flat. I know of course you've always hated such places. I simply ask you to let *me* have one. I know nothing would induce you to spend more of your time in town than you can help. But I don't see why you should prevent my doing so."

"Because I don't choose to spend my money in that way, and I do what I like with my money."

Anne would have liked to make no reply to that domineering remark, for she knew perfectly well she had better let the matter drop. But she was driven on by that incorrigible sense of having right on her side which prevents many a woman from tactfully holding her peace, and she rejoined, in a voice which even her own ears warned her was growing sharp: "Well, you needn't take such an unreasonable line. You're not *fair* to me, you never have been. You *knew* I always hated the country and I never expected to have to live in it…"

As her tones rose slightly Charles interrupted, more rudely than before.

"We've had enough of that. Can't you, for heaven's sake, stop raking things up? I tell you I will *not* have you argue about it. I've decided—and I'm not going to change my mind. We've got Carron, and you'll kindly be contented with that."

The violence of his voice warned Anne not to reply and she turned away in order to prevent herself saying any more.

Silence fell between the two; angry, bitter silence. After a few minutes, Charles, who was now thoroughly roused, broke into speech again.

"And while we're on the subject of living down here, let me tell you I mean to put my foot down over Barclay. I will *not* have Pamela associating with that man."

Anne looked away, pursing her lips together in her determination not to be drawn into further speech.

Charles went on, his tone growing nastier with each word he uttered.

"She's not of age yet, and I intend her to do what I wish. She's not to see that man any more. I'll not have him about the place, and that's to be understood by all of you."

"You'd better speak to her, then," said Anne briefly.

"I certainly shall. And you'll kindly not go behind my back and encourage her. This affair has got to end, and I'll speak to her this evening!"

Anne made no reply at all, and after a furious glance at her, Charles flung himself back in his corner, slapping the pages of his evening paper angrily together, and muttering to himself.

They rushed on through the flat, luxuriant countryside, until the car turned off the high road. For a short interval they rolled along an utterly deserted by-road, with no houses, no farms, no inhabitants, until the big car turned in at a white gate and whirled down a short drive to the house. Charles instantly banged open the door on his side, while the chauffeur was preparing to climb out of his seat, and dashed out and disappeared into the house. The chauffeur stolidly came round to open the door for his mistress.

The door of the house remained open, left so by Charles in his angry passage, but there was no sign or sound of life, merely the silence of a hot summer's evening. The sun beat through the trees on to the grey stone front, the creepers hung still and straight in long trails around the windows, the bees hummed and roared softly in the mauve edgings of cat-mint that bordered the drive—beyond that all was stillness and somnolence.

For a moment Anne sat quite still. In her own way she was as furious as Charles in his. Returning to her home brought with it the familiar feeling of imprisonment, of resentment, of irritation deepening almost to hate. The mere aspect of the place, the knowledge that once across the threshold all her problems and difficulties would rise up and confront her, filled her with bitterness.

'Rural peace'—that was the phrase which seemed to pass through her mind as she slowly collected her handbag and a few small parcels and stepped out of the car—'Rural peace!' How beautiful was the sound, and how bitterly she disliked the reality! Though (her sore, angry thoughts ran on) perhaps she hated the phrase because after all there was no true peace here—only 'rural solitude' and the jangling and jarring of personalities at strife.

She went into the house, crossed the hall, and went quickly up the wide, bare, polished staircase to her own room, still absorbed in her thoughts. Perhaps it was the stillness and beauty of the hot, summery afternoon, perhaps the sudden feeling that had come over her as her eyes had taken in the outward aspect presented by the house, perhaps merely a heightened sense of the passing of time and life which the very season of early autumn seemed to bring to her each year now—but whatever the cause, she stood still in her room in a sudden passion of stormy feeling; revolt, anger, almost hatred.

She flung her hat and parcels down and walked across to the window. Mechanically she paused on her way and glanced at herself in the mirror, and a fresh access of bitterness welled up in her.

She was nearly forty, and in one violent burst of feeling she realized that here was one potent source of unhappiness, for her life was passing, she *must* make the very most of the time that remained before middle age should be upon her. At present she emphatically did not feel herself ageing, she was burning with vitality, with desire to get the most out of life, and she was determined to snatch at any happiness which came her way before it was too late.

She pushed her waves of deep auburn hair into shape, and sat down to make up her complexion, and as she did so she tried to steady her nerves and calm her irritation. For Anne was no fool, she knew well enough that Charles was on the verge of an explosion, and she knew too that she had better control herself, better try to stave off trouble for the present. She must gain a little time.

Below her she heard hasty movements, steps sounded crashing down the bare polished staircase, and a door slammed violently.

Charles, of course! giving vent to his feelings! God! what an evening they were likely to have!

Charles indeed was working himself up still further. Angry he was, furious he would be! So he flung himself out of the house and strode down the garden path, black temper in every line of his body, in every stride he took.

The house stood on a hillside, and the garden sloped away below. A terrace lay immediately beneath the window, with rose-beds and paved walks. Then beyond a hedge of lavender the field fell to the orchard, and between the apple trees showed the tennis court and a little thatched pavilion, and to the right lay the new swimming-pool. All shone in the strong yellow evening light, the flowers, the grass, the distant water all glistened and sparkled, and seemed to breathe loveliness and peace. But nothing could soothe Charles's temper, and angry thoughts flew through his head as he strode along.

Damn Anne! Damn her obstinacy! Damn her deceit! Why the devil had he ever married her! Why did he put up with her! Why didn't he put an end to it all!

His rage had made him quicken his steps, and by now he had arrived at the gate leading to the kitchen garden. His eyes fell on the figure of the gardener, stooping over some raspberry canes.

"Here, Duncan," he barked, "I want a word with you." The gardener straightened at once and came to him. "Why the devil don't you do more to keep the birds down? They're getting at all the fruit, and Jamison tells me the magpies have been at the young chickens again. Why aren't you getting them shot? and why don't you take some trouble over things?" Conscious that he was perhaps making too loud an uproar, he checked himself with difficulty, and broke off.

The man before him answered respectfully enough.

"Well, sir, I have spoken to Mr. Sylvester, but he hasn't had time, he said, to have a shot at the birds."

"Mr. Sylvester? What's he got to do with it? It's your job to deal with the garden, not his! What the devil do you mean?"

"Mr. Sylvester has a gun, sir, and since your old one went out of action we've no other for our use. I thought I should ask him to see to it, sir."

"Oh!" slightly baffled, then, with renewed irritation: "But I told Mrs. Courtley to order another gun. Hasn't she said anything to you about it?"

"No, sir."

"Well, I'll see to it myself," and curtly he turned on his heel and resumed his walk, his anger only damped down on the surface, but underneath burning as fiercely as before.

Anne! his angry thoughts went—Anne's slackness again! Always Anne at fault! What a useless wife she was to him now! He should never have married! He'd have done well enough to stay as he was. He should have known better. A middle-aged man had no need to make a fool of himself. He should have had more sense—and more self-control. Why did people say it was better to marry a young wife? Fit herself in to one's ways indeed! Precious lot of that Anne had done! She'd never tried to adapt herself, even at the beginning—and now things got worse and worse. And children—a curse and a nuisance his were! Better without them, they only led to more trouble.

Still, one thing he'd got, and here his mouth set in lines of grim satisfaction. For all their yowling and grumbling he'd got this place, and here he'd stay, and here *they'd* stay! And Anne need make no grievance about it. She'd known from the first he meant to live in the country, and in the country *they would* live.

He stopped, and looked round him, and there swelled up in him that supreme satisfaction, the power to exercise his choice to live as and where he wanted. No town life for him! Country, land, property, possession! That at least he had. Fresh energy seemed to pour through him with the realization that here at least he had his way. Then, as sounds rose up through the clear still air, and laughter echoed from behind the screen of orchard and hedge, his black eyebrows came down again over his angry eyes, and he once more strode crossly forward.

Meanwhile Anne, in her peaceful bedroom, was still sitting before her mirror lost in her thoughts. Her eyes looked almost unseeingly out, beyond the glass, to where through the wide-open casement lay the spread of the countryside. Mile upon mile lay there, fields, copse, and slopes, laid out like a vast patchwork quilt, stretching away to the distant line of downs.

Deep in her thoughts she pondered and planned, and while she gazed her mind worked busily, wondering, hesitating, calculating risks.

The stress and worry which showed in the lines of her face, the faint tension reflected from her stiff upright bearing, were again at variance with the countryside without, and the sophisticated interior of her room. Discord was as marked as it might have been unexpected. For beauty was all round her, without and within the walls. Certainly as far as material welfare went she had no cause to complain.

The room behind her was as lovely, and as peaceful in its way, as the somnolent countryside which lay beyond the windows. Every piece of furniture in it was perfect, though in accordance with modern taste, there was not very much of it. Spaciousness and beauty of line were the characteristics of that room. The bed, which stood against the opposite wall, was a beautiful little antique four-poster, very light and elegant. Valance, frieze, and counterpane were all of the most exquisite embroidery, with faint colours of red and green on a pale background. A walnut tallboy, dating from William and Mary, and a few lovely old chairs stood against the wall. The dressing-table before her was a converted spinet, beautifully inlaid. The floor was polished parquet, with one or two superb Persian rugs laid on its glinting surface. There were no pictures, nor were there in that room any ornaments of any kind—in short a room of bareness and simplicity, almost of austerity.

But as she sat lost in thought, mechanically playing with her dressing-table fitments, a sudden outburst of sound floating up from the garden made her fling down her lipstick and go quickly to the window again. From the swimming-pool there came up, clear in the still warm air, sounds of a man's voice raised in angry argument and a child's almost hysterical reply.

Anne leant out of the open casement, biting her lip in vexation and suspense, and straining to hear the cause of the commotion.

"Do as you're told! Do as I tell you! Do you hear me? Do what I tell you to do!"

Harsh, angry with a rising note of dominance, showing the beating down by sheer force of resistance offered, came the man's voice.

"No! No! I won't! I won't! I won't!" in a child's shrill tones.

"Do you want me to throw you in? That's what it'll come to if you don't do as you're told!"

"No, Daddy! I can't, I simply *can't*!" cried the child's voice rising to a wail of terror.

Anne's whole figure trembled as she listened. Her fingers clenched themselves on the window-sill, her lips parted, clearly she was on the point of calling out, but clearly too she realized this would be useless, for the distance was just great enough to prevent her voice carrying over the loud noise of disputation. Even while she hesitated the child's voice rose to a scream:

"No! No! Don't touch me! Don't touch me!" She could see, as she strained from the window trying to peer through the stems of the fruit trees, a wild scurrying to and fro of figures around the edge of the swimming-pool. Even as she turned to dash from the room there came a piercing shriek and a splash and then other voices rose angrily in a storm of recrimination and abuse.

Anne tore through the house, dashed down the terrace steps and ran as fast as she could towards the outcry coming from below. But as she reached the gate which opened on to the tennis courts and swimming-pool, she checked herself, for someone had outdistanced her. Her husband, his swarthy face flushed with his anger, stood confronting an equally angry young man, who, clutching his tennis racquet, stood boldly and defiantly between Charles and the pool.

By the side of the pool a small girl in a wet swimming-dress lay crouched on the grass, sobbing and shaking, and over her bent a girl of about nineteen or twenty, whose pale gold hair caught the gleam of the setting sun as she stooped, partly attempting to soothe the child, partly trying to attend at the same time to the two angry men.

"It's abominable!" shouted the young man. "You're nothing but a bully! Frightening the child like that! You don't care a damn whether she dives properly or not! You're only trying to assert yourself!"

"Mind your own business!" roared Charles. "I'll stand no inter-ference here! What I do is no concern of yours!"

"It is! It is!" retorted the young man furiously. "It's anyone's business to see a child isn't frightened and terrorized—even if it's by her own father!"

At this point Anne decided to intervene.

"Dick! Dick! Don't speak like that! What on earth are you shouting like this for? I could hear you right at the house! Please control yourself!"

She purposely spoke only to the boy, paying no attention to her husband. The young man looked at her astonished, and his face crimsoned. He opened his mouth to speak, then thought better of it and stood silent. Anne made a move to slip past her husband, who stood stiffly blocking the path, meaning to go to the child. At once Charles turned on her venomously, and his voice broke out into a threatening note.

"Don't interfere! We've enough of that already. Kindly leave this to me!"

Anne hesitated, biting her lip. She really was almost frightened. Charles's dark face was so suffused with passion, the boy too looked so beside himself, that she really dreaded what might happen. Afraid lest the quarrel should break out into a downright scuffle, she stopped short. She looked beyond Charles towards her two daughters. The younger one, Prue, who was crouched down crying and sobbing hysterically, had not even looked up, but the elder girl, while continuing to attempt to soothe the child, raised her golden head, turned a very flushed face and addressed her mother.

"Mummy, do stop it! Don't let him go on like this! It's simply monstrous. It'll make Prue ill. Daddy says she's got to dive—and she *can't*—she's got so frightened she simply *can't!*"

Anne said nothing, but looked at her husband. She was exerting every scrap of self-control, for she felt if she were not careful this scene was going to lead to a really terrible explosion.

Charles stared at her, then as if recognizing that she meant to leave things to him, he, with a faintly triumphant smile, but with a distinct lowering of his tone, turned to the boy who still stood facing him. He spoke slowly and clearly.

"Now that my wife is here and can herself look after Prue, perhaps you'll kindly leave us alone. We can settle this matter between the family."

The young man looked past his opponent towards Anne. He paused irresolutely, glanced towards the elder girl, and then as no one spoke, slowly turned away and going round by the pool let himself out by the gate into the meadows. As he disappeared among the trees the man stepped forward until he stood by the side of the two girls. Anne followed him but she neither spoke nor made any gesture towards her daughters. A brief silence fell, filled with an electric tension. While the younger one crouched lower, the elder girl had drawn herself up as her father approached and fixed her eyes on his face.

"Now!" said Charles, with a sort of grim satisfaction. "We'll have an end to this hysterical nonsense. Prudence, get up!"

There was a metallic resonance in his voice which seemed to have a galvanizing effect on the sobbing child. Slowly she pulled herself upright and stood there, still gulping and heaving and looking neither at her father nor mother but miserably down on the ground.

"You can swim perfectly well. You know you cannot drown. Stop this childish fuss! I don't believe for a moment you're nervous. Do as I tell you—dive in again!"

The child neither moved nor spoke, but stood there beside the pool. Another pause.

"Do you hear what I say? Do as I tell you, *Dive in Again.*"

Still no movement and no reply. The older girl deliberately looked at her father and a mocking little smile came to her lips.

As if that smile set him in motion, the man stepped forward, and with a sudden rough gesture seized the child's shoulder and pushing her violently sent her staggering backward into the pool.

"Very well, if you won't *dive* in at least you'll *go* in!"

Spluttering the child came to the surface and began to swim to the side of the pool, impeded by the hysterical sobs and cries she was now uttering.

Anne stood perfectly still and looked slowly from the swollen tear-stained face of the child in the water to her husband's equally red countenance. She said nothing at all. The older girl, however, had less self-control. She turned with renewed fury on the man.

"You utter coward! You bully! You send Dick away because you think you can torment a child! Oh, how I hate and loathe and despise you!"

Her mother spoke now, for the first time, coldly and severely.

"Pamela, you do no good speaking to your father like that. You'd better go up to the house. I'll stay here."

The girl paused, clearly on the verge of another outbreak, and then with a glance of passionate contempt at her mother: "You're as big a coward in *your* way as he is!" she burst out. "You won't even stand up for Prue!" And then, as if measuring her father's strength against her own and realizing the futility of further resistance, she snatched up her racquet and sports coat, and running as fast as she could she too dashed through the wicket gate and disappeared into the fields.

The man still took no notice of his wife but walked towards the end of the pool where the child, panting and hysterical, was now approaching the edge.

"Pull yourself together," he snapped, "and swim back the length of the pool."

The child below clearly realized she had better accept her ordeal and get it over. She turned and swam towards the far end where the diving-board was fixed. Arrived there, as if aware there was now no escape, she clambered up the steps and paused miserably.

"Go up and dive," came the order. She obeyed, and after a moment's hesitation, made a bad and bungling effort. "Do it again," as she came up to the surface. Her sobs had stopped now, and in sullen silence, she repeated the performance. Only after the third flat smash on to the surface did the man turn away contemptuously.

"Well, perhaps you can't learn to dive, but you *can* learn to obey me." And without a further glance at his wife, he went up the path towards the house.

During this performance Anne had stood silent and motionless, holding herself in with all the power of self-restraint she could call up. Now, as Prudence came slowly out of the water and went towards the thatched dressing-rooms at the side, she followed her. Silently she helped the child out of her wet swimming-suit and handed her a towel. Prudence had stopped crying and only cast shamefaced glances towards her mother while she dried herself. Anne, who had clearly decided on the line she meant to take, offered no sympathy. She waited while the child dressed, with clumsy shaking fingers, and then the two set off together towards the house with just a few casual remarks passing between them as they climbed the steep little path. As they reached the top and before she opened the garden gate, Anne paused.

"Now, Prudence," she said, quite kindly, but with no warmth in her tone, "I'm afraid this has been very disagreeable for you, and I'm sorry you've been so upset. But at the same time, I do think you must behave more reasonably. We all know you can swim and dive quite well—and you know your father has always said that it was a condition of having the pool made that you should learn to dive. It's very foolish of you to work yourself up like this. It's no good setting yourself up against your father"—and here a bitter note crept into her voice—"you'd better make up your mind to that and try to show more sense."

The child made no reply. She seemed ready to burst into fresh tears and turned quickly away to go into the house by the side door. Her mother stood still and as she watched the child go her expression changed. In place of the self-control which had kept her voice cold and her face stiff, a flash seemed to come into her eyes. Her lips tightened, and her look seemed to harden into bitter resolution. No one seeing her now could accuse her of being afraid. She did not look a coward—nor indeed was she one. She was a woman faced with a difficult, almost an unbearable, situation. She was determined to find a way out, but she hesitated as to whether the moment had yet come for decisive action. Yet, she inwardly resolved that however much she was obliged to give way now, she would act in her own good time, and as she turned up towards the house, Charles Courtley might have had further cause for dissatisfaction had he known the tenor of her thoughts.

Chapter II

WHY THEY MARRIED

S o the fierce little scene was played out, and the actors dispersed. Charles went up to his room feeling that at least he had achieved two things—he had got his own way and he had partly relieved his temper. Anne for her part decided that she would try to ignore it all, as she had so often done in the past. She only hoped Pamela would by now have seen this was the only line to take. Rather apprehensive on that score, she too began to dress for dinner. Luckily, she reflected, it was still early and dinner would not be before eight—by then everyone would have had time to calm down. A meal created a sort of bridge over which one could walk to safety sometimes.

So, having dressed, she made her way downstairs to join the others before dinner.

Pamela, for her part, had flung off almost beside herself with helpless anger, but she too had had time to reflect. She had rushed away from the pool and gone up to her room. There, by herself, at first she had raged up and down. A girl of twenty, she had all the impetuosity and all the reckless courage of her generation. Warmhearted and generous she loved her little sister and could not endure to see her brow-beaten and frightened. Between the girl and her mother there was less sympathy, indeed though each loved the other in their own way, yet in some respects there was a sort of antagonism between them. Pamela was well accustomed to her father's temper, but that made it no easier to bear. She thought her mother should stand up to him more, and now as she grew older she was both less able to bear his tyranny, and felt herself more capable of opposing him. Friction between them was growing worse. The girl had inherited something from Charles too, and it was perhaps a touch of his violence which now made her burn with such furious resentment. But, as she reflected bitterly, she was after all living in Charles's house, she was dependent upon him, and though she could defy him, he really had the whip hand in that household. So, her first furious storm of feeling having abated, she too prepared to face Charles with the best composure she could muster. She tried to steady herself and to regain her confidence by taking extra pains with her appearance. She was an extremely pretty girl with unusually pale gold hair and very bright liquid dark eyes. Her slimness and delicate features gave her an air of fragility, rather strange in the child of parents who both possessed marked vitality and strength. She slipped on a pale green frock, raked out a pair of gold brocade shoes, and as the gong pealed through the house, snatched up a pair of long gold and green ear-rings. She ran down the passage, fixing them to her ears as she went with a defiant little smile on her lips, for Charles specially disliked 'anyone of her age' as he put it wearing such sophisticated ornaments.

She met her mother on the staircase. Anne, too, was looking remarkably handsome. She had put on a silver frock which made her stand out clearly against the background of the dark panelled walls, her beautiful hair with its reddish lights, and her eyes with reflections and flecks of the same tawny copper made her and her shining frock a symphony in russet and silver. They were an arresting pair, each full of individuality and character.

Anne sighed as she saw her daughter, for the heightened colour in the girl's cheeks, the angry sparkle still lingering in her eyes, brought out and intensified the girl's beauty, and to Anne gave an additional pang—Pamela deserved more happiness than she seemed likely to obtain. She smiled slightly at the girl, but Pamela made no response, and in silence they both went on downstairs.

The Courtley's house, Carron Cross, was situated in one of those remote and lonely districts still to be found in parts of East Anglia. Charles liked the district, partly because it was so unspoilt, partly because it was fairly accessible to the City where he had large financial interests. He had originally bought the place for holiday purposes, but now that he was retiring from business he meant to live there altogether. It was an old house, and very picturesque, having originally been a small manor which had gradually sunk to the status of a farm, and now had been promoted again to be the expensive hobby of a wealthy man.

In the process it had been altered and transformed almost out of recognition. True, the old part of the building still survived, but wings had been thrown out, rooms added on, until the newer part far exceeded the old. Inside it still showed clear signs of its diverted purpose, in its irregular levels, its draughty casements, its unexpected turns and twists. It seemed to have lost the unity of purpose of a house lived in by people with a definite end in view, and to have taken on the incoherence born from the whims of a rich man's fancy. Yet wealth had helped to give it certain elements of beauty and of taste. The rooms held good furniture, the walls were hung with good pictures, nothing here was ugly, or shoddy, or cheap.

So, the dining-room where all were now to meet was in itself a charming room and summed up both the history of the house and the tastes of its new owner. Charles had chosen all the furniture in the dining-room with the idea of keeping the character of the old room, for this had been the farmhouse kitchen. The great open hearth remained, with its old Sussex-iron fireback. The black oak rafters still barred the ceiling and the stone floor still showed beneath the Persian rugs. The high mantelshelf had some beautiful pieces of blue and white porcelain, and the shelves of the high dresser held pieces of pewter. The table was a large round gate-leg, a very nice antique piece.

Set round the table were places for six people, and here the 'old farmhouse' atmosphere grew thin. For the laying of that table indicated the high standard of life of the modern rich. An array of wine glasses stood grouped for each person, with heavy cut-glass goblets for the abstemious who might prefer long soft drinks. Small battalions of knives, forks and spoons indicating a dinner of many courses kept the glass company, and the table mats were expensive hand-coloured French prints, glazed and framed in gilt. The middle of the table was taken up with a vast bowl filled with late-flowering lilies. This was Pamela's handiwork, for arranging flowers was something she loved and did well.

It might have been anticipated that dinner that night would be an impossible meal. How could people who had flung such epithets at each other meet within an hour and sit down together? But life in the household of a really bad-tempered man runs on other lines than those of more ordinary families. Consequently, where others might have stayed away and left empty chairs, all Charles Courtley's household assembled as usual and no one considered that the stormy events just passed need cause them to absent themselves from the meal.

True, Charles scarcely opened his lips, he sat in glowering silence, eating and still more drinking his way through his dinner in silence; but this did not appear to upset his family unduly. They were fairly well accustomed to his ways and pursued their usual policy of ignoring his temper.

The rich score too in these exigencies, by the actual adjuncts of their wealth. The family was not left to itself, they had guests, they had 'secretaries,' they had as usual 'the servants,' before all of whom appearances must be kept up. These third persons, of course, being acquainted with Charles and his ways, knew what was to be expected and combined to deal with the situation. Even the butler played his part, being quicker than usual in filling his master's glass, handing plates with extra speed and deftness, and obviously helping to remove any further possible cause of friction by ensuring that the service at least should give no grounds for complaints.

Nor was Charles obliged to sit next to any of the individuals who had so angered him. Prudence did not dine down, she was young enough to have her supper upstairs. Her champion had clearly been warned and instructed to show discretion. He came in rather late, apologized to his hostess and sat down mildly enough in the place between her and the elder girl—well separated from his sullen host by the rest of the party. Naturally Pamela took her place with a faint tremor of excitement. Besides the ear-rings, she had also chosen to mark her lack of repentance by making up her face rather more startlingly than usual. Charles was fanatical on the subject of make-up, and Anne had battled long before she could induce him to accept any concession to fashion. Usually his daughter kept her lipstick within bounds. To-night her brilliantly scarlet lips were meant to be deliberately provocative, but for once Charles refused to be drawn, and ignored her.

On Charles's right sat his mother-in-law, and she proved a tower of strength. A handsome grey-haired capable-looking woman, she lived up to her appearance; and by her valiant conversation, aided and encouraged by her daughter and by the sixth person at table, the meal was got through comparatively well.

This sixth person was Freddy Wadham, Charles's secretary, who came in apologizing for his lateness just as the others sat down. Freddy was, of all the people gathered in that room, the most striking in appearance. He was a man of about thirty, thin, dark. His whole face radiated intelligence and energy. No one glancing at him could doubt that he was a person of ability and force. Yet there he sat, occupying no more exalted position than that of secretary to Charles Courtley, and clearly to be secretary to Charles meant that one must be prepared to exercise tact, to bear with much unpleasantness, to be in fact in a subordinate position to a man who would not make that an easy affair. There was an apparent incongruity between Freddy's appearance and his position.

Mrs. Mitcham, Anne's mother, let her mind turn to this puzzle, as she glanced from the face of her son-in-law, dour, angry, and powerful in its set lines, to that of the younger man, so quick and animated and agreeable. True, she reflected, Freddy liked comfort and the good things of life, and in a measure he got them. Charles was, with all his faults, a generous employer when he thought it worth his while. He recognized Freddy's ability and paid him an excellent salary, and in addition put in his way many opportunities of picking up 'inside' information which might help anyone with Freddy's known inclination to speculation. Yet neither of these facts would really account for a man of Freddy's ability being apparently content with his prospects and his job. There must be, so Mrs. Mitcham concluded, some weakness in Freddy which made him lacking in ambition or even in the resentment many people of his calibre would feel in the treatment he so often had to endure.

But puzzling as Freddy's ultimate motives might be, one thing was clear, he knew how to deal with the situations his employer created. To-night, for example, he obviously set himself to relieve the strained relations of those sitting round that table. He talked cheerfully, and volubly to Anne, to Mrs. Mitcham, and when he got the chance, to Pamela or to Dick. Thanks largely to his efforts, the meal was got through without further unpleasantness.

True that Pamela and Dick insisted on talking only to each other, true that the remarks exchanged by the so-to-speak 'neutral' members were commonplace in the extreme—still, conversation there was, not deadly silence.

The light gleamed on the polished table and on the great bowl of lilies which helped to screen Charles's forbidding face from his companions. The wine glowed in the clear glasses, the excellent food disappeared into the mouths of the diners, and on the whole the meal progressed not too uncomfortably.

Yet while social custom kept these people sitting placidly enough, talking apparently with calm friendliness, the thoughts which ran through their minds would, if revealed, have made clear all the complexities of a horrible situation.

Mrs. Mitcham perhaps could have made the nearest guess at what was passing in the minds of these people, all so well known to her, and yet all so cut off by the barrier each individual can and does raise to protect their secret thoughts. For she knew the train of circumstances which had brought this husband and wife together, and which now forced them apart. As dinner drew to a close and the need for talk grew less, she let her mind turn anxiously to a consideration of these circumstances. When Anne rose to go to the drawing-room, her mother followed her rather wearily and sinking down in her chair gave herself up for the moment to the dreary going over in her mind of her own responsibility in the matter.

Anne and Charles were miserable together. That, of course, was definite. And Charles made his children miserable, that too was evident. The marriage in fact was a failure. Yet could it not be put on a new footing? Was the situation too hopelessly tangled or could this family even now make a fresh start?

She looked at the unpromising side first. Charles and Anne were ill-assorted. He was, after all, both too old and too set in his ways.

She thought of the past, when Charles had first come 'courting' her daughter. Anne had been a girl of eighteen, not pretty, no, her mother reflected, one could not call her that for then she had too snub a nose and too square a chin. But she had a promise of charm, her slim figure had grace, and her chestnut hair together with her really remarkable tawny eyes with that touch of fire in them had given her subtle attraction. She was clever too, and her parents had given her as good an education as they could afford. It was quite easily to be understood why Charles had wished for her then. He had known them all so long, he had seen Anne grow up, and they had all been such good friends, none of them had foreseen the dangerous possibilities latent in that friendly familiarity.

She sighed. One learnt from experience too late. Perhaps she had been too ignorant herself; it had never occurred to her that Charles, her husband's friend, a settled bachelor of forty, should suddenly have changed his ideas and resolved on marriage. She could dimly see now that in him had moved some obscure dread of middle-age, some desire to ally himself with youth, which had caused that disastrous flare of passion in his heart.

His intelligence, strong and clear, had always made him rather formidable. His marked character had always set him a little aside from ordinary men. The very carelessness of his manners, the untidiness of his clothes, had been—had they but seen it—an indication of the fact that he considered himself a law to himself. He believed he need pay no attention to the feelings of others. Despite the passion which suddenly swept him towards Anne, with her vitality and youthful exuberance, he was essentially a cold man too. The heat of desire which had inflamed him then had not lasted. It had died away as soon as he had satisfied it by getting what he wanted. He had beaten down their opposition, forced on partly by a genuine wish to have Anne as his wife, partly by the determination to have his own way. Mrs. Mitcham had, as far as she could, discouraged the match. She remembered so well the anxious talks with her husband, their doubts, their fears lest they were letting Anne make a mistake. The disparity in age, more than twenty years, was too great, and Charles was not only close on forty when he first wished to marry, and thoroughly set in his bachelor ways, but those ways even then had caused her uneasiness. Though she had liked him, admired him, she had, as she now acknowledged, been secretly afraid of him. He had been even then a little formidable in his determination and in the resolution with which he always bore down opposition.

She sighed, for there had lain the cause of the whole catastrophe. Charles had got his way. He had overridden her objections, and more readily those of her husband, who found it easier to see the good points of his own friend. He had won over Anne herself too, and persuaded them all that he would make a good reliable husband and that it was sensible for a girl to marry a man so settled, so well known to the whole family, and so rich!

Here her conscience gave a sharp jab. That had been the decisive factor, the wish for security for Anne. They had been so poor, and the girl's prospects so uncertain. Anne at eighteen had been rather a problem with her unusual character and her strong, difficult nature, and in view of the poverty which made it hard for her parents to give her many opportunities, it had not seemed at all sure that she would have many chances for marriage. They could not afford to give her any expensive training such as would open out to her some career; her father's health had always been bad, and there had lurked in the background that constant dread as to what would happen to them all if he were to die young—as indeed he had, at the age of forty-five.

No, those material anxieties had been real and heavy then. It had seemed best to play for safety, to take what was offered, and not expose Anne to the chance of missing marriage altogether. As a family, they had known too well how difficult and dreary life could be for people of small means. They were bound to be influenced by the prospect of prosperity, even of wealth. As a mother, she had come to welcome the thought of winning for Anne a secure and prosperous future. She might have been expected to be happy enough with Charles, especially if children came to supply her life with the element of real affection.

There had been a risk, of course, but surely a risk which all parties had been justified in taking? Then why had everything gone wrong? Why had Charles and Anne, instead of growing gradually together, drifted steadily apart?

It was partly the coming of the children, those children whose birth might have been expected to draw the parents together. Charles had not cared for them, and had resented his wife's joy and pleasure in them. He had, apparently, no warm family feeling himself, and the children had only upset the one thing he did desire, a well-ordered home centring on himself. When the babies had absorbed his young wife's attention he had at first been jealous, then indifferent, and that indifference marked the departure of such affection as he had been capable of feeling for his wife. They had drifted apart—and too soon quarrels had sprung up over the way in which Anne brought up the little girls.

Yet that might have been got over—indeed as the children grew older, and needed less of their mother's attention, she and Charles might have come together again. Parents often did, as they found themselves thrown back more on each other when children grew up and went their own ways.

But in the case of Charles and Anne matters had not improved; indeed, they had grown worse.

She must be fair, she must do Charles justice. Here her conscience reproached her. Charles had been very generous to her. He had insisted on giving her a good allowance when her husband's death left her so poor. He was always free with his money when he was in a good mood, and often insisted on her accepting handsome presents. The beautiful dress she had on at that moment had been his last present to her, sent when one of his business deals had proved marvellously successful. He and she had always got on quite well, and she freely admitted to herself how much she owed to him.

No, difficult as he was, Charles had his good points. The worst side of him came out if he were thwarted, if he were opposed in anything he wished to do.

That was why things were going so wrong now. It was this fatal move to the country! Mrs. Mitcham involuntarily glanced out on the wide landscape, now veiling itself in mist as night began to draw in. Anne had been happy enough in London. Born and brought up there, she had her friends, her interests, her familiar scene. But the country! No, that had been a disaster. Why need Charles have uprooted them all? Why could he not have gone on as they all wished, in his comfortable house in the big London square? It had not been fair on Anne, dragging her down here to the wilds!

Here again Mrs. Mitcham, being an extremely honest woman, felt herself obliged to pause. Charles had lived in London for years, true enough, but from the days when Anne and her sister were small girls and when as their father's friend he had come to spend every Sunday evening with them all, he had always kept them amused with tales of the country. How many times had the little girls begged him to tell them of his home, had asked for the 'story of the time you shot the bull,' how often had he described the incidents of his life as a country child to enchant these little dwellers in a city? Of course, he had often enough shown his deep and real love for country life, and perhaps it was not to be wondered at that as he grew more towards old age he should resolve to go back once more to the country he so deeply loved? And when chance had brought to his attention a place on the market in the very district he had always fancied, it was not to be wondered at that he had decided to buy, and to give up the work which he had begun to find trying and monotonous. Having made his money, and made indeed so much more than they had expected, he was, of course, entitled to retire. That was to be understood. But what was so stupid, so misguided, so unkind, had been his sudden decision to abandon London altogether. A country house, yes; Anne would have borne that for part of the year, the summer perhaps or for holidays—but to come down here for good, to refuse to keep on even a tiny flat, to bury Anne all the year round in this remote spot—no! That had been Charles's selfishness, and for that he must take the blame for the ruin of his married life. He *had* been selfish, utterly reckless of Anne's feelings. Why, he need never have insisted on this actual house, no decent man would have forced his wife to come to such a place... so lonely, no village, no neighbours, no society—of course, Anne hated it. Hardening her heart, Mrs. Mitcham thought, "Anne *isn't* to blame!"

And as she came to that conclusion, her animosity against her son-in-law blew into a brighter flame. It *was* Charles's fault. He'd been so harsh, so arrogant, so unwilling to consider anyone's feelings but his own! That came from his making so much money! His wealth had spoilt him. Because he'd done so well, made so much, he'd grown tyrannical. He thought his money gave him the right to dominate—and so he'd alienated Anne, come to bully his children, spoilt his family life, his bad temper was due to his arrogant development, and Anne was not to be blamed for that.

Well! Perhaps it was useless to try to apportion responsibility for this or that. The mistake had been made, disaster had gradually come nearer and nearer. Yet for the sake of the children, for the sake of Anne herself, some effort must be made to put things right.

What could be done to improve matters? On the one hand a naturally bad-tempered man, made arrogant now by the acquisition of great wealth, unable to adapt himself to the ways of the young generation, violent, unbending, harsh.

On the other a dissatisfied woman, disliking her home, feeling her youth gone, longing for some outlet for her thwarted possibilities. Mrs. Mitcham sighed, for these were hopeless ingredients. At this moment Anne's voice startled her.

"Mother, where is Pam?"

Mrs. Mitcham, shaking off her weary thoughts, answered vaguely: "Pam? Well, she didn't come in here with us. I think she went straight out into the garden."

Anne got up and moved across to the coffee-tray.

"She's not had her coffee. Why do you suppose she's gone out like that?"

"Oh, gone with Dick as usual, I suppose. Probably they've thought it nicer out of doors. It's such a lovely evening and quite warm."

Anne moved restlessly to the window. "I do think Pam is silly about that boy. She doesn't care for him and she's only making him thoroughly silly over her."

"Well, my dear," said her mother tolerantly, "she can't do him any real harm, and I think it's something for her to have anyone to amuse herself with."

"Yes, I should think so!" came the bitter response. "Poked away in this hole, with no one to see day in and day out!"

"I didn't quite mean that," answered her mother. "What I really think is, it's better on the whole for her to be taken up with Dick rather than with any of the other people she is thrown with here!" She looked meaningly across at Anne, but her hint met with no response. Anne turned away, took up a book, and flinging herself carelessly into a chair began to flick through the pages in a bored listless way. Clearly she did not mean to be dragged into any discussion with her mother.

Chapter III

WHO WAS IN THE YARD?

M eanwhile Pamela had, as the elder woman surmised, slipped
out of the house, avoiding both her mother and father. When
the ladies had left the dining-room, Dick too had seized the opportunity to escape, and scurrying across the hall had overtaken Pamela
in the flower garden which sloped from the front door up to the
little country road. The two paused for a moment in the shade of
a tree, while Dick lit the girl's cigarette and his own. As he flung
down the match his eyes turned towards the house, where a bright
square of light marked the dining-room. Clearly lit up they could
see every detail of the room, and they saw Charles, still sunk in
angry sullenness, raise his glass of port without even glancing
round at the depleted table. They saw something else too. Wadham
suddenly leaning forward and with a confidential air breaking into
his employer's gloomy reverie.

"Rotten hypocrite, that fellow!" exclaimed Dick. "I know perfectly well he really loathes your father, yet look at him now! Just
making up to him for all he's worth!"

Pamela in turn looked towards the two men, every detail of
whose faces and expressions showed up clearly in the brightly lit
room. Charles, apparently roused by what his secretary had said,
had swivelled round in his chair, and with one hand holding his
cigar was now talking earnestly and with animation. He bent slightly
forward, dark and formidable, intent on bringing something before

his companion. Wadham, though equally intent, yet with his more animated face, his glinting eyes, his quick smile, showed up as somehow insinuating, intriguing, false.

The girl and boy, outside in the darkened garden, both felt themselves as it were spectators of a drama, and both instinctively found something to dislike in the attitudes and expressions of the men inside the room. Perhaps it was the apprehension which came to Pamela of the fact that her father, so morose and silent all dinner, was now choosing to expand, to confer, with Wadham, perhaps it was a perception that there was something afoot, something shared between those two, from which the rest of the household was excluded. In any case she stared hard for a moment, then shaking off the impression made on her, with a shrug she turned away.

"Oh! Come on! Come on! What does it matter what he and Daddy discuss! Money, I suppose! Money and business! Freddy's like everyone else, he wants cash, and he has to take it where he can get it! He makes up to Daddy because it's worth his while! As most people seem to do. I only wish—" but breaking off abruptly she took her companion's arm and drew him on up the path away from the house.

"Look here now," and pouring a rapid stream of words into his ear the two wandered away into the dusk.

Time passed. The hot still evening went on. Silence pressed down round the house. The rising moon began to cast deep velvety shadows across the open space in front of the porch. Charles, emerging from the front door, began to pace up and down the path which lay between the door and the gateway on to the road. The stillness, the warmth, the beauty of the night would have soothed most minds. But Charles was too deeply disturbed even to notice the peace and quietude around him. He paced slowly to and fro, mechanically

turning as he reached the vague glimmer of white which marked
the gate, overshadowed now by the great elms which bordered the
lane. To the right, reaching almost from the gate to the house, lay
the great barn and the former outbuildings of the old farm. The
barn was actually more beautiful than the house itself, for it was
one of those vast ancient structures which have stood for centuries,
so well were they built, so perfectly adapted to the countryside.
Carron barn was made of timber, its roof upheld by vast rafters
and baulks, its tarred sides reinforced with stout posts of oak. In the
middle wall were huge double doors, and within was space enough
for a dozen cars. For it was used now as a garage, and the gravel
sweep had been diverted up to its doors and its floor concreted. On
the far side another pair of doors led out into what had once been
the cattle-yard and which was now used as a yard for washing and
cleaning the cars.

Charles's mechanical pacing went in an unconscious round, up
to the gate, then round by the barn door back to the front of the
house, and so on, over and over again. He walked with head rather
bent, his long arms and powerful clumsy hands hanging at his side.
His mind was filled with conflict. First he thought with a sort of dour
satisfaction of the scene by the pool. That to-night in turn led to his
children. The bullying turn of his temperament was satisfied with
the success he had met with in imposing his will on his little daughter. He had shown himself, as usual, master in his household. This
child should be brought up as he thought right. Discipline would
toughen the fibre of her character, give her the qualities she lacked.
He was confident in the rightness of his aims and of his methods. Yet
behind his minor triumph of the afternoon lurked discontent. Anne,
he knew perfectly well, had not approved. Too many quarrels left
him in no doubt whatever as to her attitude. She thought his whole
treatment of the child wrong. She herself would have humoured

Prue's timidity, let her yield to it, made excuses for what he called cowardice. She would never have attempted to induce the child to overcome it, and she would never see that it was in the child's own best interests that he wished her to struggle against and overcome her fatal lack of grit. Yet how could Anne fail to see that her indulgence had proved disastrous to Pamela? He had let things slide in the case of that first child, and what were the results, now staring them in the face? Pamela had no self-control, no stability, she rushed from one mistake to the other, frittering away her energies and her emotions, spoiling her life. Look at her endless flirtations and love-affairs! And philandering with that odious fellow Barclay! But he'd put a stop to that, anyhow! What was the use of this futile young puppy Dick hanging about her now? Pamela could never think of him seriously, yet she spent all her days and apparently part of her nights with him! He was sure he had heard her slip past to her room very late the night before. Had it been two o'clock that he had heard the garage clock chime? To-night, in any case, he'd be on the look out. But Anne would never admit that Pamela's unsatisfactory behaviour was due to her spoiling! Anne backed Pamela in everything. Anne was disloyal in this, as well as in other things!

His bitter thoughts dwelt on his wife. He began to consider the very problem which had earlier occupied his mother-in-law, but of course from his own point of view. Why had Anne ever married him? Many years younger than himself, clever, with an ambition to have what he contemptuously called 'literary friends,' a confirmed lover of towns and town life, why had she ever thought she could be happy with him? Of course, he thought cynically, she had never even considered whether she could make him happy, never tried to adapt herself to his ways! Why had she made so little effort to please him? His natural arrogance kept him from giving the answer which stared him in the face. He did not want to believe that Anne had married him not from affection, but simply for his money. He was fully aware of his own abilities, he knew that he was respected in many circles. He believed that physically he was in his way attractive. True, he was older than she, but age had, he thought, improved his looks; his iron-grey hair was becoming to him, in conjunction with his piercing grey eyes, his dark, strong, confident face. And Anne knew all about him, he had been no stranger to her. For years he had been her father's intimate friend. He had come to their house from the days when Anne was a schoolgirl. When, at last, having made his money, amassed a fortune indeed, he decided to settle down and take to himself a wife, it had seemed quite natural that he should think of the girl whom he knew so well. Anne had known perfectly well what she was doing. Why then did she seem so bitter and resentful now? What had she expected that she had not received? He was a good husband to her, she had a luxurious home, children, good health, what more could the woman want?

Just as his pride emphasized his good points, and turned away from the knowledge that Anne had been poor, her circle limited, her chances of a wealthy marriage almost non-existent, so the same stubborn refusal to recognize his mistakes kept him from dwelling on what he knew to be the source of discord now—his determination to live in the country. Anne was town-bred. She neither knew nor cared for the country. She had married him, thinking of life with him in London. When he first had told her that he was buying a country place she had believed it would only prove a whim, a passing fancy. He would soon tire of it and they would return to London, the place where both had spent their youth. She had never, his harsh thoughts went, recognized the difference that their respective ages meant, even in this. Charles had lived for many years in town, but now he was tired. He was turned sixty and he wanted to spend the last part of his life in the country. After all, the fact must be faced that he was now setting out on the slope of old age. He wanted peace, and the quiet of the fields and woods.

Anne on the other hand still wanted the bustle and gaiety of town. She was not even within sight of the phase of approaching age. Life still burnt brightly in her. Well, she must put up with it, she must accept his choice.

There was the sore place! Anne never had tried to adapt herself! Never had tried to see his point of view. She always thought she could get her own way if she stuck out for it. Well, she was mistaken—and always had been. That was why they had quarrelled so often and so bitterly. For if she would not give way, still less would he! He had always been master in his own house, and no efforts of hers had ever deflected him from his ways. From the outset she had failed to win any power to influence him. Her youth, her charm, the intimacy of marriage, had all gone for nothing when they touched his self-will. What he wanted, that he had—and always intended to have. Anne could not change him, and it seemed that she could not adapt herself to him. Well, he would win this battle, as he had won so many others in the past.

It was now close on midnight, and as Charles's steps led him to the strip of grass bordering the great barn, a sudden sound checked him. The night was very still, and that 'click' had struck sharply on his ear. It seemed to him it was the latch of the farther door of the barn. He listened. Yes, someone was there. He could distinguish two voices, whispering, a man's and a woman's surely? He thought too that he could smell tobacco smoke, and to confirm his suspicion came a faint clink, which to his sharpened attention was unmistakably the sound of nailed shoes on the bricked floor of the yard. Who was it? He realized it must be members of his household, for Carron Cross was too far from the village for any local people to be using his barn as a rendezvous. Annoyed lest it should be Pamela and Dick—for why must they be out now? and why must they whisper like that?—he began to feel for the latch of the door on his side. Softly he pressed it down, but the door did not open, it was duly and safely locked. He thought a moment. He must creep round through the dairy, that would bring him out to the far side and he could catch the couple there. But even as he decided on his plan of action, the latch, which he had released cautiously, now shifted and clicked back into place quite audibly. The hurried whispering stopped, there was a slight scuffling noise. Abandoning caution Charles hurried towards the dairy, but by the time he had made his way round and through to the far courtyard, he was too late. In the bright moonlight the door of the barn swung softly to and fro, but the culprits had vanished. Only the trace of tobacco still lingered on the air. Charles sniffed, trying frowningly to decide—if he could—what had produced that aroma. Then, with his gloomy lowering expression deepening, he hastened back towards the house.

Again he felt his angry dissatisfaction rising. He knew instinctively there was something afoot, something secret and furtive, and a second sense made him believe that whatever was going forward was based on opposition to himself.

As he went in at the front door the bright moonlight glinting from behind him struck a shaft across the narrow old staircase in the corner. Courtley started. Surely the beam had caught the fluttering skirt? He sprang forward, caught his foot in a rug which slid across the polished floor and stumbled heavily. He saved himself from falling flat by clutching at the table in the window, but that tilted in his grasp, and a torrent of tennis racquets, books, magazines, fell to the floor. Cursing and swearing to himself he shovelled them on one side.

He shut and locked the door behind him and hurried on upstairs. Dodging quickly along the dark twisted passages he came to Pamela's door and knocked.

"Who's there?" It was Pam's voice, and at once he felt angry disappointment that he had not caught her out of her room.

"I thought you hadn't come in," he snapped. "Wasn't that you out there in the barn?"

"No, it was *not*! I came to bed ages ago!" And Pamela flung open her door. She was not only ready for bed, dressed in her pale yellow pyjamas, but her face was duly 'creamed' for the night, and glancing beyond her Charles could see her clothes, even to her stockings, neatly folded and arranged on a stool. For one of Pamela's redeeming qualities was her extreme neatness in anything concerning her own personal belongings. There was not the faintest sign of any hurried undressing, no disorder, no haste, all looked as if Pam had come leisurely to bed.

Baffled, and annoyed with himself for feeling so, and with the girl for her triumphant self-righteous expression, Charles turned away with an ungracious grunt. If it were not Pam, who had it been? One of the maids, or—Anne?

The maids were less likely to have gone up the great staircase, if indeed that had been a woman's skirt he had glimpsed. Yet what would Anne have been doing in the yard? A suspicion rushed into his mind, and he acted promptly upon it.

He went across to Anne's room and knocked, and entered without waiting for an answer. Instantly his heart gave a thump. It *had* been Anne. She was standing by her dressing-table, her face turned towards him. The brilliant flush in the cheeks, the sparkle in her eyes, the quick breathing which she could not disguise, all told their tale.

Violent black rage rushed over him. He walked towards her, head thrust forward threateningly.

"You've been meeting him again!"

"No!" She retorted at once, facing him without the slightest hesitation or fear. "If you mean Peter, I've *not*."

He was checked by the steadiness and sincerity of her tone. He looked at her again searchingly, and began to hesitate. He did not think she was lying.

She was wearing a thick heavy white satin wrap, the cord tied round her waist. He stepped nearer and pulled the front of the wrap apart. She did not check him, though her flush burnt more angrily than before. She had only taken off her evening dress, and apart from that was wearing her evening underclothes, complete to her stockings, and still had on her brocaded high-heeled shoes. The toes showed a faint darkening, damp or stain.

"You've been out," he said accusingly and with certitude, pointing to the tell-tale shoes.

She turned away from him, angry and contemptuous.

"To the yard!" she answered tauntingly.

"Why?"

"Because I heard voices out there and I went out to see who it was."

Charles hesitated. He had himself done just what she alleged she had done, yet he did not believe her. If she had gone innocently, why did she look so stirred, so... so exalted?

"I don't believe you," he said sullenly. "Why should you care who's about? You don't keep the maids in order, anyhow!"

Anne made no reply to this. Instead she sat down on the broad low stool before her dressing-table and began to brush her thick gleaming hair. There was a moment's silence. Charles, being no fool, saw the possible alternative. Had she too suspected Pam? If she had, she was silent now for fear of giving her daughter away to him.

"It wasn't Pam," he said grimly, watching the face reflected in the mirror.

At that she rounded on him.

"Very well then. Think what you like. I don't care a damn *what* you think. I've told you I was not meeting Peter, and you must take my word for it."

Again a threatening silence. Then Charles moved slowly towards the door, paused, and turned.

"Well, so you say. Perhaps I can't prove anything yet. But I tell you now what I've told you before. If I get proof you're being unfaithful, I'll divorce you—and I'll get the custody of the children. I warn you. You know what you've got to face."

Silence met him. Anne would not answer. He looked full at her, triumphant in the knowledge that she dared not face divorce—or, to tell the truth, dared not leave her children alone with him. The law would give him full control of them, he had that supreme advantage.

Proud of this power, which he knew must check and control her, he left her. She sat still, her hands fell to her lap. Silent, brooding, intent, she stayed motionless. But no one studying her face and her poise would have reckoned her a desperate or a defeated woman. Pride, resolution, something almost triumphant shone in her eyes as she finally turned away from her glass.

Chapter IV

BREAKFAST PARTY

Morning came, the morning of September 5th. Carron Cross, like every other household, gradually awoke. Maids got up, curtains were drawn rattling along their rods, steps clattered on the polished stairs. Outside, the gardeners and the farm hands came bicycling along the lane and turning in at the gate swirled cheerfully round to the back regions. Talk and noise began, the ordinary happy workaday noise of daily life. Everything seemed to mark the beginning of a completely ordinary day in the life of an ordinary affluent country household.

Yet perhaps to the observant even the start of that day was not, after all, completely ordinary.

To begin with, the weather proved exceptionally hot. Early September even in England does sometimes bring with it a heat, a burning, still golden heat, almost more oppressive than the gay sunshine of July. The sun beat down, seeming to gather strength and fierceness each hour, and the earth, already dry and itself radiating heat, made the air quiver above the stubble in the fields. The dark heavy foliage of the elms hung in welcome clumps of shade. Keats's 'season of mists and mellow fruitfulness' seemed far away, for this was still apparently the time of glowing, invigorating summer sun.

Charles got up early, as was his habit in the country. He put on a dressing-gown over his pyjamas, and when his early tea was brought to him he took it downstairs and went out on to the terrace at the back to view the landscape and decide on the probable weather for the day. There, slightly to his surprise, he met his mother-in-law. She was not usually out and about so early, but in fact, knowing his ways, she had deliberately got up and come out, in the hope of finding him before the day's friction and irritations had roused his temper.

"Charles," she began at once, determined not to let her resolution fail her, "I want to talk to you for a few minutes if you don't mind."

"Well," said Charles, seating himself and beginning to sip at his tea. "I've a few moments before I need go back to dress. What is it?"

Mrs. Mitcham looked uneasily at the hard lines of his face. He did not meet her eyes, and her heart sank as she realized something disagreeable was already afoot.

However, she had come here with her mind made up, and she decided to stick to her purpose. She was a woman with plenty of grit and resolution.

"I'm afraid," she began, as reasonably and in as conciliatory a way as she could achieve, for long experience had taught her that this was the only way to deal with so violent and obstinate a man as Charles, "that you and Anne aren't getting on as happily as we'd hoped?"

No answer came. Charles went on sipping his tea, his eyes determinedly roving over the countryside spread out below them, brightening now and taking on colour under the morning sun as the mist drew up, promise of a scorching day.

"I was wondering," she went on, "whether perhaps you'd let Anne bring Prudence to spend a week or two with me at the sea? I'm going on from here to Sidmouth, you know, and I'd love to have them with me—and I think perhaps a little break might make things easier for you all."

Charles laughed at this, a sneering, disagreeable snigger. "Anne's last 'little break' didn't do much good!" he said contemptuously.

Mrs. Mitcham flushed, and felt herself growing angry too. "It's no good us going on with that, Charles," she said, sharply, "we've gone over it often enough. I tell you again, as I told you before, you're utterly wrong in your suspicions. Anne was with me, and with no one else."

She spoke so resolutely and with so much sincerity that her son-in-law relaxed a little in his hostility. He put down his cup and faced her squarely.

"Well, I should like to believe you, but you see I know Anne was having a love-affair last autumn with that fellow Sylvester. I know it. She's practically admitted it. And I know he was away from home when Anne cleared off to you."

"But that's the point," interrupted his mother-in-law eagerly. "Anne *did* come to me. She didn't go away with him. Charles, I assure you, she came to me the very day she left here; she came up to my flat, by herself, and she never once even saw Mr. Sylvester the entire month she was with me." Again she tried by the urgency and sincerity of her tones to bring some conviction.

Charles looked at her sharply. He pondered, a strange look on his face. Finally he spoke, abruptly and harshly.

"Well, that's as it may be. I'll take your word for last year's affair. But I don't trust Anne. And on one thing I'm completely resolved. Whatever happens I won't have a separation, or at least not in the sense Anne would like one. If she leaves me, just to go off and live apart I mean, she shan't have the children. I married for a home, and I don't mean to let her break up mine and set up one for herself. And of course," he added savagely, "that applies even more if she goes off with another man. I'd not be one of these husbands who take the blame. I'd put her through the divorce court, and I'd see she didn't set eyes on the children."

He stopped, as if he had said more than he meant, seeing the look of anger and disgust in his mother-in-law's face. He seemed to pull himself up, and in a different, more reasonable tone, said: "But we needn't talk of that now. I'm only warning you, for Anne's sake, to use your influence with her. I don't want Anne to leave me." He spoke slowly, but there was a queer, indefinable threat in his voice. "I've a position in life, I hoped I had a home and children. Anne and I haven't got on for a long time past, but I've no wish to smash up our home. Only," and here his face darkened and the sullen, angry look overspread it again, "I'll not put up with her carrying on behind my back. She needn't think I'll stand for that. She can go her way—as long as it doesn't lead to a secret affair with Sylvester."

His mother-in-law hesitated, then: "I agree with you there, of course. If the worst came to the worst I should have advised Anne to ask you openly for a divorce. But actually I'm perfectly certain that affair with Mr. Sylvester was quite temporary. Whatever there was between them, it's ended now. You and Anne ought, for the children's sake, to try to settle down now."

Charles shuffled impatiently. "Exactly—we '*ought* to try to settle down'—but I tell you, I don't trust Anne. She's in a queer mood. She's so infernally discontented. She won't accept the fact that I mean to settle down *here*."

Mrs. Mitcham seized her chance before he could work himself up into a rage. "You've not given her long enough, Charles. Anne has had what to her has been an emotional shock. She was in love with Peter Sylvester, but you can't altogether condemn her for that..."

"Why not?" interrupted Charles with a sort of cold bitterness. "Doesn't one blame a wife for unfaithfulness?"

"I don't want to rake up the past," replied his mother-in-law, "but, Charles, you must look facts in the face. You're a good deal older than Anne. You and she have had separate rooms for the past ten years. Like many other women, Anne isn't as cold and self-contained as Englishwomen have been supposed to be. You left her to herself, you brought her to this lonely place, and here she found an attractive unattached man of her own age living next door, and brought into close contact with you all. You were asking for trouble when you kept him on as your agent. But *don't* let's go over that," she went on hastily, "we've been over it all before and you've agreed to let all that be forgotten. She did fall in love, but it didn't last. It was a flare-up—and she got over it. And Mr. Sylvester's going away, isn't he?"

"Well, he's leaving my employment of course, but whether he'll get another job elsewhere I don't know. He's at his own house till his time is up."

Mrs. Mitcham glanced at him sharply. "Well, Charles, if he's still here and living so close that's all the more reason to get Anne away for a change. Of course he'll try for an agency elsewhere, and let's hope he'll soon go off to some other neighbourhood, and if Anne comes away with me now that will make everything easier. She's sore and wretched at present. If she gets a change and a break she can come back and begin the winter cheerfully, and he'll have gone and we can hope for better times." She spoke as encouragingly as she could, wanting to put the whole matter in a prosaic, everyday light.

Charles laughed shortly. "Well, I'm willing. We can't go on as it is. Have her and Prue for a bit if you like. Let's hope it will do them both good: nothing could be much worse than things as they are."

He reflected a moment and then, as if annoyed that he had been brought to give even this grudging consent and determined to compensate himself, he turned his dark face full towards her. "And another thing. While Anne is with you, perhaps you'll impress on her that I won't stand for any more extravagance. She's spending far too much. This house is run with the most outrageous wastefulness. If she can't reduce expense I've made up my mind to have a housekeeper who will. I shall employ a paid person, and Anne will have the running of the house taken out of her hands. She sets the girls a most appalling example," he went on. "Of course I know I've plenty of money, but that doesn't mean I want it thrown about, and I mean my daughters to learn the value of money. I won't have them get into the way of spending money like water. Pamela's spoilt enough as it is, God knows! Painting her face, and doing just what she likes. She's getting beyond all bearing, and Anne just leaves her to go her own way and helps to make her worse. Nothing but useless squandering and extravagance!" He paused, and Mrs. Mitcham sat aghast. Here was fresh trouble. She was silent for a moment, not knowing what to say. Charles followed up his advantage.

"I'm going to tell Anne this to-day. I've got to go through the accounts with Wadham. I've told him to get me out a balance-sheet. I shall tell Anne that I'll give her three months, and if she hasn't kept within my figure each week—well, someone else who can do so will take on."

He spoke with finality. His hard grey eyes seemed to bore into his mother-in-law's face, and then turning away with a sort of nod, he went indoors. She heard the clack of his loose slippers on the polished floor, she heard him go up the stairs, and then his door slammed behind him.

For a moment or two she sat still. She felt almost hopeless. No sooner was there an attempt to get things right, than fresh trouble cropped out. This new outburst was dreadfully ominous. Mrs. Mitcham knew her daughter. Anne was proud and had plenty of spirit and temper. Charles was taking a course which was bound to lead to disaster. Anne would never tolerate having control of the housekeeping taken from her. Why must Charles think of these new causes for quarrels? Well, she must see what could be done.

She got up and went slowly into the house.

Half an hour later, the household began to come down to break-fast. Mrs. Mitcham coming rather wearily first into the dining-room, decided to keep this threat of new difficulties to herself. At least she had got her way over the proposed holiday. She would not let herself think beyond that.

As to the rest of the party, the brilliance of the day seemed to have brightened not only the atmosphere, but their spirits. The sky was cloudless blue, and beyond the lattice windows the tall spikes of yellow and pink hollyhocks rose in great pyramids against the black tarred side of the big barn. Mrs. Mitcham sat down at the table facing the window. She looked at the grass sparkling with dew, she heard the peaceful clucking of the hens in the yard beyond, she smelt all the fresh scents of the country. "Well," she thought, her spirits rising insensibly, "there is something to be said for Charles and his country life, after all. London on a day like this would be only tantalizing. I hope the children will have a good day." Sensibly she decided that it was no good letting herself be depressed by things that might never happen. Charles had blown off steam to her, perhaps now he would after all let Anne alone. If she could get Anne and Prudence off with her, this other trouble might come to nothing.

At this moment her faint revival of cheerfulness was augmented by the sound of an obviously gay and good-tempered Pamela descending the staircase.

"Hallo, Mum!" as she saw Anne coming out of her room. "Good morning! Gorgeous day, isn't it?" The girl came bounding across the hall and into the dining-room, producing a pleasing effect of bright colour with her lemon-coloured slacks, white blouse, no lip-stick for once, but a cheerful glowing face to which Charles (however cross, thought Mrs. Mitcham parenthetically) could take no objection.

"Now then, Gran!" she rattled on, "how are you, old thing, to-day? Pretty perky? Ready for your bacon and egg?" Darting across the room she began to rattle covers off hot dishes, and as Dick too came hurrying in, turned to him equally cheerfully. "That's right! down to time for once! Come on, make yourself useful, do a bit of buttling, lazy!" and she thrust into his hands laden plates for her grandmother and herself. "Come on, Mum," she went on, "you buck up a bit now, have some food besides your old orange juice? What can I tempt you with? Egg? Ham? Kedgeree?"

Her mother smiled briefly, but shook her head and sitting down began to sip at the glass of orange juice which was to form her meal. Anne had obviously not shared in Pamela's improvement of spirits. She looked pale and heavy-eyed and was clearly disinclined for any effort at conversation. Pamela looked at her sharply and was just going to speak, but at this moment steps sounded on the gravel outside and a shadow passed across the window. The three women with instinctive apprehension glanced out. They knew it was Charles, and each wanted to see what was the mood of the master of the house.

At once a broad grin lit up Pam's face, and she pointed a disrespectful finger to attract Dick's attention to her father. "Psst!" she hissed softly. "Dick, just look at the old man!"

Dick, passing from the side table to his place with his cup and plate, followed the direction of her pointing finger, and his face too burst into irresistible smiles. "Gosh! How marvellous! What on earth's he up to now?"

"Oh, hopping off to superintend the farm," said Pam brightly. "And let me tell you, his outfit is the converse of his temper; the worse his clothes, the better his mood! Lucky day for us to-day, I can tell you!"

Her grandmother smiled benevolently across at the young man. "Yes, Charles has his own ideas about country clothes," she said, "and when he wears that get-up, we know he's going to have a good agricultural morning." Secretly she reflected that things were as she hoped, Charles had got rid of his tantrums by venting his feelings on her.

"Sensible, perhaps," laughed Dick, "for it's going to be hot enough to-day in all conscience. I expect he'll find his kit just the right style."

His host, whose clothes had created this sensation, had indeed shown his individuality in his attire. Charles often boasted that he needed no breakfast beyond a piece of bread and a glass of milk, and he had already secured that sustenance from one of the maids and was now apparently off to his farm. He had put on a pair of khaki shorts and a shabby old shirt. His head was covered by an ancient panama hat, and his feet shod with an even more ancient pair of white sand-shoes. He cared nothing what people thought of his appearance, and in fact secretly enjoyed posing as an original. And after all, as he knew and all those around him knew, it would be more than anyone dared to criticize what he chose to wear. So, shabby but tranquil, serene and apparently amiable, he made his way up the fields, leaving his family to breathe more freely in the knowledge that he was probably in a good mood and was certainly intending to be fully occupied at a nice distance from them and their amusements.

Breakfast therefore became a cheerful meal, and then, once finished, there came the eternal problem of the country house—what was to be done to-day?

"Tennis!" said Pam firmly. "Tennis! Dick, you and I must practise for the tournament—it's only two days off. I'll ring up the Courtolds and get them to come over."

"Right—tennis it shall be! Work, not play, shall be my motto! Take example from me, Prue." He turned to the child who had come silently in and seated herself by her mother. She looked fearfully white, and great black circles under her eyes betrayed a bad night. But as he spoke he almost regretted his attempt to cheer the little girl. She had glanced at him and her lips only formed a polite mechanical smile, because Prue was a gentle little creature and always wishful to appreciate well-meant efforts. She looked as if she had hardly the spirit to respond even to kindness.

Anne glanced quickly at her little daughter, and then decided to leave her alone, judging that the catastrophe of the previous evening was too recent and too devastating to be recovered from at once. Mrs. Mitcham, too, looked thoughtfully at the child and then turned to Anne.

"Could I have the car? If Charles is busy on the farm he won't want it this morning, and I'd like to go to Marple and do some shopping. Perhaps Prue would keep me company?"

Prue herself did not answer, she went on steadily with her breakfast. Anne, realizing that in her mother's opinion even a short escape from Carron, a change even of such a limited character, might brighten the child's listlessness, hurriedly agreed, and was just getting up to go about her household ordering, which should include arrangements for the car, when Wadham came in.

Anne paused, startled, and gave a quick glance up at him. Freddy did not to-day look his normal self-contained, cheerful self. True, his colour was no different from his usual healthy pallor, and his dark eyes were bright and clear. But somehow he looked haggard, uncertain, jumpy. He was evidently aware of the surprise caused by his late appearance, aware too that he was not able to present his usual equable front to the world, but at the same time he clearly did not wish to let his strained face betray him. He spoke quickly and briskly.

"Sorry I'm so late, Mrs. Courtley. I overslept for once—a thing I never do as a rule. So I'll make up as fast as I can for wasted time," and turning his back he busied himself at the side table, quickly carving himself some ham and pouring out his coffee. He came back to seat himself with his back to the window.

Anne paused, her hand on the back of her chair, glanced at her mother, at Prue's still downcast face, and then said lightly: "Well, you need not hurry; Charles has gone off up to the farm, so I don't suppose he needs you very promptly this morning."

Wadham paused for a moment, and then with a perceptible effort: "Oh, that's rather unlucky. I'm afraid he's forgotten, we've some important stuff to get through this morning. I'd better hurry up and go and catch him."

Instantly Anne's face clouded. What sickening luck! Just when Charles had gone off in a good mood, and might have been relied on to potter happily about all morning, and leave his family in peace. Rather stiffly she answered:

"Yes, that *is* a misfortune. Charles can't have remembered at all. He's put on his old kit and been up and away already. Do you think you need fetch him back before twelve? Surely you can get on with things till then without him?"

But Wadham shook his head. "Not a hope! Mr. Courtley specially told me we must get a particular piece of work done this morning— he's something else on this afternoon, and this stuff can't wait."

There was a curious note in his voice—hesitancy or urgency? Mrs. Mitcham glanced at him, then firmly told herself she must stick to her determined policy, she must not try to see beneath the surface in this house-hold! She got up. "Well, Mr. Wadham, I gather in any case, if Charles is dragged away from the farm it will only be to the study? Prue and I can have the car? He'll not be going out anywhere?"

"Why, yes, Mrs. Mitcham, that is so. I'm afraid it's he and I for a stuffy indoor session!"

Undoubtedly he was nervous. His over-bright tone betrayed him. Both women could tell that. Well, each of them knew that for Freddy to be nervous probably meant an end to the prospect of a serene day, and each resolved to remove themselves from the scene. Charles recalled from the farm, Charles shown to have forgotten important business, Charles thus irritated, to be cribbed up indoors on this hot, glowing day—no! Let Freddy dree his own weird.

Anne turned quickly to her mother. "It's going to be very hot, Mother, so will you start soon? Then you'll get in to the shops before they are busy."

Mrs. Mitcham nodded. She knew that the sooner she and Prue were off the safer, and resolved too that they would find time to visit the milk bar so beloved of Prue, where the consumption of ices might prolong the time before they need return.

"Why, yes, Anne, I'll get ready at once. Prue and I will be down by the time the car's round, if you'll order it now," and she bustled out of the room and up the stairs.

Prudence, who had listened without a word, followed her grand-mother in the same listless silence she had kept throughout her meal. Anne, after a moment's hesitation, gave one brief glance at Wadham, and seeing him intent apparently on hastening through his last piece of toast, turned too and vanished into the kitchen quarters of the house. Wadham, left alone, gulped down his coffee, lit himself a cigarette, and then, with a sort of shrug, shook himself together and resolutely and briskly set off in pursuit of his employer.

Charles, as he walked slowly across the fields, felt in rather a better temper. He thought he had impressed his mother-in-law, secretly he was relieved at the idea of Anne going away for a while. He hated the consciousness that his married life had come to such an unsatisfactory stage. He hated to fail in anything, and though he blamed Anne entirely for their disagreements, still he was willing enough to think that if she fell in with his ideas they might yet tide things over. A break now might be politic. Anne had made a fool of herself over Sylvester, but he believed that was ended, and if it were not—well, he had made up his mind what he would do.

It only remained to see that Peter got a job elsewhere, and did not get taken on by anyone in the neighbourhood. And, more important still, perhaps, he must without delay clear up that matter of the letters. He halted. He must set Wadham on to that job.

Once that had been dealt with and Sylvester got out of the way, he must see what could be done about Barclay. Instinctively he glanced at the pointed roof of the oast-house showing above the trees, just at the head of his drive.

Barclay! A foul fellow! That family were all a perfect nuisance. He'd been unlucky there, a pity he'd not found that out sooner—a fellow like that, wasting his time trying to paint! Charles despised artists and meant to stick to his contempt, though he knew it was more up-to-date nowadays to treat them as superior beings. But he'd no use for them. And Barclay was the more to be disliked for sticking to that piece of land. Only did it out of spite. Charles had offered him far more than the place was worth, he only kept it to be an annoyance. Well, Charles would get even with him! Running after Pamela was he! That could be used against him, no doubt!

At this stage he caught sight of Wadham crossing the fields towards him. Clearly he was wanted and he halted till the other should come up to him.

Fairly soon a perceptibly dreary procession of two returned to the house from the meadows. Charles slumped along in front, grumpiness once more proclaimed in every line of his body. Wadham followed behind, his cheeks slightly flushed, flicking nervously with a long switch at the shrubs and tall hollyhocks as the pair passed through the garden. They disappeared into the study.

The car came round and departed with Mrs. Mitcham and Prue. Faint screams and shouts came drifting up at intervals from the party below on the tennis court, and time passed on.

Chapter V

SCENE WITH A SECRETARY

I n the study the two men sat facing each other across the writing-table.

Charles looked most grim, his face set in hard lines. Wadham showed some agitation, he wiped his forehead uneasily, he turned away from his employer's sardonic gaze.

"Now, Wadham, don't be so scrupulous! You've got something to tell me. Out with it."

Wadham decided to plunge. "Well, sir, I've followed out your instructions. I've been on the look-out for Mr. Barclay, and I've got to tell you he was here last night."

Charles said nothing, and forced to go on, Wadham continued nervously.

"I went out for a stroll last night, lateish, it was so hot. As I went up across the fields I saw Barclay climbing over the fence at the top. I stopped to see where he went. I was under the trees and he didn't see me, but he was in the full moonlight and it was as bright as day. I could see him quite distinctly. I saw him come across and go into the garage yard."

Charles nodded. "Yes. I know someone was there last night. Who was he meeting?"

He shot this out sharply, but Freddy evaded his gaze.

"That I don't know. It was a woman, I just saw someone in a light frock; but I stayed where I was, and I was too far off to see the face."

"Now look here, Wadham. Don't be so mealy-mouthed. You're my employee—and with the record you and I know of, you can't afford to be too particular!" Charles spoke with a savage sneering tone that brought the blood to Wadham's face.

"You've got to get this information for me. Are you *sure* it was Barclay you saw, not Sylvester?"

A short pause. Then Wadham answered hesitatingly and he still avoided looking Charles in the face: "I was pretty sure it was Barclay—coming out of his own house; it looked his build and walk. I didn't actually see his face, but I thought at the time it was Barclay."

"That's not good enough," interrupted Charles harshly. "You know he's as thick as thieves with his cousin. Sylvester dines there three nights out of four. They're the same height, and they're very alike. Can't you be more definite, man? Which of them was it?"

Wadham shook his head. "I can't be positive. I can only tell you that at the time I thought it was Barclay." He was now thoroughly agitated and nervous. Quite obviously he didn't want to commit himself to the statement that it was Sylvester he'd seen. Whether truthfully or not he wanted to convey the idea it had been the other man.

"Well!" said Charles, trying to curb his annoyance, "that's not much use to me! What I want is something sounder to go on. What have you done about that gun? Did you tell Sylvester that gun was bought for him to use in his capacity as my estate agent? Now he's no longer employed by me, he must hand it back, just as he'll hand over the papers and vacate his agent's house."

"I spoke to Sylvester about it. He said of course it had been a birthday present from Mrs. Courtley to him. He says he won't give it back. He says it's a personal thing, and nothing to do with his official job as agent."

Charles reached out his hand and opened a drawer. He took a paper out of it, and handed it across the desk to Wadham.

"Take that and show it to Sylvester. A receipted bill from Hilman, made out to me, in my name, showing that the gun was debited to me. And here"—he took out a long yellow envelope and rapidly flipped through a wad of cancelled cheques returned from a bank—"here's the cheque itself which Sylvester will see was written out by you, signed by me, payable to Hilman for the exact amount. Perhaps that will convince him the gun was bought and paid for by *me*."

Wadham took the bill and the cheque. "Yes," he said quietly, "I think, sir, he'll hand the gun over when he sees this. He told me Mrs. Courtley had ordered the gun herself, when he was with her, and of course he'd concluded she paid for it."

Charles laughed. "Doesn't the fool know my wife orders things but I pay for them? She's not a bean of her own! I imagined he knew that well enough."

Wadham kept silent. He knew the underlying inference, that had Anne possessed any money of her own, she and Sylvester would before this have gone away together.

The mention of money clearly roused a new train of thought in his employer's mind.

"Now then, Wadham. See this fellow over the gun, and get it back. I've no intention of letting him keep it. And while you're about it, tell him I want my wife's letters back too."

Wadham looked up quickly, obviously taken aback by this totally unexpected order.

"Yes," went on Charles, "don't look so gaping! You know—and I know—and everybody knows, that my wife has written often enough to Sylvester, and I don't choose that he should keep letters of hers!"

"But, sir," stammered Wadham. "Mrs. Courtley... I mean," he stuttered, "it's for her to ask for any letters, isn't it?"

"Don't be a fool! I tell you, I'm asking for them, and I mean to get them. Wasn't I always seeing papers and notes in the hall here addressed to him? He was utterly moonstruck over her, and I'll be bound he's sentimental enough to keep everything she wrote! Sylvester's got to hand over any he's got. Make that clear to him, and if he shows signs of jibbing, just make him realize that I'm his last employer, and without a reference from me he's no chance of another job!"

Charles spoke triumphantly, for here he knew he had a sharp weapon. Jobs were difficult enough to come by, owing to universal depression, and without a reference any man's chance of a livelihood was poor in the extreme.

Wadham sat still, with his dark eyes studying the surface of the table. He tapped out a tune on it with his fingers, heedless for once of Charles's presence. Then, emerging suddenly from his preoccupation, he looked up, his decision made. "Very well, sir. I'll do my best about it." He had grown rather paler but he spoke with calmness and determination, as though, once resolved to tackle a disagreeable job, he was confident he could carry it through.

"Right. See the fellow to-day—now, there's another matter. I want you to go down to the police station and tell the sergeant from me I'm going to stop the people from coming into Fosse Wood. There's no right of way, and I'm closing the forest paths. I'm going to put up boards, and I'll prosecute everyone found there.

"And go down to Smithson, and tell him if he finds people around there and doesn't turn them off, he can look for another job too. I'm selling some of that timber, as you know, and I may replant. If I do, I'll have no one in my woods. People are too damned careless, they set the place alight with their cigarette ends and matches, and if I've gone to the expense of young plantations on a big scale, I'm not going to have my money wasted by a pack of careless fools."

Wadham looked thoughtfully at his employer. He knew, and Charles knew, that this question of the woods was a very sore one. The beautiful forest was a source of pride to the whole of that district, where trees were comparatively scarce. These woods, planted many years before, were a glory to the countryside. Charles's decision to cut down and sell some of the grand trees had roused great ill-feeling. If in addition the right of the public to use the forest paths was curtailed, there was bound to be trouble and great ill-will.

He tried to be diplomatic.

"But, Mr. Courtley, there'll be trouble over this. Oughtn't we to consult your solicitors first? We want to be sure of the legal position. People always resent the closing of country paths..."

"And I resent their using my private paths, and I intend to stop it. Of course I've discussed the matter with Lawson's and they advise me I'm within my rights. So get on with that. That'll do." He turned abruptly away to show that he considered the subject closed. He picked up some papers, but as Wadham prepared to leave the room, called him back. "And remember, Wadham. You'll find it worth your while," he stressed the words meaningly, "to get me those letters—and to pass on to me any information you think I'll care to have." He spoke with emphasis, and Wadham, colouring slightly, nodded his comprehension. He went out, his face altering as the door closed behind him. He let his real feelings show now—anger and sullen indignation.

Coming away from the study, he crossed the hall towards his own little office at the back, when he saw Anne coming down the staircase. He waited for her, and in a low voice asked:

"Mrs. Courtley, could you come to my office for a moment? There's something I want to talk to you about."

Anne looked at him attentively, then, without speaking, followed him. Once in the little room, looking out on the back, Wadham came to the point at once.

"Mrs. Courtley, something very disagreeable has happened. I think it may be better if I tell you about it."

Anne glanced at him, and then quickly looked away. The hot colour came into her face. She realized at once that her husband had given Wadham some piece of work to do which involved annoyance and humiliation for herself.

"Do please believe me," went on Wadham, with an earnest, friendly tone. "This is a hateful thing for me, and I do honestly want to try to prevent it from being too unpleasant for you." He paused.

"Well," said Anne, with a faint smile touching the corners of her lips, "be brave, get it over. Tell me what's gone wrong now." She spoke calmly, for both of them knew quite well how much she had endured in past scenes. There was nothing to surprise either of them in any behaviour on Charles's part now. Wadham shifted the paper in his hand uneasily. "Well, it's like this. You remember the trouble we've had over the guns?"

Anne nodded, her face hardening.

"And you'll remember Mr. Sylvester had no piece suitable for the duck-shooting?"

"Yes, of course," said Anne shortly, "and I ordered one for him. I did that myself a couple of months ago."

Wadham looked still more confused. "Yes, yes, of course. But, unluckily, Mr. Courtley considered that the gun was intended to be *his* property. I mean, it was only to be used by Mr. Sylvester as agent, it was in fact lent to him, as it were."

"Nonsense!" said Anne sharply. "I ordered that gun myself in my own name, not Mr. Courtley's. It was meant to be a personal present for Mr. Sylvester—a birthday present—he's a first-rate shot, which no one else is here. Mr. Courtley doesn't shoot, as you know, and—well, anyhow, this is a matter of a present made by me, it's nothing to do with the estate."

"That's just it, Mrs. Courtley." Wadham brought all his conciliatory tones into play. "It's very unfortunate, but the account for the gun was sent in to Mr. Courtley, not to yourself—and he paid it—so that he can now claim the gun was, and is, his property."

Anne grew pale with humiliation and anger. So that was how Charles had got to know! How imbecile the gunmakers had been! She was sure she had told the man to send the bill in to her. However—what was done couldn't be helped now. She looked at Wadham.

"Well, if that's so, I suppose Mr. Sylvester will return the gun. I'll send him a note."

A strange look crept into Wadham's eyes. "That would put things right, Mrs. Courtley. If you like"—he caught her eyes, fixed on his, and glanced quickly out of the window—"I'll go over myself and see him. I've some other messages for him from Mr. Courtley that I've to deliver at once, and I can give him your note." He added with bitterness: "You know, I'm not able to do what I want always, I've got my job to think of, and I simply can't afford to quarrel with it."

Anne moved a little nearer towards him. "I understand that. None of us can do quite what we'd like." She paused, and then letting a faint warmth tinge her voice: "Thank you very much, Mr. Wadham. I'm sure you mean to be kind. I'll write that note now if you'll wait." The two looked at each other. Both knew quite well the situation which her words implied. They each belonged to the brotherhood of those who, having no money, are bound by their limitations to give in to those who have. Each in their hearts knew that it was their own qualities, or lack of courage perhaps, which prevented them from claiming independence. Wadham and Anne alike could not face being thrown on the world on their own resources. They knew that Courtley held them by the power his money conferred. They knew that they both resented their position. Each was resolved to act in their own individual interests, but they recognized too that their interests need not conflict. Anne, the subtler of the two, perceived that Wadham's approach held some special significance. Some "tide in the affairs of men" had been set in motion. Well, she would do her best to see that it "bore her on to fortune."

She went out of the room, and into the drawing-room, deep in thought. She sat down at her writing-table, and for a moment rested her head on her hands. She sat and stared unseeingly at the wide landscape, now shimmering in the heat.

She realized that Charles was acting intentionally. He meant to humiliate her, and Sylvester too. With a swift movement she opened her blotter, took a sheet of notepaper from the stand before her, and began to write.

When she had done, she sealed the envelope with wax, took it back to Wadham's office. She found him there, clearly waiting for her return.

"Here's the note," she said briefly, holding it out. He took it, slipped it into his pocket, and caught up a small file of papers from the table. These he stuffed into a leather brief-case. "I'm going now," he said quickly, as if to reassure her there was no possibility of Charles getting hold of that letter, and stepping out of the French window on to the grass he walked rapidly across the side-lawn. She stood and watched him as he crossed the drive and vanished up the lane. Then she too stepped out of the window and walked down towards the garden below.

The hot morning wore on, and at length lunch-time came.

Once more the cool dining-room filled, but this time no place was laid for Charles. He rather enjoyed being erratic over his meals, liked to pose as though food were a matter of indifference to him, though actually he exacted a very high standard in cookery. To-day, however, he was apparently leading the simple life, for he sent word to say he was not coming to lunch, he merely wished for 'bread and cheese and beer' to be sent in to him. He was 'too busy,' it was to be inferred, to waste time on a lengthier meal.

So a relieved family, glad of further respite from his company, enjoyed a noisy merry meal. Pamela was still in the best of spirits. The tennis had gone well. She and Dick had shown themselves in good form. She laughed and joked and teased her grandmother.

After lunch the whole party strolled out on to the lawn. They sat down in the shade of the big elm that stood at the end of the old black barn. The lovely afternoon must not be wasted. Anne made a few tentative suggestions, for she knew Pamela's abounding energy. She hoped no one would think of using the bathing-pool, for Charles's study faced that way and she dreaded a repetition of Prue's ordeals.

Apparently the others felt the same, for though it was an ideal afternoon for the water, yet no one even mooted the idea, until suddenly Pamela said, "I tell you what we'll do. Let's take the little car and go over to the sea and have a bathe. The water will be glorious to-day. Daddy's been shut up in the study all morning instead of pottering on his beloved farm. He'll emerge simply spoiling for a row. We'll all hop off and keep out of his way. Don't you think that's a good scheme, Mummy?"

"Yes," said Anne, "for you certainly. But I won't come with you. I've lots of odd jobs I'd like to get done. Granny would like it I expect, wouldn't you?" and she turned to her mother.

Mrs. Mitcham nodded. She partly guessed Anne wanted to be alone, but her love of the sea was notorious, and she answered quite sincerely, "Yes, I'd love to come. I always like to get an hour or so on the beach, you know."

Anne had been considering something and now she turned to Pamela. "I think you might just go into the office and ask Mr. Wadham if he would like to come with you. He's been hard at it with Daddy all the morning, and he's so keen on proper bathing, I expect he'd welcome the chance of a good swim."

"Oh, Lord! We don't want that blighter," interposed Dick. "After all, it's his job to work, he's paid for it—let him get on with it! He'll only be a pest to us with his beastly superior ways and his marvellous skill as a swimmer!"

Anne glanced at him with annoyance, but merely repeated to her daughter: "I think you ought to ask him. Just go in, Pam, and see if he's free now. He's not with your father, I heard his typewriter going as we came out. It's so hot too," she continued, "he must be grilling in that little room. I dare say he can make up his work later on when it's cooler."

Pamela laughed with some surprise, for she knew that whereas Dick openly disliked the worldly-wise and sometimes patronizing Wadham, her mother, she half suspected, had no greater fondness for the tactful and efficient secretary, and she saw no need for this solicitude.

"Oh, why all this bother about dear Freddy, Mum? We don't really want him, you know."

Anne only reiterated her request. "Just ask him if he'd like to go with you, he didn't seem himself at breakfast and I think you ought to give him the chance of a bathe."

Pam, ready to oblige, got up, strolled round the side of the house and poked her head in at the open casement window of the little study. She returned to the group on the lawn. "Not there," she reported, "and everything all tidied up and put away. Marvellously neat man, our Freddy! But no sign of him there. I expect he felt it a bit hot too, and has gone out himself."

Her mother hesitated. "Well, you know, Pam, I always worry a little over Prue and the sea. She's so nervous, and if you and Dick go swimming off she might get into difficulties. There are always such currents in the bay."

Pam glanced at her mother and then said lightly: "Well, I tell you what we'll do. We'll hop in to Mr. Barclay's as we pass and see if he'll come. He often likes a bathe, you know." Seeing doubt in Anne's face she added impatiently: "Oh, don't be so tiresome, Mum! Daddy won't know!" and for Dick's enlightenment she added, turning to him: "Barclay's the man who lives in the oast-house. He and Daddy are always having terrific rows, but Mum and I like him."

While she spoke, Anne made up her mind. "Well, I don't much like you asking him, still I'd rather that than have Prue with no one responsible about, so go off and ask him and I'll be answerable to your father."

She did not look at the girl, for both of them knew perfectly well how furious Charles would be at this invitation.

Mrs. Mitcham opened her mouth to speak, then decided against it. After all, Charles was not likely to know, and his temper had habituated his family to deceitful ways.

Pamela had waited impatiently for her mother's consent. Now she scrambled lightly to her feet.

"Splendid! On your head be it!"

She flew up the drive and vanished round the clump of trees by the gate. There was a sleepy silence. The others all waited lazily for her return. In a few moments she came back, but the spring had vanished from her step. She walked slowly down to them.

"No good," she said briefly. "He says he can't come. He must go and finish some wretched picture or other. Says the light's just right."

Evidently she was disappointed, for all the brightness and gaiety had gone out of her face.

"Well," said Mrs. Mitcham cheerfully, "if that's so, of course he can't come. His paintings matter more than your bathe. Anne, don't worry, I'll be there, and I'll keep a good look out and I'll see the other two don't go swimming out while Prue's in the water."

"Thank you, Mother," said Anne. "It'll be all right really I expect, so be off, all of you!" She rose to her feet and went with the two girls towards the house.

Within a short time Dick reappeared ready before the two girls, his bathing-kit over his arm. He busied himself opening the doors of the great barn and bringing out the Rover used for these occasions.

Presently Mrs. Mitcham came from the house and then Pamela and Prudence. They all packed themselves in and waved gaily to Anne who had come to the door to see them off. Dick, who was driving, started the car. It roared up the short drive and turned off to the left in the direction of the road leading to the coast.

Peace settled down on the house and garden once more.

Chapter VI

LAST APPEARANCE OF CHARLES

The bathing party had set off for the sea-shore just before three o'clock. Shortly after the hour Smithson the gamekeeper came out of the side door, and very red in the face and stiff in his bearing, turned across the drive towards the barn.

The cook and parlourmaid, standing together by the back door, noticed him striding along.

"He's been catching it!" remarked the cook.

"Yes, he has," reflected Nelly. "I heard Mr. Courtley shouting away at him. I don't know how he stands it, I'm sure."

"Ah, well, he knows which side his bread's buttered. He's a married man with children—he wouldn't want to find a new job at his age, there aren't many for his sort to be got in this neighbourhood nowadays, you know."

"No," said Nelly reflectively. "Odd, isn't it, to think how things change. Here are you and me able to pick and choose and go where we want—and neither of us in the least intending to stay stuck down in the country. Yet here are all these men, got to hang on to their jobs for dear life—and all of them, as far as I can see, as keen as mustard on staying in this dead-and-alive hole."

"Well," responded Cook, "that's one way country people are different from Londoners. They like their own neighbourhood and their own people round them, they don't like the idea of shifting to a new part. It isn't as if men like Smithson could get a job in a town, you know! Gamekeepers and all them have to stick in the country and they don't like strange places and new ways."

"That's right! And it's not only the keepers," Nelly contributed. "Look at Mr. Sylvester and Mr. Barclay. How they can want to stay stuck away here I don't know. Yet Mr. Barclay won't budge from his old oast-house, no matter what Mr. Courtley offers him for it, and Mr. Sylvester—well, look what he's put up with in the past so's he could stay on here."

Cook smiled. "Well, he'd his own reason for *that*, you know, and anyhow he's got to go now. Got his notice all right."

"There you are! He's got the push from here, but has he gone off yet? Not he! After the awful row he and Mr. Courtley had, you'd have thought he'd have taken the next train and gone somewhere else. But there he is, still hanging about when you'd think the last thing he'd want to see would be Mr. Courtley walking around owning the place, and he himself sent off to find a new job."

"Yes, I can't understand *that*," said Cook. "I must say, if I'd had to sell up my place I'd have gone right away and not stay to see others in what had been mine—much less worked under them; but it's what I tell you, country people don't feel happy out of their own place. And after all, he'll not be here long. He's only staying, I expect, to work out his notice so to speak and until he's heard of something else, and he's got his cousin to be with and they're as thick as thieves together."

Nelly nodded. "Yes, that's right, they do stick together, those two. Real friends they are—and I'm not surprised. They're a fine pair, you know, and both of them as good-looking as they're made, don't you think?"

"Yes, I do," responded Cook heartily, "that's the style I admire. Real English, like they have about here, though actually I think Mr. Barclay's the one for me—he's got 'something other people haven't got' all right!"

Nelly laughed, and hearing the clink of footsteps on stone, glanced round. "Talk of the devil! Here's the gentleman himself!"

Someone had turned in at the gate and had paused for a moment to exchange greetings with the gamekeeper, who at that moment had emerged from the barn and walked up the drive. The two tall men stood together for a moment.

"Good afternoon, Smithson," said the newcomer. "Mr. Courtley at home do you happen to know?"

"Yes, sir. He's in his study. I've just come from him!"

The man's curt, abrupt manner was noticeable. His companion glanced at him curiously. Then, perceiving that something disagreeable was afoot he smiled to himself, gave his shoulders a little impatient twist, and with a brief nod to the gamekeeper came on down to the front door. The two maids vanished as he approached.

He was indeed what they had summarized as 'real English.' In this man the Saxon stock seemed to survive in all its primitive force and beauty. He had the corn-coloured hair, and bright fierce blue eyes which bring to mind vague thoughts of Viking forebears. His whole body radiated strength and vitality. Yet he was no rustic, there was intelligence and sensitiveness both in his face and in his whole poise. It was possible to suspect that this man had gifts out of the ordinary run of country squires, and easy to see that he had force and energy enough to belie any theory of an anæmic decaying family. He had in one way full measure of what the French call 'beauté rustique,' but shot through with a fire and resolution not so common in country dwellers. Were he to be stood side by side with Charles Courtley a strange comparison could be made—the one emphatically the town dweller, the financier, the intellectual Viking perhaps of modern days; the other, an older race, as tenacious and as resolute, but beaten down by the modern weapon of money. Incapable perhaps of winning any victory in the struggle for material prosperity, but still able to hold its own in another sphere.

The gamekeeper—child, too, of this same country-side—perhaps had a glimmering of this contrast, and this contest. He stood looking back at the tall, golden-haired man walking firmly in the sunshine up to the old grey house. His own bitterness against the upstart townsman welled up. "Ah," his thoughts ran, "he'll stand up to that bullying foreigner! He'll give as good as he gets. Mr. Courtley'll get more than he bargains for from him! And he's not under his thumb, thanks be. He can snap his fingers at the fellow!"

With a sardonic grin he glanced at the oast-house, whose tall spiked hood glimmered through the trees, its red bricks flaming in the westerning sun. He chuckled to himself. "Rare angry Courtley'll be every time he looks at that there oast-house! And glad on it I am! Right glad I am!" Quite heartened up by these reflections he strode away.

As Barclay approached the front door his firm foot-steps sounded clearly on the gravel. Anne was seated at her writing-table in the drawing-room window, and at the sound of those steps she glanced up. She looked startled and then apprehensive. Charles would not welcome a visit from anyone with whom he was on bad terms, and the quarrel between him and Barclay was notorious.

She hesitated, looked over her shoulder, and then rising hurriedly, walked quickly to the window. Before the man outside had time to reach up and ring the doorbell, she opened the casement and leaned out.

"Why are you here?" she said softly but hurriedly. "Charles won't see you, you know."

"Apparently he will," came the response, and feeling in his pocket the man produced and waved a note. "He's written to ask me to come in and see him 'on an important matter.'"

The two looked at each other in silence for a moment.

"Pam, I expect," said Anne. "I know he's furious with her over seeing you—and he's been working up to something since yesterday."

The man's face hardened. "Well, I'm quite ready to deal with him—and the sooner the better. You know I'm perfectly ready to have everything out with him."

"Yes, yes," said Anne quickly, "but not now, not to-day. Do go back. Don't come in this afternoon."

The urgency of her tone was not lost on the man. He paused and in his turn looked round. At that moment a burst of laughter came from the maids' corner of the garden and at the sound he frowned slightly.

"No good discussing anything now," he said, "and it's no good putting things off. If he wants to see me I'm quite ready."

He looked straight at Anne with a glint in his bright blue eyes, and then with determination, disregarding her faint gesture of protest, put out his hand and pressed the button of the bell beside the door.

As the sound shrilled through the house, Anne sank back in her chair. She heard someone cross the hall and open the door, she heard Barclay's steps sounding firm and loud on the polished boards, she heard the study door close behind the visitor. Then, shaking whatever doubtful thoughts she had out of her mind, she bent over her desk and tried once more to occupy herself with her letters and accounts.

For a time she wrote busily, straining to keep her attention on what she was doing. Every few minutes she glanced at the clock uneasily. Charles's study lay across the hall, but on this still afternoon sounds carried far, and she could not altogether keep herself from wondering what was passing between the two men. When the sound of their voices came to her every now and then she could not refrain from listening, try as she would to fix her attention on her own letters.

The bursts of speech seemed to grow louder. As her husband's angry tones rose, she bit her lips and paused to listen. Suddenly there came the sound of a crash, and immediately the door of the study flew open.

"Clear out! Clear out of this! And keep away from my house in future! Understand, I forbid my family to have anything further to do with you!" Charles's furious voice echoed across the hall.

For a second Anne hesitated, uncertain whether her presence would act as a restraint or as a spur, but swift steps outside told her that Barclay was not waiting to provoke his host to further outburst. She turned to the door as if to intercept him, but she was too late. Even as she rose to her feet his shadow moved quickly past the window. She ran to look after him and saw him hurrying away up the drive. She stood still, hesitating. Then, making up her mind, went after him. As she stepped across the drive she heard the telephone in the study begin to ring. It seemed to ring loudly in the quiet air. On and on it went, until its continuing whirr maddened her overwrought nerves. Why did Charles not answer it? For she knew by the sound that it was his study telephone ringing and surely he was still in the room. She took a few steps backward, thinking she must send someone to answer it, for Charles's calls were usually of importance and must not be left. At that very moment the sound stopped and she heard a man's voice. She listened a moment, then, eager to seize the chance of getting away unseen, and realizing that whoever was on the telephone would now be occupied, she stepped on to the grass that edged the drive and silently and swiftly went up the lane.

The clock in the empty drawing-room chimed four.

Chapter VII

THE SHOT IN THE WOOD

T he day wore on, hot, peaceful and sleepy. As the sun crept round, in the late afternoon, the maids left the hot kitchen, and went to sit idly in the shady patch of garden to the left of the house, which was specially kept for them. The sound of the gate banging loudly against its post, caught their attention. One of them glanced up.

"Mr. Courtley. Wonder where he's off to?" she said idly.

The cook looked up from the crossword in which she was absorbed. For a moment she contemplated the figure now passing out of their view.

"What a sight he looks in those clothes! Can't think how he can like to go out of the grounds in them! Bad enough on his own premises, I think!"

"Yes, and to-day there'll be a lot of people about. It's this Show over at Horsley you know, and there'll be a lot of people on the way there," said the other. "Oh! well, I expect most people round here know well enough what he's like!"

They could see Charles quite clearly, the bright rays of the late sun were striking full on him, as he walked with head slightly bent up the road. A strange shabby figure he looked, to be the master of the well-kept building, the immaculate drive, the glowing flower-beds which he had just left behind. He had put on an old tweed jacket, and he still wore his faded khaki shorts, his old panama hat, and his grubby white sand-shoes.

The cook shrugged her shoulders and turned to bend once more over her newspaper. "Does it partly to annoy the family, I think. Made of money, but'll only part with it as *he* thinks fit!"

And they ceased to trouble themselves further about their employer, quite unconscious that they had seen their last of him as a living man.

He plodded steadily along. Past the hedge which ended his garden, past Barclay's house, along up the hill where the great ricks caught the full blaze and glare of the yellow sun.

He met a few groups of people, villagers making their way cheerfully towards the fair, which according to ancient custom was visiting the little country town a couple of miles away. He paid no attention to them, never raised his head to nod, and made no response when one of his own men bicycling quickly home after his work saluted him politely as he flew past.

At length he turned off the road into a little lane which led through the shade of a copse out on to a piece of rough ground bordering larger woods beyond. The woods stood silent and dark on the far side of the little stretch of moorland.

Here for the last time he was seen. A little girl from the village, loitering about while she waited for some of her companions to set out with her for the fair, saw him pass close by as he entered the open stretch. She was a timid little girl and she knew his bad temper. So she scurried to the side of the path and pressed herself into the tall bracken as he passed. She need not have troubled for he never noticed her small figure shrinking away from him. Later she described what she had noticed.

"He didn't seem to see me at all. He was looking on the ground and muttering to himself. I was frightened of him. He looked so angry."

She noticed that he carried in his hand a 'sort of switch' or small walking stick, as she thought. She noticed him cross the rough patch, striking at the tall bracken as he parted its stems. The bracken closed behind him, swaying its golden fronds in the glowing mellow blaze of the autumn sun. He went on from the bright sunny patch into the cool shade of the trees.

The child watched him go and then ran off on her own way. Stillness settled down in the solitary little glade. The bees hummed busily in the purple heather, a bird twittered softly. Suddenly a heavy explosion shattered that peace, a loud crash of sound which rolled and muttered in the still hot air. Then its echoes died slowly away. It was the sound of a gun.

Away over at Carron the members of the family began to drift together in preparation for dinner. The bathing party had come back, tired but content. Mrs. Mitcham reported that all had gone well, Prue had enjoyed her bathe, and she herself had had a delightful afternoon.

Anne listened to her rather absently, and her mother noticed her silence. "Are you tired, dear?" she asked, sorry that Anne had not been with them to share the refreshment of beach and sea.

"I've rather a headache," she answered. "It's been very hot to-day."

"Yes," said her mother, glancing out at the tall elms, quite motionless, not a leaf stirring, "and it's airless here—we got the breeze down on the beach."

It was past the dinner hour, and Pamela coming in declared herself 'starving, absolutely starving' after her expedition. "So's Dick," she exclaimed, as that young man came hurrying down. "It's only dire need for food that makes *him* so punctual! Why doesn't the gong go?"

But Anne, silent and preoccupied, did not seem to concern herself with the passing time.

There was a pause while they waited for the rest of the party. As they sat for a moment, silent, Mrs. Mitcham glanced round. Really, thought her grandmother looking at the girl, Pamela was growing extraordinarily attractive. To-night she was full of gaiety and sparkle. Usually, unless made up, she was a little too pale, but to-night she had a bright natural colour. She had put on a thin filmy frock of midnight blue, which brought out her fairness. Her dark eyes were sparkling and her pale golden hair glimmered and shone and caught the light as she turned her head. She would have attracted attention anywhere, so unusual was her colouring and so brilliant the charm of her smiling face. She flung herself down on the sofa and curled her feet up under her, flinging her bright head back against the cushions.

"Oh, I'm tired," she exclaimed, "beautifully tired! We had a simply glorious bathe, Mum."

"Were you late back?" inquired Anne, leaning back and speaking rather mechanically.

"Oh, no! Dick drove magnificently, he came home like the wind! We were back quite early—I've been down to the village since."

"Whatever for? Wasn't that unnecessary?"

"Oh, I felt full of energy and I was out of cigarettes—had to get some more! But Mum, why don't we have dinner? It's long past eight, and I really cannot bear this awful internal void much longer."

"Neither your father nor Freddy are down yet," replied Anne; "we must give them a moment or two longer. Charles doesn't like us to go in without him, you know."

Pamela groaned loudly, but at that moment Freddy Wadham hurried in.

Pamela attacked him at once. "Where on earth is Daddy? We're all simply starving. Why on earth is he so late? Whatever have you both been up to?"

The secretary glanced at Anne. "I'm so sorry, Mrs. Courtley. I didn't know the time. I don't know where Mr. Courtley is. I've not seen him for some time. He told me he was going out and I've not been with him all the afternoon."

"Oh," broke in Pamela. "Then he must have gone out for a walk. Mummy, need we wait any longer? It really is awfully late now. Poor old Gran will pass out if she doesn't get some food soon!"

Anne roused herself. "Yes, he really is very late." She looked across at her mother, and noticing the pallor and grey fatigue marked in her face, made up her mind and briskly added: "Prue, just run up to his room and ask him if he's nearly ready."

Most reluctantly Prue obeyed, to return with the news that Charles was not in his room. "And his things are all laid out so he's not dressed or even come in," the child added.

Anne looked slightly worried, then: "Well, if he's not in yet, he'll be so late we really won't wait." She exchanged looks with her mother. Both knew she was risking a storm later, but Anne strengthened her determination by the conviction that Mrs. Mitcham was thoroughly over-tired.

They went into the other room, they dined, they moved back to the drawing-room. No Charles. Anne, wondering as to whether dinner should be kept or not, said aloud: "He may have gone down to the estate office. He's got a lot on hand over the forest just now. I'll ring up and see if he's been kept there."

She went across to the telephone and dialled a number. The others listened, vaguely uneasy.

"Peter, is Charles there? No? You've not seen him? Oh, no, it's nothing really, only he's not come in to dinner and I wondered if he'd come to the office and stayed on with you? No, I expect he's gone off somewhere and will turn up later."

She put down the receiver and turned to the others. "It's no good bothering, Charles always suits himself. He's probably gone in to dine somewhere and just not troubled to ring up. Get out the bridge-table, Freddy, and we'll have a game."

As Freddy moved across the room to fetch the folding table from where it stood beneath the window, the curtain shifted slightly with a sudden breeze. Into the silent room came a faint sound, the patter of raindrops on glass.

"Rain," said Freddy, and pushed back the curtain as he stooped for the table. "Well, I didn't think that was coming." He let fall the curtain and the party settled down to their game to the accompaniment of that soft hurried pattering on the window-panes.

At breakfast next morning Pamela's first inquiry as she came into the room was: "Well, where was Daddy last night?"

Anne answered shortly, "I don't know, I've not been to his room this morning."

No one made any comment, for quarrels between the heads of the household were too common to excite or invite much interest.

The telephone rang.

"Just see what that is, Prue," said Anne, busy opening her letters.

"Mrs. Courtley? You must speak to her? Who is it, please? Sergeant Groves? Oh, all right."

Almost before she could turn to her mother Anne was beside her, taking the instrument. "This is Mrs. Courtley. Sergeant Groves? Yes. An accident? A bad one? Oh!" A pause which seemed long, while the reverberations of a strong male voice echoed from the telephone to the listeners struck into stillness at the breakfast table. "Very well, I'll come down at once."

Pale under her make-up, Anne turned and faced them. She spoke abruptly, making no effort to soften the news. "There's been an accident—Charles is dead. They want me to go along at once."

Absolute silence greeted this. The two girls gazed appalled at their mother. They had not expected any such news and their first reaction was of horror and shock. Anne herself stood for a moment with her eyes fixed on the ground. Then, with a scarcely apparent shudder which ran across her shoulders, she straightened herself and looked directly across to Freddy Wadham. Her brown eyes seemed to flash slightly as they met his clear, rather sardonic dark ones.

"Freddy, will you come with me, please? The police want to see me. They say I must go, but they think too——" she hesitated, then went on with a hard note creeping into her voice "they think if possible someone else should identify the body."

Chapter VIII

POLICE ON THE SCENE

I n this way, Charles's death burst upon his household, and naturally enough they took it as an event, awful in itself, but one concerning only their own circle.

They could not foresee that this death was to become famous, that every detail of their lives, every detail of the days they had just lived through, was to be studied over the length and breadth of the land. The whole relationship of the individuals who had been in daily contact with Charles was to be endlessly canvassed and discussed by thousands of whom they had never heard.

Moreover, this death was to involve not only the inhabitants of Carron itself, but the whole countryside.

For, as was soon to be remarked, part of its interest arose from the fact that the catastrophe brought into play these two contrasting forces, the interests of the dwellers in the country, and those of the people who drew their wealth from the great towns.

Charles's life and death illustrated all the problems which that contrast involved. He had come, a townsman, with his city-made wealth, and had tried to settle himself down in one of the most conservative and exclusive societies possible, that of a remote countryside. His ways were not the ways of the local people, and he had antagonized all sections. Yet he had been brought into constant contact with them.

He had, in a way which was typical, taken an old rural building which in itself represented the life of the agricultural eastern counties, and had transformed it into a rich man's home, but he could not remove it from its rural surroundings.

The men who worked on the estate were all local countrymen, the maids came from the surrounding villages. English local government managed the affairs of the district through local men, and in accordance with the customs and ways of the countryside.

But just as Charles had come in his lifetime, with his town-bred family and London ways, to strike a different note, so now his death was to emphasize this alien element. For he had not died by accident, but by murder, and a murder which was to become so celebrated that local men and methods were replaced by the higher authority of London itself. Actually, the whole drama which was now to unfold centred round that very theme, the age-long opposition between town- and country-dweller. The stubborn loyalty of the rural community to its own circle was to confront the quick wits of the city-bred. The mystery of Charles's murder hinged on that antagonism, and so did its solution.

Away in the woods where the early sun was making the wet grass sparkle after the showers of the night, and where the wood-pigeons cooed and murmured peacefully, the village policeman stood uncomfortably on guard beside a sprawled body.

Very early that morning the keeper, passing along from his home to his work, had found a body pitched on its face on the path. He had gone straight to the cottage where Adams, the local policeman, lived. Adams had rung up his headquarters, and before the family at Carron Cross had begun to appear downstairs, the police were on their way to the wood.

In the black two-seater car which tore and hustled along the country lanes, beside the local superintendent sat a man from Scotland Yard, whom chance had apparently sent to the spot. Naturally, he had not been 'called in' as yet—though secretly the superintendent meant that he should be, if the authorities could be induced to take that action. He was actually staying in the locality in connection with something quite different, and he had been by mere chance talking in the local police station at Marple when Adams's call, reporting the finding of the body, had come through. Hurriedly invited by the superintendent to come along, he had jumped at the opportunity. It was always a good thing to be first on the spot at the investigation of a murder, and his interest had been aroused at the sound of Charles Courtley's name. Living in London, he was familiar with Charles's reputation as a financier and a successful figure in the world of big business. If this were murder, and not suicide, there would be a big sensation over his death.

So he sat in the little car, with the freshness of the early morning sparkling in the fields and hedges as they tore along, enjoying his drive, and really anticipating his experience, his dark blue eyes glancing from side to side. Simon Sturt was one of the new type of police. He had had the benefit of a modern training, and he had, as he considered, thoroughly studied the psychology of crime. Himself the son of a Chief Constable of a country district, he had from childhood been specially interested in that strange undertone of crime which sometimes shows itself flowing beneath the surface of the most peaceful-looking rural life.

When his education was completed, and the time came to choose a profession, he had unhesitatingly decided to enter the police force. He had done brilliantly and was now one of the youngest Inspectors of the C.I.D.

Chance had now sent him down to this remote country place at the exact moment when his special bent, his training and his profession enabled him to appreciate all the possibilities of the case now to be unfolded.

For a murder case it obviously showed itself to be. Arrived at Fosse Wood, they made their way on foot to the clearing, and there Sergeant Groves met them. He had gone direct to the spot, and the briefest scrutiny had shown him two things. He repeated briskly: "Shot, and killed, and no sign of any gun or weapon near." That of course was conclusive.

So it came about that Simon Sturt knelt by the side of Charles Courtley's body, with the slanting rays of the bright morning sun sloping through the trees down on to that wet huddled heap. Groves had not moved the body, beyond raising it a little to see if any weapon lay beneath. He had then let it slump back where it lay before, crumpled on its face.

The night's rain had soaked the clothing, and the uninjured head showed Charles's thick thatch of grey hair, wet and draggled. His arms were flung one on either side, but there was nothing in their grasp. A short switch lay a little ahead on the path.

Sturt examined the body, without shifting it. Then, still kneeling beside it, he raised his head, and glanced up at Groves, who stood silently by, with a look of growing bewilderment on his face.

"Yes, Sergeant. Here's a problem for us all right."

He rose to his feet, and contemplated the prone figure. "Of course you were right. It's murder, without the shadow of a doubt, but a real problem as to how it's been done."

He beckoned to the constable, Adams, who had been the original person summoned to the spot.

"Of course this was how you found the body?" he said briefly.

"Yes, sir," responded Adams, who was looking very pale, and whose attention was really given to wondering if he could control himself enough, for the sight at his feet made him feel sick and queer.

Sturt turned to the sergeant. "Yes, it's a regular teaser, and we'll have to go slowly."

He looked carefully at their surroundings, studying every detail with thoughtful eyes.

The place where they stood was within one of the most beautiful parts of the forest. The great trees were beautifully spaced, and had grown to great size. The oaks spread their branches wide, their rough trunks were interspersed with the shorter gleaming boles of splendid beech trees. The undergrowth had been well cleared, and the sunlight poured in through the great trunks on to the leaf-covered ground.

About a hundred yards away was a little cross-roads, made by the intersection of two rough paths, which led through the tall ranks of the great trees. The paths looked as though they were quite well used.

Beyond the crossing could be seen a clearing, where a number of trees had been felled and stacked. Obviously wood-cutting had begun here, and it looked from the preparations as if more extensive operations were to be carried on.

Sturt glanced in that direction, and then turned to the keeper, Smithson, the man who had found the body, and who was standing silently in the background. He had been bidden to stay, as clearly his evidence would be needed as to the finding of the body.

"What's going on over there?"

The keeper came a pace forward. He spoke with a surly air. "Well, sir, Mr. Courtley had sold all the timber in this part of the forest. Fosse Wood they call it. The contractor had taken down a tree or two over yonder, and this whole section is to come down soon."

"Were the men at work yesterday, do you know?"

Smithson shook his head. "No, they were not, sir. Yesterday was the day of St. Giles's fair over in Marple. It's a local holiday, and the woodcutters knocked off early."

"You yourself weren't in this part?"

"No, sir, I wasn't."

Sturt nodded, rather absently, and returned to his scrutiny of the dead body.

"When did it begin to rain?" he asked next.

"About nine o'clock, sir," replied the keeper.

Sturt's brief investigation had shown him that the ground beneath the body was quite dry, so clearly death had taken place before the showers had set in.

Charles lay sprawled out on his face, right along the centre of the path. He had been shot, that was painfully obvious, but Simon's inspection had already shown him that he had been killed in a most unusual way. He had clearly been shot right between his legs, and the charge had gone upwards and spread through his body. How could a man have been shot in that position?

It was hardly possible he could have been standing erect. Yet no man in his senses would have laid down flat on his face on the path, even though it had been dry before the murder occurred, and remained prone while someone else fired between his legs. Yet it did not look as if he had been thrown down. Charles was a powerfully built man and full of vigour, but there were no signs of a struggle. There were no broken bushes nor crushed bracken near the spot, no trampled places on the damp moist surface. The edges of the path were distinct and unbroken. The rain had washed away any traces of footsteps, even Charles's own, though as he had worn only light sand-shoes he would not have left any deep impress. Simon had examined the head and had seen that it was perfectly intact, there was no sign on it whatever of any blow which might have felled the man to the ground or made him an unconscious and prostrate victim of the shot. Nor was there anything in the nature of a ditch or pit over which Charles might have stepped and been shot at by a man crouching below. Crazy as such a supposition seemed, it had at first flashed through Simon's startled mind as a possible solution of the position of such a wound, and he had instinctively glanced round to see if any such pit or hole were visible. There was none. The wood with its trees and underbrush stretched around them, but the ground itself, and the path, was perfectly level. Further, it was clear from the pools of blood around and beneath the body, partly sunk into the earth now, but clearly originally deep and extensive, that the damage done by the shot had been terrible, and the fact that there were no drops or traces along the path proved conclusively that the murder had been done on that spot. The body had not been brought from elsewhere, it had bled far too extensively for that to be possible without leaving traces, and of such traces there were none. It was positive that Charles had been shot exactly where he fell.

Again Simon looked at the surrounding track. The scrub and bushes did not come quite close up to the path at this point, and there were no trees near behind which any man could have taken cover. The place had been well looked after. To one side of the spot where the body lay there was a little dell, overgrown with turf, and mingled with the turf there were patches of bracken, and the heather there grew very deep. It was possible that someone could have lain hidden in the heather, but directly he sat up, he would have been clearly visible, and this of course applied so much the more to anyone armed with a gun. Charles simply could not have failed to see them.

He bent down to scrutinize the edges of the path again. No—in no single place were they trodden down, their edges were perfectly intact and not so much as one sprig of heather was broken. The long grass which grew by the side was only flattened by the rain, it showed no tracks of feet.

He turned back with a sigh to the body and then looking up at Groves pointed to the feet. One foot still wore a rather shabby white sand-shoe soaked through with wet and slightly muddied, and the other had only a white woollen sock.

"You see, the sock's not stained underneath, Groves, it's only wet from the rain on it all night. It's clear that he'd not walked along without his shoe. That shoe must be quite close. Tell your men to look, but to be as careful as they can not to destroy any possible traces. Though," he added ruefully, "with the rain there'll not be much left probably, no finger-prints anyway." Mentally he cursed that rain. If the shoe had been torn off by the murderer, a fine night would have left finger-prints on the surface.

On Groves's instructions the little group of helpers, including Smithson, stepped off the path and began to scrutinize the low bushes and long grass to either side. Almost immediately a shout came: "Here you are, sir!" And from a little clump of tall bracken a few feet to the left of the path one of the policemen drew a white shoe. It was the fellow to the one on the body. Simon took it, faintly hoping the bracken might have kept it dry, but shook his head at the soaked sodden piece of canvas.

"No hope of finger-prints on this—far too wet. Still, we've got it, that's something."

He measured the distance between the little clump where the shoe had lain, and the body, marking the exact spot where the unshod foot rested. "Six feet." He stood looking down, deep in thought. Standing beside him, Groves looked more puzzled than ever.

"Why on earth should he take off his shoe?" said the sergeant. "Or why should anyone else take it off for him? Could his shoe have come off? Do you think, sir, he could have been stooping down to put it on again, and then been shot as he stooped?"

"Possible," said Simon slowly, but, glancing at the stiff rigid form, he shook his head doubtfully. "No, I don't think so, Sergeant. If he'd been stooping and was shot from behind he'd have pitched more on to the top of his head, I think, not be lying so flat on his face. But we'll have to get the doctors to give us the exact line of direction through the body before we know that."

Groves acquiesced gloomily. "Awful mess he's in. Don't see how they'll find that, sir, but I suppose it's their job. Mad the whole thing looks to me. I'm glad you're here, sir, I couldn't deal with anything like this."

"Well," said Sturt slowly, "it is going to be difficult, that we can tell. But we'll get the body moved now, and let's hope the autopsy may give us another clue or two."

The autopsy did provide further information, but on the whole it seemed only to add to the mysterious elements of the case.

Charles had been killed instantaneously. He had been killed by a shot from a gun, which had entered the inner side of his right thigh, rather low down. The wound of entry was a wide one, and from the one hole three pellets had branched off. Of these, two had gone right up and through the body, one going out at the chest. The third had remained in the body, and was recovered from just above the navel. Prolonged search found one of the other pellets embedded in the path, and from its position relative to the body, Sturt could deduce that the gun must have been fired from a level of about three feet above the ground. The shot had been at very close range, the weapon indeed must have been almost touching the body, for Charles's khaki shorts were singed and a patch of the cloth, about the size of a five-shilling piece, burnt clean through.

The three pellets, it was shown quite conclusively, afforded a most astonishing piece of evidence. They had not entered the body horizontally, nor had they gone from above downwards, they had gone from below upwards, on a diagonal rising from the right thigh to the left shoulder.

Death had probably taken place twelve hours before the body was found, that is to say, at about six o'clock the night before.

Besides the shot wounds the body was quite uninjured, there were no blows, no bruises, no signs of asphyxiation. Charles had not been drugged, he had not been clubbed or struck or choked.

Yet the state of the path showed two things. There were deep cart-ruts along it, and just behind the place where the body had fallen, a large deep puddle of long standing made the path very narrow, so that two men could not walk side by side. Ahead, the path was quite free from undergrowth with no cover for anyone. Some little distance away in the trees was a biggish clearing with patches of tall bracken where someone might have lain hid, but the fact that the shot had been fired at such close range and *from below* proved that the murderer had not lain there and discharged his shot.

Apparently the body had not been touched. Where Charles had fallen, there he had lain. His wallet, full of Treasury notes, was in his pocket, soaked through with blood from the wound in the chest. His wrist-watch was on his wrist and was still going when the body was found.

Chapter IX

THE PELLETS

These were the bare facts, and turning them over in his mind, Sturt reflected, with a sense of satisfaction he could not altogether suppress, that here promised to be the case of a lifetime. Charles Courtley's position made him a well-known man, and Simon saw at once that this crime held two distinct possibilities. First he considered two probabilities.

Either the murderer came from amongst Charles's personal associates, someone of his own class and circle with a direct interest in his death. Or, alternatively, it was the work of some local inhabitant, and the fact that the death had been staged away here in the country gave a faint bias towards that theory. A Londoner would have been a shade less likely to have chosen this lonely woodland scene.

Sturt had himself been born and brought up in East Anglia. He knew the country folk and liked them, but he was well aware that they remained an extraordinarily primitive people, more so perhaps than in most parts of England, for they were more cut off from the wide stream of English life. He knew that in them lurked a strong crude streak of ruthlessness, almost savagery, and a marked tenacity. They were slow to make friends with any 'foreigner' especially with any townsman, quick to resent any slight, and bitter in the grudges they could bear. Men of this stock were fierce and implacable under their rather surly outer crust. Shrewd too, and cunning, with all the countryman's knowledge acquired in his struggle with nature and the social system which had pressed so hardly on him in the past. Sturt was in no danger of underestimating the possibilities of any of the men of the district for determined and well-planned murder.

On the other hand, if the murderer was to be found amongst Charles's own personal associates, then again the crime was not the work of the ordinary 'criminal class.' Simon would have to pit his brains against those of someone working along well-planned lines of defence.

He did not repress in himself the zest of the hunter which now filled him. He was responsible for tracking down a murderer, he had at his service all the paraphernalia of a trained department, and he now flung himself wholeheartedly into the essential preliminaries which would, he hoped, lead on to discovery of the criminal. A sparkle came to his blue eyes, a crispness came to his voice, as he began to issue his directions.

The usual classic routine occupied the next few hours. Photographs of the body and of the scene of the crime. Closer interrogation of the man who found him, inquiries as to Charles's home. Reports from the local force who joyfully threw into the bubbling pot their contribution of all that was known through the marvellous gossip or 'news-service' of the countryside about Charles, his family, his household, his circumstances, and his behaviour.

As a result, when Simon at length sat down to go over in his mind all the information so copiously poured out to him, he had acquired a great mass of knowledge. He began at once to clarify his ideas. Method of the murder, that is to say, how that shot was fired. Well, that must wait, for at the moment it seemed hard to discover. Motive. Motive... Simon felt a little spurt of cheerfulness as his mind turned to this aspect of the problem. Motive would probably not be unduly hard to find. Charles, according to all accounts, had clearly been boiling up to be murdered. From all sides came evidence of his deep and increasing unpopularity. The only thing was to distinguish among those who hated him most, and who gained most from his death.

Take first those nearest to him. The wife. Well, in these hardboiled days, in the case of a married couple, the sudden death of one generally brought prompt suspicion on the other. But in this special instance there did seem to be grounds for paying great attention to the relations between husband and wife. Their marriage had been notoriously unhappy; on that point local gossip was unanimous. Maids, men, the repeated conversations of the local gentry, all agreed on that. The quarrels of Charles and Anne had been too frequent and too open. Certainly it seemed likely that this wife hated her husband. And though Charles had been elderly, Anne was still young enough and attractive enough to be able to envisage another marriage. If this one had failed so utterly, she might still hope for a new life. Clearly the death of Charles was likely to prove to her a relief and release. But, had she been the person to take action? There, unfortunately, as Simon found himself phrasing it, Anne could not be seriously suspected. Motive she had, but apparently not opportunity. So much was clear from the details he had collected as to her actions. Charles had been killed towards 6 o'clock the previous evening. Anne had been in the house certainly from 4.30 onwards and had been seen at intervals after then by one or other member of the household. That was speedily established. She had been alone all the afternoon of course, the rest of the family being away at the beach. She had gone out of the garden and up the road at four o'clock, but she had not been away for more than half an hour, since at 4.30 she was in the drawing-room, ready for tea which had been taken in to her there. At intervals from then on it was proved that she had been seen in or about the house. She had never been long enough out of sight to have enabled her to walk the two miles to Fosse Wood, and back. Simon tested all this in every possible way, and, as a result, he came to the firm conclusion Anne could not have been the person to fire the shot that killed her husband.

True, that emptying of the house did arouse some suspicion, Simon reflected. Unhappily married, alone in the house, her husband found dead—no! he did not like it. Yet there were the inescapable facts, Charles *must* have been shot where he was found, and Anne could not have been at that spot at the fatal time, or at all that afternoon.

Further, he was bound in fairness to admit one other little point, tending to clear Anne. The actual method of the murder was more probably the work of a man than of a woman. Very few women would be likely to use a shotgun, and the type of gun employed, the peculiar character of the wounds inflicted, all seemed to point towards the murderer having been a man.

Such was the conclusion at which Simon arrived, sitting in the office set apart for his use at the police station at Marple.

So, for the time at any rate, dismissing Anne from his mind, he decided to get more light on the problem of the shot. He rang his buzzer-bell and asked for the ballistics expert, who, summoned from London, had already dealt with the weapon and the shot. Bernay, for that was his name, came in cheerfully, his task had been more interesting than usual.

"Well, Inspector," he began briskly, "you've a nice little case here, and a bit out of the ordinary."

Simon smiled, partly amused at the enthusiasm of his colleague, and partly because he himself welcomed any unusual feature, as being more likely to help in the solving of the case.

"Sit down," he said, offering the other man a cigarette. "Let's hear the good news."

"Now," began Bernay, "in the first place I can tell you definitely the weapon used—it was what is called a 'fowling-piece.'"

"What exactly is that? A sporting gun, I conclude!"

"Yes, of course, but we can get it a bit narrowed down in addition. The gun was what is generally used for duck-shooting—takes a bigger pellet, you know. And of course that would be quite a common type of gun to find round here. There's excellent duck-shooting in this part, and most men round here are keen sportsmen."

Sturt nodded. "I see that. Nothing special in the gun then. But," as a sudden thought struck him, "if it takes a big pellet, wouldn't that make it a specially useful weapon if murder were intended?"

"Yes," said Bernay. "I think that is so. It would be easier to kill with the heavier shot. But our murderer has done better for us than that. He meant to make dead sure of killing this man. He'd tampered with the cartridge and he used a specially made pellet."

Here he paused, and Sturt waited expectantly, for he saw this was important.

"Actually," went on Bernay, "any man who was a good shot could have done the trick, even at some distance, using ordinary duck cartridge. But here, in addition to firing at such extraordinarily close range, our man did something to make death an absolute certainty. He'd opened the ordinary cartridge and taken out the pellets, and put in specially made large ones."

As he spoke he laid on the table the two pellets, one extracted from Charles's body, the other from the path. The two men bent over them.

"Look," said Bernay, "you can see for yourself something else, which gives the show away. These aren't ordinary pellets at all, they're hand-made, in a mould!"

Sturt was no expert, and he admitted to himself that he could not have distinguished these blobs of lead from any others. To Bernay, however, the fact was obvious. "They were specially made, to kill. Made of an extra large size, quite skilfully done."

"Can anyone but a gunmaker do that sort of thing?" inquired the Inspector.

"Oh! dear me, yes!" replied Bernay. "It's perfectly easy if you've a mould, and plenty of sporting people have those—gamekeepers, too, they quite often have them."

Sturt looked thoughtful. "How do you know they were specially made for the purpose of the murder?"

"Well, actually I deduce that from their size. They're far too big to be used on any bird. Blow anything to pieces. They're not meant for sport at all. As you know, they did terrible damage to your corpse."

Simon nodded agreement. The injuries inflicted by those heavy shot as they tore their way up through Charles's body had indeed been very extensive. This evidence raised his spirits. It would he hoped be easier to trace an unusual shot manufactured in this way than the ordinary everyday ones.

But Bernay had not finished yet.

"I've more still for you," he continued cheerfully, and proceeded now to arrange a neat little row of exhibits on the table. At first sight they seemed a collection of small blackened blood-stained lumps, but Bernay pointed to them proudly.

"This is the wadding," he explained. "This was packed into the cartridge case round the substituted pellets, of course with the idea of fitting them into the cartridge. And, as you'll have realized, this means the murder was premeditated, and prepared beforehand."

Simon nodded; he had grasped that directly he heard the cartridges had been doctored.

"Well, you'll draw your own conclusions, Inspector. But obviously this has been done by someone familiar with guns, and at the same time by an amateur—for he's used newspaper as wadding."

Something in Bernay's tone caused Sturt to glance sharply at him.

"Yes," went on the expert, answering the unspoken question, "the wadding may give you a clue. Most of it was blown right into the body, and was too torn and stained to be deciphered. But I've succeeded in getting you one possible clue!"

He pointed triumphantly to a very tiny piece of print, carefully flattened out and laid on a sheet of clean paper. It bore the letters O U Y.

The two men bent over it.

"Not much there," sighed Simon disappointed, for he realized too well that so few letters could hardly carry him far.

"Not much, but something!" said Bernay. "Don't despise my 'good gift,' you'll probably be thankful for it in the end."

Sturt smiled. "Anything else?"

"No, that's the sum total. Fowling-piece used; big pellets substituted; newspaper wadding: that's my list of items."

"Well, thanks very much, Bernay; no doubt I'll be thankful for all this, as you say."

Cheerfully as he had come, so Bernay went and Simon thoughtfully gazed at his meagre exhibits.

This tampering with the cartridges cut both ways. It pointed to the fact that the murderer had a certain familiarity with sporting weapons. It meant too that either he mistrusted his own aim, and so meant to be sure that if he was obliged to fire from a distance, the heavier pellet, with its far greater deadliness, would make him more certain of killing his victim. Or, as an alternative, that a skilful shot was 'camouflaging' his own proficiency, and meant to convey the impression of a man doubtful of his skill.

"Well," thought Sturt, "that must be borne in mind. But in any case, this shows it wasn't a sudden quarrel, it's true premeditated murder."

He put Bernay's contribution carefully away, and picking up his paper and pencil, once more began methodically to consider his suspects.

Anne, of course, was probably sufficiently familiar with guns, though he'd have to find out if she were a good shot. But in any case, he told himself, it wasn't necessary to do much investigation on those lines in her case, for the time-factor had let her out.

The maids had seen Charles go up the drive at 4.45. Less than fifteen minutes later Anne had been in the drawing-room, ringing the bell for tea to be cleared away. That fixed one end of her time-alibi.

At the other, came the evidence of the child in the wood, the last person to see Charles alive. Luckily that evidence was precise, for the little girl had been waiting impatiently for her companions to set out for the fair, and so had been intent on the time. She had seen Charles enter Fosse Wood, had heard the heavy report and the echoes soon after and had then gone back to her home to see how much longer she should wait for her little friends. The church clock had struck six just as she ran home, and that was a distance of nearly a quarter of a mile from the clearing.

Taking 5.45 to 6 then as the proved time of the murder, Anne must be dismissed as a suspect.

Well then, who came next on the list?

Sticking to the 'nearest' Simon went on methodically to the daughters.

First the least likely, Prudence. She was so young, and could never surely have done anything in the way of manufacturing the pellets? True, some children were extraordinarily clever with their hands. True too, that a morbid child of that age had in past cases been clearly capable of crime. Poor Prudence had always shown a hysterical dislike of her father and this to a slight extent counterbalanced the improbability caused by her youth. None the less, Simon mentally crossed her off his list. He did not believe the murder was her work.

Then Pamela. Here Simon paused longer. She too had been on bad terms with her father, so Groves had informed him. She also had possibly special grounds for a violent quarrel, since she was said to be carrying on a love-affair with Barclay, in defiance of her father. But again Simon shook his head as he meditated. He must see her of course, and go into her whereabouts, but contrary to some modern theories, he felt it unlikely in the extreme that any daughter, however provoked, would plan and execute her father's death.

Mrs. Mitcham? He paused, and before his mind's eye summoned up a picture of that lady. Well, her resolute face, with its clear determined lines, its steady eyes and self-controlled lips, was the face of a woman capable of strong action. Yet, could anyone so dignified, so sensible, fall into any measure so desperate and so terrible as premeditated murder? Mothers, so he knew, ran the accepted belief, were capable of any action when roused on behalf of their children. He recalled, almost with a smile, a famous play and the story of an American novel, where in each case the murder had been the work of the devoted and to all outward seeming, the gentle, amiable, elderly mother. Was this a case where a mother had not hesitated to kill in order to protect her daughter? He decided that he must not put such a possibility aside. He must investigate Mrs. Mitcham's own history, and he must check her movements. As to motive, the case itself would probably resolve that problem as it unfolded. Unlikely—but possible—was his conclusion. Once more he decided, this shooting was probably the work of a man.

What men had been most closely associated with Charles, who could be suspected, and how could their actions be investigated?

He decided that local knowledge must be enlisted here again. Groves, called into consultation, was already prepared.

"I've been making inquiries from the staff at Carron," he began at once, "and I think Mr. Wadham's affairs will bear being looked into. He's the secretary, and from what I hear, a bit of a dark horse. No one seems to trust him. They *say* he's keen on Mrs. Courtley, but that may be just romancing, made up after the event. He's a good looker, and one of these smart clever men women seem to go mad over. There's been some hanky-panky up, so the staff say, but they don't know what. Opportunity he may have had, for he was out somewhere or other all afternoon. Now, that's suspicious, for he's usually in his office then. But he wasn't in it at three o'clock, and he wasn't heard about at all. He came down late to dinner, and he'd been out in the roads somewhere, for his shoes were dusty, we got that much from the maids."

He paused triumphantly, and Simon nodded approval. "What about the gun? Does he shoot, does he own a gun, or had he access to one?"

"Yes, he can shoot, but he's not said to be any too grand at it."

Simon cocked an eye thoughtfully, for surely an indifferent shot was more likely than a good one to have tampered with that cartridge? The object of the change of pellet had clearly been to make certain death would follow the shot.

"But," went on Groves with rather a worried air, "there's no way of connecting him with a fowling-piece. I've been on to the keeper who, of course, knows all details of this sort. Mr. Courtley had one, and used it a while back to go off after the duck in the Fosse pools (there are some big ponds in those woods, you know), but latterly he'd given it up, from what the keeper says, and the gun had gone out of action and hadn't been repaired."

"H'm," said Simon. "Well now, let's stick to that line. Who in this circle had a fowling-piece? I take it you've thought of the keeper himself?"

"Yes," replied Groves promptly, "but he's out of it. He was at home yesterday from before six o'clock, and his gun itself in his cottage. He and his wife and the gardener, Duncan, can all swear to that. Duncan lives in the next cottage and spoke to him when he came home at five, and saw him at his tea."

"Well, then, we must trace any others you have on the records," replied Simon. "Get a list for me and we'll go through that. There's another line to follow up too," he continued. "Why was Mr. Courtley at that particular place at that time? Had he gone there to meet anyone? He hadn't been running along that path, or he'd have left some signs in the tracks. It looks as if he hadn't been expecting any attack, for the murderer had come right up to him—almost touching him. That doesn't look as if he'd been pursued, or taken by surprise by some unknown person.

"We ought to find out, if we can, if he'd any known reason for going to that place. Well, possibly someone will be able to tell us whether he was in the habit of walking there, or if he'd business there in connection with the felling of those trees."

Groves hesitated. "There's been trouble about that wood, that I do know. The people hereabouts always use that path, but there's been some fuss over it. Mr. Courtley threatened to close it, and that made a lot of talk. And again, people were vexed he was felling the timber. It's such a beauty spot, they say, and it wasn't liked that a newcomer should spoil one of the best old pieces of forest hereabouts."

Simon was interested. He had an instinct that the locality of the crime was important, and here was at least an indication that the spot had a local significance. He got up, feeling more cheerful.

"Well, we'll try to find out more on that line, Sergeant, and now I'll be off up to the house. I want to interview the family myself."

Chapter X

THE HANDSOME AGENT

U p at Carron he asked to see Anne, and was shown into the cool drawing-room. Outside it was very hot, with an airless brazen heat, the September sun shining more fiercely down on the enclosed space in front of the house. The drawing-room was empty. Simon felt refreshed as he looked round, and his eyes rested with pleasure on the bowls of flowers, late-blossoming sweet peas and tall spikes of gladioli. The bare polished floor, the fresh green and white chintzes seemed delightful. Then with sudden revulsion he thought with horror of the contrast between the silent peaceful room and the torn and shattered body of the man who had been its owner. Hatred had been the atmosphere of the house, not peace. He hardened his heart as he thought of the bloody death which Charles had met.

At this point his train of thought was interrupted by Anne's entrance into the drawing-room. She came in quickly and Sturt looked carefully at her, for his mind still worried away over the personality of this woman. He had an inkling that this whole murder turned on Charles's personality, and he believed that in the relations of Charles with the people surrounding him, the clue to his death would be found.

The first thing he recognized about Anne was the strength of her character. Her firm resolute face, the determined lips, the steady eyes, her complete lack of agitation or nervousness, struck him immediately. Then he appreciated her physical make-up. Certainly she had no obvious beauty or prettiness, she lacked colour and sparkle. Yet her thick auburn hair, springing crisply back from her forehead, had the attraction of vitality. Her rather square face, the marked edge to her lips, even the lack of any specially beautiful trait, seemed in an odd way to emphasize the attraction and force of her individuality. This woman was unusual, arresting, and subtle. Simon recognized that in her strength and unusualness lay a very powerful charm. He knew she had been unhappy and he saw that she was a strong and resolute woman. It seemed to him more than possible that, finding her married life to be unendurable, she had decided to end it, and he believed as he looked at her, that she was the type who would not draw back from any decision. He believed her to be a woman capable of anything—and his worldly wisdom told him that though murder seemed a drastic remedy for an unhappy marriage, yet it was one which people sometimes sought. Divorce would have been insufficient, for divorce of a wife meant the loss of her position, and in this case of wealth, and the companionship of her children.

At least, so he believed. It remained for him to make sure that Anne had no probability of re-marriage with a wealthy lover. Short of that, his impression was that here was one possible source of the trouble which had culminated in the removal of Charles. She might not herself have done the deed, but she was perhaps the motive which lay behind it.

Anne for her part realized as she looked at Simon that here was something new in her experience. She had taken for granted that the investigations by the police would be in the hands of the local force, and she vaguely recollected such dealings as she had had with them had been with severe precise men possibly radiating efficiency, but certainly lacking in charm. Now with Inspector Sturt she perceived, for Anne was a good judge where men were concerned, that here was someone with a marked and highly attractive personality. The thin dark face, the bright clear eyes under well-defined brows, the mobility and intelligence which marked his features, all made up a composite whole which produced an extraordinary impression on her. Strung up as she was, aware of the position into which she was forced, she yet felt a slight, pleasurable tingling in her nerves as she faced this man. Something leapt up in her, and she was aware that in the contest of wits which she foresaw there would be an element not only of excitement but of pleasure. She knew a faint thrill of exaltation as she realized that life still had a potent attraction for her—and she knew that she still had the power to evoke and to respond. She summoned her forces, prepared to contest the power of this man to investigate her private life, and to baffle his inquiries as far as she could.

She sat down in the armchair to the right of the great open fire-place, and Simon settled himself beside her.

"Mrs. Courtley," he began, coming at once to the point, "I want first to ask you if you know at all why your husband went up to Fosse Wood? I'm anxious to have that established, if I can."

Anne looked at him, her slow gaze seeming to estimate silently the powers and intelligence of her questioner. She was perhaps astonished at the point he had chosen to attack, and slightly puzzled.

"No," she said briefly. "I have no idea."

Sturt tried again.

"Can you tell me what were his arrangements yesterday for his routine work? Was he planning to deal with the timber in this Fosse Wood, do you know? Was he in the habit of going up to that part of the forest?"

"I know nothing at all that can help you, I'm afraid," replied Anne composedly. "I had nothing to do with my husband's management of the estate. I don't know in the least what he was doing about the woods, or if he often went up there."

The inspector decided to probe a little further. Primed by the local force he had some idea as to Charles's action over the forest.

"I'm told, Mrs. Courtley, that your husband disliked people walking in your woods. He'd decided to close the paths there. Can you tell me anything about that?"

"Yes," said Anne, with some reluctance, "I have heard him speak of that. He wanted to keep our woods private. He had put up notice boards, and I know——" she hesitated for a moment, then went on slowly——"I know the local people resented it. I believe there was talk of legal action."

Simon nodded. "And being Fair Day over at Marple I understand the local people may have wanted to use that short cut through Fosse Wood on the day in question?"

Anne looked at him directly. "That isn't a short cut anywhere, Inspector. Those paths don't help anyone to get to the village."

If Sturt had laid a trap for her, she had not fallen into it. If he had wanted her to snatch at the chance of drawing attention to local discontent, she had not taken it. He shifted his ground.

"Mrs. Courtley," he began again. "We know this is a case of premeditated murder. It's not even man-slaughter—not an act done on the spur of the moment. It was, I'm afraid, all carefully planned out," he explained, his eyes studying her face, "therefore, you'll appreciate, we've got to look for motive as well as opportunity. Now, we shall end by finding the motive, but at present I want to establish opportunity. I want to find any indication as to what your husband was doing in Fosse Wood yesterday evening. Was he meeting anyone or was he on the look-out for anyone?"

Anne's composure deserted her. She looked angry. "I've already told you I know *nothing* of my husband's plans or doings yesterday. I had not seen him since the morning. I've no idea what he was going to do—or what he did!"

She ended defiantly and Simon saw he could get nothing here.

He reflected, and then decided to come out into the open.

"I don't want to distress you, Mrs. Courtley, but I must ask you something disagreeable. I know Mr. Courtley had enemies. Can you tell me of anyone who had any special cause for hatred towards him?"

Anne's angry flush deepened. "If you mean, you know my husband had a terrible temper, that's true of course. He gave plenty of people cause to hate him. But if you ask me to name any special people, well, I neither can nor will. He's dead, and it's your business to find out who killed him, but it's not mine to tell you of gossip or hearsay!"

Simon kept his temper. "I'm sorry you take it like this. It's quite usual to ask near relatives if they have any suspicion of anyone. Often they can give us some clue or hint." He paused, but she made no response. He saw that she was determined not to help him, and swiftly he decided to spend no more time on her now.

He got up and said coldly:

"Well, then, I won't trouble you any further, Mrs. Courtley, as you think you can give me no help."

"None at all," she retorted. "I've nothing to tell you."

Those who try to get information regarding the personal affairs of any family will say that they first try a direct approach to the family members; failing that the household staff may be communicative; and if that resource fails too, then the tradespeople. No one can have 'private affairs' to-day. Everyone's doings and sayings are always known. Having failed with the wife, Simon decided to see if he could do better with the staff.

"Then, Mrs. Courtley," he said, "I must see if any of your household can help to establish what your husband did yesterday. So perhaps you'll send your parlourmaid in here?"

Anne rose too. "I'll send you Nelly," she said briefly. As she crossed the wide floor, Sturt felt a surge of irritation as he realized her complete self-control, her calm competence to keep her own counsel. The personal equation was a difficult one. Here he had no routine of professional criminals to deal with, he had to embark on that most difficult form of crime, based not on material gain, not on the desire for wealth or money, but on the interaction of people who hated each other.

In the brief interval before Nelly appeared he walked to the window, and stood with impatience looking at the sunlit landscape below him. How hateful life must have been in this place! For human beings do not kill from sheer inability to bear with a man's presence, until they are hard driven.

The parlourmaid came down the two little steps into the room. Unlike her mistress, she was far from composed. She was very pale, and very nervous. Simon concluded he might do better to take advantage of her agitation.

So with intentional brusqueness, he began, "I want you to give me some information which may be very important. So please be very careful in what you say. I want you to be strictly accurate."

Nelly looked at him with anxiety.

"Yes, sir, I understand that."

"Now, first, did Mr. Courtley have tea here yesterday?"

"No, sir, Mr. Courtley never had tea when he was by himself. He hardly ever had it at all, actually. Sometimes he'd just come in and drink a cup if the family were having it and he wasn't busy. Yesterday he hadn't any. He went out just after I'd taken tea to Mrs. Courtley in the drawing-room." She described how she had seen him go up the drive.

"Did anyone call at the house to see him in the course of the afternoon?" asked Simon.

"Only Mr. Barclay, sir, the gentleman from next door."

"What time did he come?"

"Just before three o'clock, and he went away in about half an hour, I think. Mr. Courtley didn't ring for me to see him out. I think he showed him out himself."

A hesitancy and shade of uneasiness in her manner caught the inspector's attention.

"Anything special you can tell me about this visit? Everything's of importance that happened yesterday, you know."

The girl hesitated, and then answered.

"They had words, sir."

"How do you know?"

"We could hear them in the kitchen, sir; not what they said, but we could tell they were having a row."

"Then what happened?"

"Mr. Barclay went away, and the telephone rang."

"Did you answer it?"

"No, sir, it rang in the study and was answered from there."

"Who by?"

"I don't know, sir. Usually Mr. Wadham answers the study telephone, but he was out. I think Mr. Courtley answered it himself."

"Why do you think that?"

"Because I thought Mr. Wadham being out, I'd better see to it, but as I crossed the hall I heard someone answering, and it was a man's voice, and Mr. Courtley was the only gentleman in the house."

Simon nodded. The girl's reasoning was clear. He decided that call must be traced, there might be a connection between the call and Charles's subsequent departure for Fosse Wood.

A few further questions showed that Nelly had no more to tell him.

He wished to see Wadham, and inquired of her where the secretary would be found. To his annoyance, she told him that Wadham was out, he had gone into Marple. Nelly looked rather uncomfortable as she said: "I think, sir, he's gone in to see about the funeral arrangements. At least, we understood that was what he was going for."

Simon recognized that the household all felt rather at a loss in attempting to arrange matters of this sort, not knowing quite how and when the law would hand over the body. He also realized it was quite natural Wadham should have gone to deal with the matter.

He reflected a moment. He still felt the vital point was to establish the reason for Charles's presence in the wood. Failing Freddy, who as secretary might have known, he could try the estate agent. The timber and its sale would have come within his province. So finding out from Nelly that Sylvester lived at present in the little estate agent's house down in the village, two miles away, he got into his car and departed to interview him.

He drove quickly along the country road, and drew up before the house set aside for the use of Charles's agent.

He sent in his card and was shown into the office. As he entered, a man who had been sitting at a desk laden with papers got up and came to greet him. For a moment Simon was almost startled. He had driven along trying not to feel prejudiced against Anne, telling himself he must not be unfair or, worse still, fanciful. Yet so strong was the impression she had made, that all the time he had subconsciously been wondering how she had lived in this sleepy remote place, cooped up with a husband whom she disliked. The moment he set eyes on Sylvester, the thought flashed into his mind—"Here was someone who'd distract her! Here was a man to interest any woman, much more a woman who was unhappy and bored."

For Peter Sylvester was a splendid-looking man. He was over six feet in height, with broad shoulders, and a strong athletic frame. His hair was a bright reddish gold, almost too bright, Simon decided, with a crisp strong wave. His eyes were blue, rather fierce, daring-looking eyes. He had force and good looks, and as Simon willingly admitted, more than the ordinary share of masculine charm. He looked as if he had been deliberately cast for the part of 'wife's lover.' At this point, Sturt pulled himself up sharply. He was letting his psychology run away with him. He must not give his fancy such loose rein. Police inspectors must look for facts, however far their fancy roams, so he began prosaically.

"Mr. Sylvester? You're Mr. Courtley's estate agent, I understand?"

"Not quite correct, Inspector," replied the other cheerfully. "I *was* Mr. Courtley's agent, and had been so since he bought this place, but I resigned my post a couple of weeks ago."

"Why was that, Mr. Sylvester? You'll understand, of course, I'm bound to inquire into these details," he added rather apologetically.

Sylvester laughed. "Oh, no offence, Inspector, I know you have to pry into all the details of our lives! Well, I'll be frank with you. I had the very devil of a row with Mr. Courtley." He paused a moment, and as Simon said nothing, went on collectedly. "You'll soon know, if I don't tell you myself. Everyone knows we quarrelled over Mr. Courtley's policy in cutting the timber on the estate. He insisted that the stretch of forest here should be felled. Now, Mr. Courtley was a very rich man. He didn't need the money the timber would bring him—and I considered it wrong on his part to destroy one of the most beautiful woods in the whole county!" He spoke with restraint, but try as he would, feeling showed through. He saw that Simon had noticed his tone, for he was no fool, this man, his wits were as quick as the detective's and his eyes and ears too... So with a sparkle of anger kindling in his eye, and a hot tone creeping into his voice he went on. "I'm specially keen on woodlands; they're my hobby, my passion really. I think a fine wood is one of the most beautiful things man can make. And when men *have* made such a thing, have planned and planted not for money's sake, but for beauty, then I think it's a crime to destroy their handiwork, wipe it all out, spoil a lovely thing for ever…" He checked himself, and went on more coldly. "Why Mr. Courtley decided to fell Fosse Wood, I don't know. As I've said, he didn't need the money. I tried my best to dissuade him, and when I couldn't—well—I'm afraid I lost my temper and let fly. I said what I thought, and he resented it, and I chucked in my resignation. Of course I admit he'd a technical right to do as he pleased with his property, but I'm one of those who think property has its duties too, and I couldn't work any longer under a man who'd do such a thing."

He ended abruptly, and looked away. It was perfectly evident that he felt intensely on the point, with a passion which had probably been totally incomprehensible to his employer.

Simon decided to test him further.

"How long had you been agent here, Mr. Sylvester?"

"For five years; Mr. Courtley bought the property then, but he's only settled at Carron for good quite lately. Before that he just came down at holidays and so on."

"And before he bought the place, had you known Mr. Courtley?"

"No. I've always lived here, but he was a newcomer and a stranger to this neighbourhood."

"Were you agent to the previous owner?"

"No! I was son to the previous owner."

"I see. Your father sold to Mr. Courtley." Simon tried hard to speak as impersonally as he could, for he could glimpse the pride and unhappiness behind the curt replies.

"My father died, and… the executors were obliged to sell. He'd left his affairs in a mess."

"Had you been trained as an agent?"

"No. That was one of the things that made it difficult for me. I'd not been brought up to any profession, and I'd no special qualifications. But of course I knew this estate in and out, so I'd some qualifications for managing it."

"You had acted as agent for your father?"

"I had been brought up here. I understood the people and the ins and outs of this particular property. Mr. Courtley was a townsman. He offered me the job of acting as his agent and I took it. He didn't pay me what he'd have had to pay a fully qualified man, but it suited him, and it suited me."

The blue eyes stared uncompromisingly at Sturt.

The inspector paused, he wanted to get to the bottom of this, but felt he must go carefully.

"That arrangement worked satisfactorily?"

A silence. Then—

"I'd better tell you clearly, Inspector, I did not get on well, personally, with Mr. Courtley. But I stayed here because I love the place, and the people, and I wanted to do my best for them. Mr. Courtley was what you might call a 'strict' employer." A tinge of irony broke through here. He went on quickly. "I was able to make things go a bit smoother."

Simon wondered inwardly why anyone who looked as pugnacious, as full of repressed power as this young man should wish to act the part of peacemaker. Then decided to put the direct question.

"Why were you anxious to do that, Mr. Sylvester?"

"Because I tell you I'd been born and bred here—and so had all my people for generations back. We had to sell, but I'd no wish to leave. This is the place I choose to live in." Curtly and harshly the words were spoken, and Sturt felt he had better not press the point.

"You ran all the business side of the estate of course?"

"Yes."

Sturt inwardly collected himself. He wanted to press what he hoped might be a vital point.

"So that you would have had the management of the woods and the sale of the timber?"

"Yes, of course." Peter too knew the dialogue was approaching a crucial point.

"Then I conclude you arranged for the sale of the Fosse Wood? The contract had been made, I understand, and sample trees cut down?"

"Yes. That's so. I acted under protest as I've told you. I resigned my job, but I had to carry out my instructions and do the business part of it."

"Now, can you tell me what arrangements Mr. Courtley had made to go to that place yesterday afternoon?"

"No." The negative came firmly. Then, "I haven't any idea why he went there. The arrangements with the timber contractor had been completed, felling had begun, and Mr. Courtley had nothing further to see to."

"Did you by any chance telephone to him yesterday afternoon?"

"No—I did not."

Sturt's brain registered a faint hardening of the tone. He was sure there was something here. He said sharply: "Did anyone at all telephone from your office?"

"No one as far as I'm aware."

Sturt knew of course that on this point Sylvester would hardly dare to lie. Had the call been put through from this office, it would be traced.

"So," he summed up, "you can't tell me of any reason, so far as you know, why Mr. Courtley should have gone to the timber cutting?"

"None," the other answered firmly. "There was no reason at all as far as the business of the timber felling was concerned."

Simon was obliged to accept that. After all, he had no grounds for suspecting this man, beyond the fact that he had recently quarrelled bitterly with his employer, had felt very keenly over the property, and was obviously a fierce pugnacious individual. But it was early yet in the investigation. He took his leave, and as he turned away from the house he mentally suspended judgment. His dramatic sense told him that he had now interviewed 'the man' and 'the woman,' but his common sense bade him collect more facts.

Chapter XI

FINDING TRACES

Once more he turned in at the drive of Carron Cross, hoping now that he would be able to interview the man whom Sergeant Groves suspected, Freddy Wadham.

This time he was in luck. Nelly informed him that Wadham had just come back, and was now in his office. So to the office Simon went.

Freddy looked very pale. He was obviously much shaken by the terrible events of the day.

His face showed signs of strain, he looked haggard and anxious. Simon inspected him with interest. A clever face, he thought to himself. Plenty of intelligence there—but a bit shifty.

He came to the point at once.

"Mr. Wadham, the first thing I am trying to ascertain is whether Mr. Courtley had any reason for going to the Fosse Wood yesterday? Had he any appointment to meet anyone there?"

Freddy shook his head. "No. He had no appointment at all for yesterday. He'd kept the whole day free to go through some rather important accounts with me."

"No appointments at all?"

"No, none."

"What about his interview with Mr. Barclay?" Wadham glanced at the inspector, clearly he was thinking: "Got on to that already, has he?" Then he answered: "I don't know anything about it. I did not know Barclay was coming in."

"Can you tell me anything of Mr. Barclay's position with regard to Mr. Courtley?"

"Well, yes. I can tell you what everyone knows. Mr. Courtley wanted to buy the oast-house. It would complete his frontage, and being next door he wanted to make sure of the site. Barclay wouldn't sell and that gave rise to friction."

"How came it that Mr. Courtley didn't own that piece of land? I understand he owns everything else round here."

"Barclay is the nephew of the late owner. His mother was the sister of the late Mr. Sylvester, who owned that bit of land and left it to her."

"Oh!" said Sturt, "then he's related to Mr. Peter Sylvester?"

"First cousin," said Wadham briefly.

"They seem to stick to their traditions," mused Sturt. "Mr. Sylvester told me he didn't want to leave the neighbourhood, and here's Mr. Barclay living next door to the old home?"

"Yes," replied Wadham. "That is so. The Sylvesters have had this land since the days of King John, I believe. They can't face cutting themselves adrift altogether."

"Any hope of their buying back the property at some future time?" queried Simon.

Wadham hesitated, then made up his mind. "No. Neither Sylvester nor Barclay has any money. But they may have had other ideas. You'll soon hear the gossip. Mr. Courtley had daughters, but no son. You've seen Sylvester. He's a good-looking chap. So is Barclay—very like him in appearance. Barclay and Pam Courtley see a lot of each other."

"And how did Mr. Courtley take to *that* idea?"

"Not at all kindly. He objected strongly. In fact, that egged him on to quarrel with Barclay."

Simon nodded his comprehension. He could well imagine the effect on Charles.

"You say you didn't know Mr. Barclay was coming. Did you hear anything of the result of the interview?"

"No," replied Freddy, and hesitated a moment. "Actually Mr. Courtley had sent me off to get some papers he wanted from the estate office. Mr. Barclay came while I was out."

"Do you think he got you out of the way on purpose?" asked Sturt, mindful of the maid's report of the angry voices and of the violent exit of Barclay.

Freddy shrugged his shoulders. "I can't say. He just discovered some figures he wanted weren't there."

"Did you come straight back from Marple?"

"Yes. I got the papers from Sylvester, and brought them back at once."

"Did you see Mr. Courtley then?"

"Yes. I gave him the papers, and he told me he'd go through them."

"Now, Mr. Wadham, a telephone call came through to this house, at four o'clock. Did you answer it?"

"No. After I got back Mr. Courtley told me he would not want me any more for the afternoon, and I could go off. I was out of the house by four."

"And where did you go?"

"I went over to a little inn, the 'Broken Bough.' It's a nice walk, and I felt a bit stuffy after doing accounts all day. I rather wanted to see Sylvester too, and he'd told me he was going over there about tea-time."

"Why did you want to see Mr. Sylvester? You'd just seen him, hadn't you?"

"Oh! that was just for a moment, dashing in and out. Sylvester and I are by way of being rather friends, you know," he added, striving to speak easily. Simon thought to himself this assumption of ease was not quite natural. He was himself so acute, his powers of observation so highly trained, and he had a suspicion that Freddy's careless manner did not ring true.

"So you went with him to this inn."

"I met him there. It's a nice little country place. As a matter of fact, he and I used often to go over there for tea. I get a bit fed-up with always being with the family, and he gets a bit sick of his office and rooms. We've got into the way of going over there. It's quite a nice little place, and gives us a bit of a walk and a change."

Simon was not altogether convinced by this; somehow it did not ring quite true, but he let it pass, though making a mental note that there was something odd about these meetings.

"How long were you there?"

"I should think till about half-past six. We had tea, and sat and smoked, and then came back fairly slowly through the woods. It was a lovely evening, you know."

"You realize, I'm sure, Mr. Wadham, that from five o'clock to about six o'clock is the crucial time I am trying to check. You say you were at the 'Broken Bough' then?"

"Yes," rather nervously.

"Anyone to confirm that?"

"The people there, I think. I'm sure one or other must have seen us—we had our tea early, but I expect they saw us sitting on there."

"When you got back, Mr. Courtley, of course, was not here? Had he left you any note, or message?"

"No, none, nothing at all."

"No message about that telephone call?" persisted Simon, "which he must have taken, I gather?"

"No, none." Wadham had summoned his resistance in response to that faint pressure, his denial was resolute.

"You've heard about the call?"

"Yes. But Mr. Courtley must have dealt with it himself. He left no word with me, nor with anyone else. Nelly would have left a message on the pad if she had answered it."

Simon reflected. This call had come, and been answered from the study. Anne and Wadham had been out. Charles had answered it. Shortly afterwards he had gone up to Fosse Wood, where he had no apparent reason to go, and there he had met his death. That death had been planned beforehand. The telephone call must surely have been part of a decoy? Well, so far he could get nothing from these 'suspects'—he would try the one name remaining on his list, Hugh Barclay. Briefly telling Wadham there was nothing further required of him, Simon himself got up and left the office. He crossed the front hall, and picked up his hat from the hall-table preparatory to going out. But as he laid his hand on the latch of the front door, a voice spoke apologetically behind him.

"If you please, Inspector, Mary wishes to speak to you."

Sturt turned to find Nelly with another younger girl. He knew Groves had been hard at work taking statements from the staff, and being himself anxious to get on with his own task of interviewing the major suspects, inquired: "Do you specially want to say anything to me? The sergeant is seeing you all in turn, you know."

"Yes, sir," replied the elder woman, "but Mary has told me something, and we both think it better to come straight to you—you see, it's something rather private and personal."

Sturt grasped from her intonation that in all probability this was a piece of news which neither of these two wanted the local man to hear, or at least they did not want to be the ones to tell him of it, but preferred to come to the outsider. So, reflecting that anything positive was, after all, more important than the possibility of getting something out of Barclay, he turned back to the little sitting-room and sat down at the table.

Having taken down Mary's name, and noted that she was one of the under housemaids, he then asked her what she had to report.

"Well, sir," she said rather anxiously, "it may not matter, of course, and it mayn't be anything at all, but it's something I saw the night before Mr. Courtley was killed, and as it was all rather queer, I told Nelly, and she said I'd better come to you about it."

"Yes, that's very sensible of you. Of course I want to know of anything at all out of the way that's happened lately. Well, now, just tell me what it is."

"Why, you see, sir, that night, late, I know there was something going on, out in the yard, one of the ladies from here was meeting someone, a gentleman, I mean, and on the sly—and I know Mr. Courtley was on to it and nearly caught them." She spoke rather confusedly, blurting it all out in a hurry, partly ashamed of repeating such gossip, partly doubting whether, after all, such an episode were really worth bringing to the inspector's notice.

Simon, however, had no doubts on that score. Any line to the hidden happenings at Carron was welcome. He only hoped the girl could tell him something definite.

"You say you know one of the ladies was meeting a man, secretly? Now, tell me just what you saw and when it all was."

So Mary told her brief tale. She had been awake, and had heard people in the yard beyond the barn; she explained that this was possible because her bedroom, unlike that of the other maids, faced on to the front of the house. The yard lay to the right, quite close to her room. She had gone to bed early, and gone to sleep, but had woken up. The moon was very bright that night, and its beams, sliding through a chink in the curtain, had fallen on her face and woken her. She had lain awake for a little. In the stillness of the night sounds carried very far. The outbuildings of the farm lay not more than fifty yards or so from her window. She had distinctly heard footsteps. She was sure they were a man's because she had caught the click made by nails on the cobble-stones. The farm enclosure still retained some of its cobbles from old days, and the girl had often noticed how distinct were the sounds made when the farm men moved about in it. She had wondered who was afoot, for, of course, none of the farm-workers would be there so late—none of the farm animals was ill, no cow was expected to calve. No one ought to have been there.

She had turned over these ideas in her mind for a minute or two. "For," as she explained confidentially to Simon, "I'd only just woken, and I felt comfortable and a bit drowsy still."

Then she had realized that the moon, moving across the sky, was likely to throw her bright beams across the pillow for some little time to come, and aware she would not sleep while that was so, she had reluctantly got up to draw the curtain tighter.

"When I got to the window," she said, "I just looked out just casually as it were. I thought I'd have a peep to see who was in the yard, though I didn't bother much. No one could steal anything there, and I half thought it would just be a tramp looking for some-where to sleep. I knew the garage was always locked at night, so no one could get in there."

She had been surprised to see, however, that she was wrong. The garage was open on the side towards the yard. She could distinctly see that one half of the great door was slightly ajar.

"I thought it must somehow be the chauffeur," she went on. "You know how if anything is a bit odd you always try to think of some ordinary explanation. I thought perhaps there was something wrong with one of the cars, and he'd forgotten to put it right and didn't want to get into trouble in the morning. So he'd come in quietly, as it were, to do it then. Mr. Courtley was a person who'd be very angry if anything were wrong and hadn't been put right when he wanted the car. He'd have given the chauffeur a terrible dressing-down. No one would want to get in a row with him if they could help it."

"Where did the chauffeur sleep?" interjected Simon.

"In a room on the ground floor at the back," replied the girl. "Near the garden door. He had his own quarters there, bedroom and bathroom. So I knew he could have slipped out and round to the garage. Mr. Courtley's room faced the other side of the garden, away at the far end. No one would have heard him if he'd taken care.

"Then," she went on, "I got a bit of a shock. I suddenly saw Mr. Courtley himself. He was round on the house side of the barn. I could see his white shirt-front, it just caught the light. He was standing by the near door of the barn, as if he were listening. I thought he must have heard the man inside too, and I waited to see what would happen. I saw him put up his hand as if he were trying the lock, but it was shut all right, he couldn't get in.

"Then, I saw the far door opening—the one into the yard— and a man and a woman came hurrying out. They went across the yard like lightning, and ran out into the field up by the oast-house. I couldn't see who they were, but the woman was in an evening frock, that I do know."

She paused for breath, and seeing Simon's deep interest, hurried on, pleased with the sensation she was making.

"Mr. Courtley had run round into the house, and they'd hardly got away into the field before he came running out into the yard where they'd been only a moment before. But he turned towards the garage and went inside, so they'd plenty of time then to make off. He'd not got round in time to see them dash out. I waited a bit, and then he came back into the house, and then I went back to bed."

"You didn't wait to see if the woman came back?"

"No. I'd been out of bed long enough, and how was I to know when she'd be back?"

"But you did think it was someone from this house?"

"Well, yes," reluctantly. "I was pretty sure it was. I saw the dress sort of shine and glimmer in the moonlight, as if it were silk or satin, and I could see bare arms and her bare neck and shoulders. I knew it must be either Mrs. Courtley or Miss Pamela."

Nelly gave a queer little gasp at this, and Simon turned to her in a flash.

"You're the parlourmaid, you waited at table that night."

"Yes, sir."

"Well, then, what coloured frocks were the ladies wearing?"

"Mrs. Courtley, she'd a silver frock, and Miss Pamela a pale green and silver, and Mrs. Mitcham——" Nelly was determined to leave no one out—"she'd on a pale grey satin."

Again Simon felt how unkind Fate was in petty details. All three in pale light colours! No hope of differentiation there!

He turned again to Mary.

"Couldn't you tell at all from the build which it was?"

"No. They're both tall, and whoever it was seemed to run so quickly, I really couldn't say who it was. And I was startled too, and looking at Mr. Courtley more than at the lady."

"Or the man? Couldn't you tell who he might be?"

"Oh, no! He was running too—just dark clothes he had on. It might be anyone."

"Didn't you think it all very odd? Didn't you talk about it to the others?"

The girl grew red. "No, I didn't feel like talking. Mr. Courtley led them all such a life. I'd not blame anyone for doing things behind his back."

"I can quite see," said Simon slyly, "that you'd expect Miss

Pamela perhaps to be out flirting without her father's knowledge, but you know it would be a more serious matter if it had been Mrs. Courtley. Why do you think *she'd* be meeting anyone?"

The girl hesitated.

"I didn't really think it was her, at the time, but then I heard Mr. Courtley come upstairs." She paused and, glancing at Nelly, hesitated.

"Go on," encouraged Sturt. "You must tell me everything, you know. Remember this is a very serious affair, you mustn't keep things back."

Clearly rather ashamed, the girl went on reluctantly: "I heard him go crashing along the passage, and I just wanted to know what he was saying, so I got up again and listened. I heard him in Miss Pamela's room, but he didn't stay long there. He burst in on her and snapped something, but it didn't seem to come to anything. He went off to Mrs. Courtley, and I heard him shouting at her like anything."

"Could you hear what he was saying?"

"No. Just the noise of his voice. And that didn't really prove it had been Mrs. Courtley outside," she went on quickly, "because they have words often enough and he'd always put the blame on her for anything he didn't like. We've often and often heard him storming away at her."

"You didn't think of looking at her dress in the morning?" inquired Sturt. He could not help thinking that this girl must have been inquisitive enough to wish to find out as much as she could. "I mean, if whoever it was had on a long evening frock, it would surely have got damp or stained in the garden or in the field, or torn even? Didn't you think of looking?"

But Mary shook her head. "No, sir," with a touch of righteous indignation. "I never thought of such a thing. It wasn't my business.

It didn't matter to me. I just thought no more of it, till all this other trouble came along."

With that Simon had to be content. He thanked Mary for coming forward, and told them both to keep this strictly to themselves. When they had gone, he sat thinking with satisfaction as he reviewed the episode, slight as it was in itself. For at least here was some sort of indication that an intrigue was on foot at Carron. Courtley had evidently been close to the discovery of some secret meeting. Either his wife, or his daughter, had been meeting some man by stealth, and he had been on their track. Surely both the fact of such secrecy being observed, and that Courtley was aware of it, must link up with the death that overtook him the very next day?

He pondered for a moment as to the direction in which Mary had said the couple had disappeared. The field beyond the yard bordered the oast-house. He knew, of course, from what Wadham had told him that Barclay was supposed to be wishful to marry Pamela Courtley. It was possible that the maid had seen a surreptitious meeting between those two. It was not, however, a foregone conclusion. Any couple, running out of the garage, would make for that field. From it they could either get out on to the road beyond Barclay's house or if the girl wanted to get back into Carron Cross, she could come right round through the fields to the other side of the house. The garden-door by the chauffeur's room was there, and had anyone wanted to get in or out it was easy enough to manage. No, there could be no certainty that Pamela and Barclay were the two concerned. But the incident had made him revise his plans. He would see the girl now, and then tackle the man.

Chapter XII

PAMELA AND THE INSPECTOR

He sent word that he would like to interview Pamela, and waited for her to come with great curiosity. He wondered what Anne's daughter would be like. She came into the room jauntily enough, and Sturt did not know whether to admire or condemn her for that. She had made no attempt to put on mourning, but as a slight concession she wore a gay green and white linen frock instead of her usual slacks. Her pale gold hair was beautifully waved up from her forehead into sophisticated little curls, each in its most effective position. Her lips were carefully reddened, her cheeks just becomingly touched up.

She advanced with a cheerful smile, and sat down with a sort of mock correctness in the chair opposite to Simon. Yet his keen look detected a faint tremor in the hands she folded on her lap, and he was not quite certain whether all this self-possession and apparent freedom from any sort of emotion were not bravado.

"I've not a great deal to ask you, Miss Courtley," he began, "and of course I don't want to trouble you more than I can help in this distressing affair!"

Pamela at this point struck a light and lit her cigarette, as though to emphasize the fact that she was not at all distressed, and needed no sympathetic handling.

Simon found it rather difficult, in these circumstances, to deal with the details of the death of this matter-of-fact young woman's father, but he continued to do his best.

"First, I must ask you——"

"As a matter of mere routine," interjected the girl, and gabbling on madly, "to account for your whereabouts on the day and at the presumed time of the murder. Isn't that what you want to ask? Well, I'll save you all the trouble I can. I wasn't here. I was miles away, bathing down at Horming, accompanied by Granny, Mr. Dick Moore, and my sister Prue. I've a perfect alibi and you really need not bother about me."

Simon began to feel both annoyed and even a little disgusted. He was accustomed to people showing nervousness in all sorts of odd ways, but he really thought this girl was betraying complete callousness, and he thoroughly disliked her for it. He did not think this was nervousness, he took it to be mere impudence and resented it as such.

With a perceptible coldness he corrected her. "I wasn't going to ask where you were on Tuesday afternoon. I was going to ask where you were on Monday night?"

Pamela opened big blue eyes in complete surprise. "Monday night? Why, here of course! We all were."

"At between eleven and twelve midnight?" queried the inspector, and noted at once a change in the girl's face.

She tried to cover her feelings, but for a moment undoubtedly surprise and uneasiness had shown.

"Between eleven and twelve—let me think—well, what did we do that night? We played a little bridge, but Granny was tired and so we all went up to bed early. I'm pretty sure I'd be in my bath about that time!" This with a resumption of her impudent smartness.

Simon pressed a little further. "At what time did you see Mr. Courtley that night?"

She was silent, her cheerfulness vanished. After a brief pause she replied, "I hadn't said good night to him downstairs. I'd been out with Dick for a stroll after dinner. He, Daddy, came along to my room after I was in bed."

Sturt noted to himself that she was deliberately giving him a false impression. She spoke as if Charles had come to bid her good night, whereas he knew from the maid's evidence that he had come in anger to pounce on her.

"You were ready for bed then before twelve o'clock?"

"Yes, of course."

"And you remained in your room, you didn't go out again?"

Something like fear touched her. The blue eyes were frankly anxious now. "No, I didn't. I went to bed and I stayed there."

"Very well. Now, one other point, Miss Courtley. Your father objected, I understand, to your friendship with Mr. Barclay?"

Bright colour flamed in her cheeks, obliterating her artistic make-up.

"Yes, he did. But that's nothing to do with it. Mr. Barclay isn't mixed up in this."

Simon regarded her hot indignation. She must be very much in love to fire up at the slightest hint implicating Barclay.

"Had you and your father quarrelled over it?" he continued.

"Yes! We had! Just as we quarrelled over pretty well everything! But you needn't make a mountain out of a molehill! I'm nearly of age, and I can marry if I choose and whom I choose! Daddy couldn't prevent me once I was twenty-one."

Again Simon looked at those hot burning cheeks, and despite himself a faint uncomfortable feeling crept over him. Why this vehemence? 'The lady doth protest too much,' he thought. He went on relentlessly. "And had he quarrelled with Mr. Barclay over this matter to your knowledge?"

She rose impatiently to her feet and moved to throw her cigarette out of the window. When she turned back to him, she was calmer. He suspected she wanted to gain time.

"Yes, he had. He'd told him not to come here any more. But that didn't matter. Hugh and I could always meet when we wanted to, and I'm in no hurry to marry. I can quite well wait a year or two. None of this was serious," and sensing Simon's inward disagreement, she went on in an eager rush. "You must understand this. Daddy quarrelled with everyone. He always had rows. It wasn't in the least odd or out of the way for him not to be on speaking terms with Mr. Barclay. It really didn't mean *anything*. You must believe that." Her bravado, her impudence, had deserted her now, she was frightened and anxious.

Simon thought her rather pathetic. In her anxiety to clear any possible suspicion away from her lover she did not care how much she told of her home life. He thought rather sadly how little happiness she could have had in that home.

"Well," and his voice was kinder, "we'll leave that now. But I'd like to know if you have any idea why your father went to Fosse Wood when he did? I'm asking everyone this. It's important, you know."

She shook her head. "No. I don't know at all. He didn't come to breakfast, or lunch, with us that last day. So I never saw him to speak to. He was in his study when we went off to bathe, and he'd gone when we came back."

"Very well. That'll be all then," and he rose to open the door for her. She hesitated for a moment, then with a quick whisk of her skirt, seemed to shake herself back into her earlier mood. "No reflection on my character—you give me a clean sheet." She smiled cheerfully, and went lightly and gaily out of the room.

Simon waited for a few moments. The girl had been ready enough with her denial that she had been out that Monday night. Yet, if there were anything in this secret interview, and Simon thought that there was, then she would have been prepared to deny it. He decided he would tackle Barclay next. He might glean more there.

As he prepared to leave, and began putting together brief notes he had made, he was surprised by a knock on the door, and by the entry of Anne. She looked rather ruffled and he noted the hardness of her lips and the angry little twitch she gave as she closed the door behind her.

"I'm afraid my daughter has been making rather an exhibition of herself," she began. "Please don't take her too seriously, Inspector. She's rather an excitable young woman and lets her tongue run away with her."

At once Simon was on his guard. What on earth was she driving at? Why had she come in like this?

He said nothing, hoping she would be led on to explain herself. His silence achieved its object, for she went on: "I'm sorry you have to be bothered with all our private affairs. There was nothing really in this business of Pamela and Hugh Barclay. She just hadn't quite pleased her father in the way she behaved. He really didn't take the matter too seriously. I thought I ought just to warn you not to think too much of what she says."

"Mummy, how odious of you to say such things," burst in an indignant voice. Unperceived by either of them, Pamela had followed her mother back into the room. With flashing eyes she confronted the older woman.

"It's perfectly horrible of you to speak like that! You *know* Hugh and I are fond of each other—and you know I'd have stuck to him whatever Daddy said!"

Sturt was surprised to see the change that had come over the girl. All that hard bright impudence had faded away. He saw that it had only been a pose to conceal the depth of her feelings. She looked at her mother with clear blue eyes, frankly and honestly.

"Why, Mummy, you *know* I really care for Hugh, and though you say I'm so young, I'm sure I know my own mind. I've only agreed to keep it to ourselves to please *you*—you begged me not to get you into further trouble with Daddy over it. I'd have been honest with Daddy, I've hated keeping it all secret—only you said he'd take it out on you. How can you say now I'm exaggerating and making a fuss over nothing?"

There was such a hurt, puzzled tone in her voice that Simon felt terribly sorry for her. It seemed to him that a gulf was opening at the girl's feet. Clearly she had trusted her mother, against her own better judgment. Anne had persuaded her to hide her love-affair from her father, probably for her own ends, thought Simon cynically. Now the girl was realizing all was not straightforward on her mother's part.

Pamela turned to him. "Don't think I'm silly, please. I'm only afraid you mayn't know what Hugh is—he's so honest and splendid, and it's been my fault we've concealed anything. You must blame me, not him—and don't think he's a secretive person, he's not," she added naïvely. Then, with a touch of indignation, she looked at her mother. "There! I've said what I want to say, and I hope I've prevented any injustice to Hugh."

Anne had grown paler as she faced the girl.

"That's not the point, Pamela. I simply want the inspector to know your father had no serious quarrel with Mr. Barclay over you."

"But that's what I *said*!" burst vehemently from Pamela. "That's what I *told* him—I said Hugh wasn't mixed up with Daddy."

"Oh!—" And Anne looked thoroughly mortified. "I'm sorry I've interfered then. I thought you seemed in such a state when I met you on the stairs just now, and really you were so hysterical and incoherent, I couldn't imagine what you'd been saying. I merely wanted to remove any unfortunate impression you might have made."

Her last words were almost a sneer. Pamela looked at her intently. Then, with real dignity, she turned to Simon who had remained a silent spectator of the scene.

"I'm sorry. I *was* upset. I tried not to show it before you. My mother misunderstood me—" She broke off, for she was dangerously near tears. Then she turned abruptly, and ran out of the room.

Anne looked after her with an odd angry expression. She glanced at Simon, evidently thought the less said the better, and followed her daughter out, shutting the door behind her.

Sturt waited till she should have left the hall outside, then snatching up his hat and his case, went out, determined now to see this last person in the drama, Hugh Barclay. His feelings towards Anne grew more and more unfavourable. He thought she was a hard, selfish, scheming woman—and he believed, after this episode, that she was one of those women who, as they age, grow jealous of their daughters. Towards Pamela, too, his feelings were changing—but in a favourable sense. He began to admire the girl in more ways than one.

Chapter XIII

A TOUGH CUSTOMER

G oing up the short steep drive, Simon turned to the left. Beyond the great black barn lay a yard, and beyond that a low wall. Rising through a grove of young ash trees showed the top of the oast-house. It had been converted into a dwelling, but the old red walls remained, and the round base with its tall pointed roof.

As he stood for a moment after knocking on the door, Simon realized that from this particular place a full view could be had over Carron Cross, its drive, its front door, and even into the windows along the front of the house. Whoever lived in the oast-house could know all that went on at Carron.

Steps came from within, and the door was opened to him by Barclay himself.

Again, Simon's first reaction was that here was both a fine specimen and also a tough customer. Tall, with the same shade of reddish gold hair as that of his cousin Sylvester, Barclay gave a similar impression of force and virility. Sturt had already realized that Charles Courtley had been a violent and difficult personality. Now the thought came to him that in these representatives of a ruined landed family Courtley had not met with weaklings or the last feeble members of an effete and worn-out stock, but with men every bit as bold and vigorous as himself.

"Inspector Sturt? I know why you're here, of course. Come about the murder, I conclude. Come this way, will you?"

Barclay went across a small flagged hall, followed by the inspector, and into the big studio which filled the old round oast-room. The windows on the opposite side showed a wonderful panorama, the whole countryside seemed to fall away below, dissolved on this lovely September morning in faint blue mists. The harvest had been carried and here and there the stubble fields shone palely gold.

Barclay pointed to a chair, and Simon sat down, resigning himself to what he foresaw would be a difficult interview.

"Mr. Barclay," he began, "I've come to see you because, as far as is known, you are the last person to have seen Mr. Courtley alive."

"Well," said Barclay deliberately, "that's for you to say. I parted with Courtley at about three o'clock. I know nothing as to what he did after that."

"He saw no one after that in his own home," retorted Sturt, "and he left his home at about four-thirty. No one spoke to him after you had been with him as far as we have been able to trace."

"Well?" Barclay's interrogation was almost a sneer.

"Can you tell me the subject of your conversation?"

"Certainly. I'd gone to see him on business, but actually we never got to it. He was in a foul temper when I arrived, and began straight away on an old grievance, my friendship with his daughter. He objected to it. He had some while ago forbidden me to go to his house, and I told him that no doubt in these circumstances she would come to visit me in mine. Since then, he and I hadn't been on speaking terms. Yesterday afternoon he accused me of meeting her the night before, in his own grounds—which I had great pleasure in telling him to his face was a lie."

"When had he forbidden you his house?"

"Oh, a few weeks ago," Barclay replied carelessly.

"Then you hadn't been to Carron Cross for some time?"

"Correct."

"And why did Mr. Courtley ask you to go and see him yesterday afternoon?"

The blue eyes stared hard for a moment. Then, with a defiant laugh:

"Well, in the circumstances I suppose you've a right to pry into all our affairs. He wanted to do a deal with me."

"A deal?" Simon was surprised.

"Yes. Courtley was always ready for a deal, and always believed he'd get the best of one! Just as he firmly believed everyone and everything had its price. He was set on getting this house and piece of land, and I imagine he thought once he'd 'warned me off' his daughter I'd perhaps be readier to quit." He laughed sardonically. "He didn't realize that after the way he behaved I'd have cut my hand off rather than sell to him. I took the greatest pleasure in baffling him, I can tell you."

A queer note had crept into his voice. Triumph? It sounded like that to Simon's acute ear.

"Why, feeling as you do, did you agree to go and see him?"

Barclay shrugged. "He wrote that he'd something really important to discuss with me; a purely business matter, he said. Well, I'd no reason to refuse to talk business with him—and I wasn't afraid of him, and didn't choose he should think I might be!"

Simon looked at those fierce blue eyes, that firm mouth, and decided that it was natural combativeness which had sent Hugh Barclay down to confront Charles Courtley. He reflected for a moment.

"You and your cousin came from the family that formerly owned this property?"

Barclay nodded. His face grew dark, and he turned away his eyes. There was a brief uncomfortable silence.

Simon decided to plunge.

"You disliked Mr. Courtley perhaps partly because he'd bought your property?"

"Not mine," corrected Barclay. "Strictly speaking, my cousin's. And I didn't dislike Courtley because he'd bought the place. I disliked him for what he was."

Simon smiled. "Well, so far I've failed to find anyone who liked him, for any reason at all."

Barclay looked at him curiously, then: "So you've realized the kind of man he was? Good for you." He paused, then went on coolly: "You won't find anyone in this neighbourhood very willing to help you to catch Courtley's murderer, Inspector. A better-hated man hardly lived. His family—well, they detested him, and with reason. His work-people feared and disliked him to a man. We're country folk here, you know, and we don't in any case usually take to strangers; Mr. Courtley had really earned himself the hatred of the entire countryside."

"Why?"

"He was a bully and a money-snob," returned Barclay savagely. "He thought because his dirty money bought the place, it made him master. Well, people here don't believe any man's good enough to be another man's master. They had to stick his bullying, poor devils, because once you lose a job now it's hard to find another. And people don't leave their homes if they can help it, especially country people. But he's got across everyone, and no one will regret him or lift a finger to point out the one that did it."

He ended on a note of defiance and Simon recognized only too clearly the truth that lay behind the outburst. In any land country folk hang together. Peasantry will very rarely betray anyone of the soil. When in addition their solidarity is invoked against an outsider, there is little hope of getting them to break that apparently sullen and stupid silence which is their last and surest refuge. Sturt remembered a case he had once read about, the murder of a Frenchman, Carrier, a prominent writer in the days of the Orleans monarchy. A whole countryside then had known how that man came to his death, had known and talked amongst themselves, but never a word to outsiders and never a breath of the truth to the police.

"Well, Mr. Barclay, can you tell me anything at all likely to throw any light on this murder? Whatever Mr. Courtley may have been, I'm investigating his murder, you realize, and you're bound as a citizen to give me any help you can."

Barclay remained silent, only his sardonic smile showed how little he was affected by the inspector's platitude.

"Did you hear the telephone when you were leaving Mr. Courtley's house?"

"Yes, I did," replied Barclay. "I heard it ringing as I came up to my own door."

"Did it ring long?"

"No, someone answered it at once."

"Well, that helps me to some extent," replied Simon meditatively, but did not explain how.

He sat for a moment wondering how to go on to the next subject he wished to tackle, and his eyes wandered casually round the studio. Subconsciously he took in the various canvases, a few hanging on the walls, more stacked round the room. Then his eye fell upon Barclay's hand, which was bandaged. "What have you done to your hand, Mr. Barclay?" he inquired.

"Hurt it cleaning my gun."

"Oh! How came that about?"

"Keen on the trail, aren't you? Well, we all shoot round here, you know, Inspector. But I'm careless. Didn't clean my gun properly and it exploded. Luckily it's no more than a baddish burn. Nothing serious at all."

Simon looked keenly at his antagonist. "Your right hand, I see! What part is damaged?"

Barclay grinned. "*Not* the finger-tips, Inspector, the palm and side. Doctor Williams can tell you all about it."

Sturt nodded. He felt no sort of vexation. This man was perfectly open and above board. He and the inspector were playing a game, and he meant to concede no points. But neither had any animus. Now he must tackle his opponent over the midnight interview.

"I'm sorry to have to ask you a very personal question," he began, "but there's one other aspect of this affair I'm bound to investigate. Do you mind telling me if you are engaged to Miss Pamela Courtley?"

The bright blue eyes stared at him without any extra sparkle and Barclay's voice answered without any sort of changed intonation.

"I don't mind telling you that I am not."

"I know, of course, there's no open engagement, but I must ask if there is any private understanding between you."

"There's none," was the brief definite reply.

Sturt paused. Of course it might not have been Barclay that night, but he must see whether he could catch any sign to help him in his decision.

"Yet you met her very late at night?" he said, purposely putting a query into his voice, hoping he might provoke some reaction.

"Met her late at night? I certainly did not." His denial was emphatic, and there was no sign of any confusion or hesitation. "I've told you that Courtley himself asked me that, and I told him what I tell you. I did not meet her."

"Oh!" responded Sturt, "but I'm told you were seen leaving Carron grounds at some time after midnight on the night before Mr. Courtley's death, after having met Miss Pamela."

"Stuff and nonsense, Inspector! I tell you I did nothing of the sort! Who's been filling you up with such a tale?"

Simon smiled. "Information received, you know."

Barclay shrugged. "Well, it's wrong information this time. That's all I have to say."

Sturt looked at him with a hard direct gaze. "You weren't then in Carron grounds that night at all?"

"I was not."

Well, that was final, and whether true or not, must be accepted for the time being.

"Then I've nothing more to ask, and must get on. Good-bye, Mr. Barclay." And rising to his feet, Sturt went thoughtfully away. He bore no malice to Barclay for his thrusts at him. In fact, he felt slightly invigorated by his encounter.

Chapter XIV

FRESH DISCOVERIES AT AN INN

One duty he felt he must undertake at once. He must verify Wadham's alibi. Of all the three men whom he had interviewed, Wadham was the one who inspired him with the least confidence. He was basing his investigation of the case on the proved fact that Charles had been shot at very close quarters. That implied that some person familiar with Charles was the murderer, for it was unlikely that any stranger, or any person whom he had cause to fear, or any person whose possession of a sporting gun was unusual, could have come up so close as to be touching the body of his victim.

The keeper had an alibi. Anne also had an alibi, and in addition, had no access to a gun of the type used, for the only fowling-piece at Carron Cross was out of order.

There remained, therefore, as chief suspects three men: the cousins Sylvester and Barclay, and Wadham. Wadham had alleged he was out of the house, and with Sylvester over at Marple during all the crucial time. Well, this must be proved.

Simon accordingly decided to set off for the place where Wadham had told him he had gone—the 'Broken Bough' inn.

The postman, whom he met as he turned out of the oast-house, told him that the inn was a little place at a cross-roads about two and a half miles away.

"There's a nice path through the forest," remarked the postman, and Simon, feeling the need for exercise and hoping that, as sometimes before, a solitary walk would clear his brain, set off on the path indicated.

As he made his way along the little by-road, the inspector could not but be struck by the apparent emptiness of the countryside. The tall hedges, still green and with very little sign of approaching autumn, rose on either side. An occasional gap caused by a gate gave him glimpses of the wide rolling expanse which lay below the ridge. The country was almost entirely pasture, and save for a few cattle dotted here and there, the fields were empty. There were no cottages in sight and no farms lying on the fertile slopes. It was a dull sort of place, Simon reflected, not enough character for beauty. The men whom chance appeared to have brought together at this spot must have found it pretty deadly. His talks with Groves had already brought him up to date in the local gossip. He knew that Courtley's family had definitely found the place boring. No neighbours, no golf, nothing really for anyone to do. Courtley himself had frequent trips to town, on his business affairs, and he was apparently genuinely interested in the management of his estate. Moreover, reflected Sturt as he turned off the little road and crossing a stile struck into the woods, Courtley was past middle age. He'd without doubt lived a full and strenuous life. He might feel ready to settle down without further excitement. For younger men, though, it must be a very limited life. Hard though it was in these days for a man to get a job and stick to it, still, he could not but wonder how and why anyone with any go or enterprise should be willing to stick himself down in this corner at the job of being agent to anyone as difficult as Courtley, from all accounts, had been. Sylvester must be a strange man to have borne with him, he thought.

To his surprise, after twenty minutes the little woodland path he was following brought him to the glade where Charles Courtley's body had been found. It was solitary now, with the sun shining through the leaves of the oak trees, down on to the patch where the dead leaves stained with blood had now all been cleared away. The sound of the blows of an axe resounded from the place where the woodmen were now at work felling the trees, but the intervening trunks and undergrowth prevented Simon from seeing the men themselves. He looked round. The little paths wound away amongst the sturdy stems of the trees. Not far off a beam of sunshine caught a thick patch of bracken. Simon noted that it was a dense patch, and although he knew the shot which killed Courtley had not come from such a distance, he went over to it. At once he made a discovery. Someone had lain in that bracken. The ground there formed a little dell and in its depths the fronds were broken and crushed. But search carefully as he might and did, there was no faintest sign to show who had lain there, or why. Reluctantly he abandoned his search and went on his way to the 'Broken Bough.'

The little inn proved an attractive enough place. It stood by the side of the road which here bordered the forest. In itself it was a quaint little building of old red brick, half-timbered in rusty black. Originally it had clearly been nothing but a humble pub, meant to provide locals with their routine drinks. Motor traffic had brought it additional life. Though the main road was more than a mile away, the ubiquitous motorist, always searching for quiet byways and possibilities of meals, had found out this little inn. The owner, in a laudable desire to be up to date, had cleared a small rough field beside the building, had planted a few flower borders, dumped down some of those mysterious stone toad-stools and 'gnomes' which are supposed to add to the 'amenities' of a place, added some rustic benches and tables. In fact, he had created a rough-and-ready 'tea-garden.'

The most agreeable thing about the inn appeared to be its sign. One of those new gay affairs with which enterprising brewers have sought to civilize their premises, it stood in a little cleared space opposite the inn door. In modern style it gave a bright picture of an impressive old tree, shattered down one side, apparently by lightning; probably, thought Sturt idly, it really carried on some very old tradition of some famous old tree, stricken down and made memorable by some storm or catastrophe, or even—for his desultory reading had taught him a little folk-lore—this was a piece of ancient superstition, an effort to avert the anger of Jove's thunderbolt, just as the acorn on a blind had that propitiatory meaning behind its everyday use.

Entering the bar, the inspector asked if he could see the proprietor. A tall, fair girl, acting apparently as barmaid, answered him.

"You want to see Mrs. Gwyn? She is the proprietress. But I'm afraid she's not here to-day, sir, she's gone over to Marple."

Simon hesitated. "Perhaps you can tell me what I want to know." He produced his card and held it out.

At once the girl stiffened. The colour seemed to leave her face and Simon, his attention caught by her agitation, looked at her more closely. She was a girl of a fair, colourless type. Her blue eyes were rather pale, her hair not so much fair as mouse-coloured. Yet she had good features, her slim figure gave her an elegance not altogether usual for a country girl, and her lips, set now rather closely, showed that she had restraint and control. She looked at him intently and spoke slowly.

"Scotland Yard? What is it you want to know?"

"I want some information about people who've been here," said Simon firmly. "Can I talk to you anywhere more private than here?"

The girl came from behind the bar and silently led the way to the little stuffy front parlour on the other side of the passage. There she turned and faced him. "Is it about Mr. Barclay's accident?" she said, with a ring of anxiety.

Simon's mind made a swift decision. If there were anything odd about that 'accident,' now was the moment to deal with it.

"What can you tell me about it?" he replied.

The girl looked at him anxiously. "I didn't actually see it happen. The gentlemen were sitting outside in the tea-garden. Mr. Barclay had his gun and began to clean it while he sat there. I was in the kitchen. I heard the gun go off, but one often hears guns here, so I didn't pay much attention. When I took the tea, there was Mr. Barclay, tying up his hand. He told me the gun had gone off and burnt him. I wanted to get my first aid outfit—I've taken my Red Cross exams—but he said he'd go straight to the doctor."

"What time was all this?"

"I don't know, sir. I've no watch and I wasn't thinking about the time. I was single-handed and busy. I can't tell you at all."

"Was it about four or five, or when?"

She looked more frightened than ever, but reiterated stubbornly: "I can't really say, sir. It was a good bit after four o'clock. More than that I could not say."

An utterly obstinate look came over her face. Simon recognized that expression with despair. Once let East Anglians turn stubborn and there is no moving them.

He went on to another point.

"Where was the gun?" he inquired.

"Lying on the ground beside him. It looked all smashed up round the barrel."

"Wasn't he badly hurt?"

"No. He said he dropped it before it had done much damage. Mr. Wadham said he'd go and fetch his car and run him in to the doctor."

"And did he?"

"No. Mr. Sylvester had come up just then and he said he'd take Mr. Barclay. He was going that way. So they got into the car and went off."

Simon was silent. So here all *three* men had been—Wadham, Barclay, Sylvester, all together on the important afternoon.

"Did these gentlemen often come here?"

The girl nodded.

"Yes, sir. You see, Mr. Sylvester and Mr. Barclay have known Mrs. Gwyn since they were boys. She used to be in service at Carron in the old days. Then she married and came to run the inn here. The gentlemen used often to come in and see her, or come in to have a cup of tea."

There was a tinge of self-consciousness in her voice, a faintly constrained look on her face. Simon guessed that she had welcomed the visits of such a striking pair as the cousins, and had formed one of those romantic affections, based on day-dreams, for one or other of the handsome young men.

He went on: "Did you notice what they were talking about yesterday, before the accident?"

"No, I didn't. I wasn't paying any special attention to them. I was so busy and I just wanted to get them their tea and have done."

A tinge of defiance had crept back into her tone. Simon felt a sort of baffled impatience. How irritating 'local feeling' made people. He was sure this girl would not give anything more away than she could help.

"You realize this is important?" he said sharply. "I'm investigating Mr. Courtley's murder. I want all the information I can get."

"Yes, I know all about that." Her voice, too, had hardened. "I've nothing to tell you, I'm sure."

"Well, did anyone see these gentlemen?"

She answered reluctantly: "Perhaps old Walter did. He's generally about."

'Walter' was produced. An ancient gentleman, apparently a retired hanger-on. From his looks he might have been well over eighty, but bent old countrymen are not always as old as they look, and this particular specimen was perfectly free from deafness, and his blue eyes were bright and clear and obviously observant. He, too, looked hard at the handsome dark face of the inspector.

Yes, he'd been sitting on the bench outside the evening before. Yes, he'd seen the gentlemen. Know them? Why, of course. Known Mr. Sylvester and Mr. Barclay from boys. Yes, he'd heard the bang of the gun, but he'd not interfered. Mr. Barclay hadn't seemed much hurt and he himself didn't see any call to do anything. Mary had been about and she knew how to deal with accidents.

What time had it been? He couldn't say, couldn't say at all. Late afternoon, five or six or thereabouts, he couldn't say.

What time had they gone? Well, that he couldn't say neither. Which way? Why, Mr. Sylvester and Mr. Barclay had gone off in the car towards Marple, going to find the doctor. Mr. Wadham, he'd gone back into the forest, going home to Carron he'd be.

Simon turned to the girl. "You didn't tell me that. You said they'd all gone off together."

"Indeed I did not," she retorted angrily. "You didn't ask me anything about that. I just told you the truth. Mr. Sylvester said he'd take Mr. Barclay in his car."

Simon persevered, for this 'alibi' was important.

"Come now, can neither of you tell me the time? You must keep your eye on the clock," turning to the girl. She shook her head obstinately.

"No. I can't tell you. I was busy and I didn't look at the clock. And I'm not good at guessing what the time is, ever."

"Of course," thought Simon to himself, "they're just on the defensive. I'll bet they know the time perfectly well. But they don't want to be mixed up in all this—so they're denying they know!"

And question as he could, he came up against that blank wall of alleged ignorance and no impression could he make. Finally in despair he gave up, for the time being at any rate. He must try to get his information elsewhere.

Taking up his soft hat, he turned crossly out of the inn, prepared to set out back towards Carron. But as he stood for a moment looking down the little sunlit country lane, his face changed. Where had he seen that group of trees? The oak, and behind it the strangely twisted thorn. He hesitated, then it came to him, a picture—unfinished but clearly to be recognized—in Hugh Barclay's studio.

He turned back to the girl and old Walter, who were standing side by side eyeing him with obvious distrust.

"Does Mr. Barclay come here painting?"

The girl nodded.

"Been here often?"

"Yes, painting the old thorn."

"Does he meet anyone here?"

"Well, he just comes and does his painting."

"I must ask you definitely. Has he met Miss Pamela Courtley here?"

"No, he hasn't!" Nothing could be more positive than her tone. Yet Simon had caught a flash of a glance from her to the old man. He turned to him quickly.

"You ever seen him meet the young lady here?"

"No, that I have not. Just as Mary says"—this with a half-impudent cheerfulness.

Resignedly Simon accepted defeat. That this pair knew something he believed certain, but equally certain was the fact they did not mean to tell him all they knew.

He set off back, leaving the two standing side by side in front of the inn—calm, cheerful, and, each in their own way, impenetrable.

Chapter XV

ANNE'S STRANGE STORY

A s he swung along homewards Sturt, despite the check received at the hands of Mary and old Walter, felt his spirits rise slightly. His instinct told him that he was fumbling with a clue which might lead him to the truth. Barclay, Sylvester, Wadham, all in conjunction, and just before the catastrophe, must portend something. Two of them hostile to Courtley, the usurper of their place, Wadham discontented and untrustworthy. He walked quickly, turning over the facts he had collected, pondering the theory he was beginning to form.

It was late now, and he turned in to the room he had taken in the village, tired and ready for his bed.

Next morning, he woke early, and anxious to get to work he hurried over his breakfast and set off to the police station.

Sergeant Grove came hastening out to meet him.

"Inspector! Mrs. Courtley's here. Says she must see you at once. Says she's something very important to tell you."

"Mrs. Courtley?" Sturt was quite taken aback. He had begun to visualize so clearly a drama based on property, on the hatred felt by the dispossessed for the prosperous, that he had quite forgotten the woman.

"Mrs. Courtley? What's she to do with it?" was on the tip of his tongue, but bumped back to earth by the sergeant's words, he pulled himself together, tried to clear his mind of the two cousins and their disturbing personalities, and with his most official air went into the little dull office where Anne sat waiting.

The moment his eyes fell on her his heart gave a jump. There was no mistaking the look on her face. Very pale, very wrought up, very determined, something graven deeply into the hard lines of her lips told Sturt that this woman had steeled herself to a difficult ordeal.

"She's come to confess," flashed through his mind.

"Yes," as if reading his thoughts she spoke, "I've come to confess, Inspector."

Then, before Sturt could collect his wits and begin the time-worn words of charging 'Anything you say may be used in evidence against you...'

"Oh! not of murdering my husband! But of something I know— something I've done—which I suppose will help you to catch his murderer." She paused, but Simon, restraining himself, said not a word.

"Yes, Inspector. I've made up my mind..." and her pale ravaged face showed with what anguish she had struggled to her decision. "I must tell you, I must see"—she hesitated, then went on with renewed vigour—"that you don't make any mistakes. I've come to realize I had better tell you what's been going on. Probably you'd find it out yourself, but you might get it wrong."

Silently Simon seated himself, and got out his notebook. He realized he had better let this woman tell her story in her own way.

She clasped her hands tightly, and fixed her eyes upon them, and not once in the time that followed did she as much as glance up.

"Peter Sylvester and I are lovers," she began abruptly. "That's been so for a long time, more than two years. My husband did not know. He, my husband I mean, and I have not cared for each other. We have not been happy together. He had his work—and his own life. I had mine to live, and I have taken my happiness where I could find it."

The short hard sentences went on, revealing the pressure this woman was putting on herself.

"I'm fond of my children, very fond of them. I did not want to give them up. So I never thought of a divorce—and I did not wish Charles to know of my affair. But someone suspected. Freddy Wadham suspected. I think he told my husband. I'm not sure, but I think he did. Charles has been different lately. Watching me. Watching my letters. Different with Freddy too."

She broke off, wrestled with herself for a moment, then went on with increasing passion.

"Charles hated me, and he hated Peter Sylvester. He'd have liked to ruin us both. He'd planned to dismiss Peter—and he knew Peter would never get another job, without a reference, and saddled with a scandal. So he wanted to catch us somehow. But we'd been careful. He'd no proof. And he wanted proof. So he set Freddy on. Freddy's treacherous. He's hard up too. He's been trying to help Charles to trap us. And he's got caught himself." A flash passed across her white strained face. She went on.

"Charles had some hold on Freddy. I'd always guessed that. Freddy's clever and ambitious. He'd never have stayed here if Charles hadn't got a hold on him. Well, Charles meant to squeeze him further, to make Freddy spy on us, to make him get hold of our letters—something—anything—I don't know the details. But I do know this." Here she raised her eyes for the first time, and looked full at Simon. "Charles trusted Freddy. Of course he didn't trust Peter Sylvester. He'd have let *Freddy* go near him with that gun. And Freddy has been lying to you. He wasn't out of the house that afternoon when the telephone rang. *He* answered the telephone. I was only just outside the garden window when it rang. I turned back to answer it. And I heard Freddy's voice. And I heard him say: 'Yes, certainly I'll meet you at Fosse Wood. The little cross-road by the timber cut? Five-thirty—right.' You see, he's deceived you. *He* was the one who was in. *Charles* was the one who'd gone out, down to the estate office. The maids weren't out in their garden then, it was before tea. They'd not see Charles go and come back. Don't you see that must have been what happened?"

She repeated breathlessly, "It was Freddy himself who met Charles, there in the woods." Her eyes were blazing and she came to a stop.

Sturt, who had been scribbling down her words, glanced up. His impersonal look met her eyes, fiercely sparkling, lit with deep feeling.

"You realize what you've told me is of the greatest importance, Mrs. Courtley?"

"Of course, I do," she answered impatiently.

Now Sturt knew something about Charles's secretary which Anne herself did not suspect. The business which had originally brought him to the neighbourhood was connected with Freddy Wadham. A victim of blackmail had at last in utter desperation gone to the police. Sturt had been put in charge of the case, and his investigations had led him to Freddy Wadham. He had ample grounds for knowing that gentleman was lacking both in cash and in principles, and he had here a possible confirmation of Anne's story. If Charles Courtley knew of Freddy's shady activities, he had indeed the power to bring pressure to bear. If he needed a tool to use against his wife, he could almost certainly utilize his secretary. And if that secretary were pressed too far he was perhaps capable of a wild desperate effort to free himself, even if murder was the only way. Simon found all his ideas assembling themselves, with Freddy as the possible villain of the piece.

But was there sufficient evidence? Motive? To prove that involved solid proof of Charles Courtley's knowledge of Freddy's evil past. Opportunity? Well, that rested on Anne's report of the telephone conversation.

Why had Anne told him? He looked at her more searchingly than ever. He was quite sure she had not told him because her nerve had failed—no, she had come forward deliberately. Why did she wish to incriminate Freddy so fatally? Well, he would ask her!

"Now, Mrs. Courtley," he began. "You realize, of course, this is a most important piece of information. Why did you not give it to me before?"

"I did not want to help to hang a man," she answered, not pausing for a moment at the harsh word.

"Then, why tell me now?"

"Because I felt you were suspecting Peter Sylvester," she answered at once. "And that I could not bear. I had to come forward to clear him."

"To clear him?" said Simon, rather puzzled. "Why do you say that?"

"Because of the letters," replied Anne, growing if possible whiter than before. "I thought Freddy had met Charles out there to hand him the letters."

"The letters?" queried Sturt, now quite at sea.

"Oh!" gasped Anne, to whom his tone had evidently brought enlightenment. "Haven't you got them? Oh, my God! What have I done?"

And without more ado, she slid from her chair to the floor in a dead faint.

Chapter XVI

WHAT WAS IN THE LETTER?

When the excitement and commotion which follow upon a fainting attack had somewhat died down, and Anne was once more able to sit up in her chair, Simon at first thought he would press home his advantage.

"What letters were you speaking of, Mrs. Courtley?" he began firmly, hoping that a frontal attack might prove successful.

Anne, however, was fully equal to him. "I can't answer your questions now, Inspector," she began. Simon almost thought she was embarking on the classic phrase 'without the presence of my solicitor,' but she went on: "I really feel too ill. It's impossible for me to talk," and she closed her eyes, with every apparent intention of relapsing again. Simon had enough sense to see that if she chose to stick to that line he was helpless, so without any further effort to extract information he sent for her car and despatched her home, telling her that he would ring up the doctor and ask him to call at Carron Cross at once.

"But I must warn you, Mrs. Courtley," he went on seriously, "that I must see you as soon as the doctor agrees that you can be questioned. You must realize your statement is so important it must be followed up at once."

Anne nodded acquiescence. She was duly taken home, and though Sturt took the precaution of having both Carron Cross and Sylvester's house watched, and the telephone tapped, she made no effort to communicate with anyone.

The inspector puzzled over this new information. How did it fit in with the facts? Was it even true? If Anne had indeed overheard the telephone conversation, then it was clearly of great importance. Granted that she had—and he could not see why she should deliberately invent such damning evidence—then what was its bearing? Anne had asserted that Wadham had been telephoning to Charles himself. Well, that was impossible, but there was an alternative. He might have been speaking to some other person. Indeed, if the alibi of Mary and Walter were accepted, he *must* have been speaking to some other person, and that the murderer.

If Wadham, Sylvester, and Barclay had all been at the 'Broken Bough' up to six o'clock, then had Wadham telephoned to the murderer? It was impossible to get proof. Inquiries from the postal authorities had shown the call was put through from the call-box which stood in Marple village.

No, he only had Anne's word to go on.

As to these 'letters,' why on earth should Wadham be arranging to go out to Fosse Wood to hand over letters to his employer which he could have passed across the table in the study at any moment? It did not make sense. No, either Wadham was going to fetch this 'letter' from the mysterious person who had telephoned, and Courtley was to be present, or the whole story was an invention. But why should Anne have burst out in this way? And why, above all, should she have been so genuinely agitated as to faint on realizing that Simon had not been aware of this 'letter'? For her faint was genuine enough. Therefore, he argued, there *was* something genuine behind all this. Well, he must find it out.

Early in the afternoon a message was telephoned through to tell him Anne could now receive him.

Taking Sergeant Groves with him, he set off.

"You'll see, Groves," he said as they turned in at the gate, "this is our first real connecting link. We must try to screw out of her the full information which I'm dead sure she can give us."

The two men were shown up to Anne's bedroom, for she was declared not well enough to get up. Certainly she now looked really ill, her face wan and haggard, purple rims round her eyes, and a look of strain and anxiety impressed on her whole face.

Anne did not keep him waiting. She began at once.

"Inspector, of course I've thought and thought. I've been going over everything in my mind. I know now I was a fool, but I thought you had got hold of some fearfully important letters of mine, and I was terrified."

She paused, interrogatively, but Sturt kept silence. She went on:

"As I've said so much, I may as well tell you the whole story."

('I wonder,' thought Simon sardonically.)

She pulled herself into a more upright position, and went on in even, unhurried tones which betrayed how truly she had described herself as deciding what she should say.

"I told you what the position was between Mr. Sylvester and myself. I told you we had been careful to keep our affair a secret. But of course, we occasionally wrote to each other."

She broke off, then went on: "I may as well make my story complete. Two months ago, I was so unhappy, I left my husband. I thought we might possibly separate amicably. I hoped he might agree to let me have the children—he didn't care for them. But I found he would not, and Prudence is so young I could not leave her with him."

Again she stopped, and Sergeant Groves, who as a local man knew all the local gossip, could not refrain from casting a look of sympathy towards her. He knew how Charles had bullied and terrorized his little daughter, and Groves could at least understand the reluctance any mother would feel in leaving her child to such treatment.

Pulling herself together Anne went on: "My mother persuaded me to come back, and to try again. I tried to break off with Peter, I tried to get on better with my husband, and I failed. When that failure was clear to me, I wrote to Peter. I believed"—her voice hardened—"that Freddy Wadham knew of my letters. I believe he was trying to get hold of them. If he had got them, my husband could have divorced *me*. I only suspected this lately, and I went yesterday to Mr. Sylvester's house to warn him and to beg him to destroy anything I'd written. I'd asked him before," she added simply, seeing something in Simon's expression which betokened his surprise that any man should keep such letters, so fatal to a woman he loved. "But he'd always said he only kept each one as I wrote it, and burnt the others. He was obstinate, he wouldn't listen, he said he must have something from me to keep when I wasn't able to see him. That awful afternoon, I looked but couldn't find any letter. I thought he had it on him. But when I heard you'd been questioning him, when I heard you'd been asking about letters, I was terrified. I thought perhaps Charles had got my letter, that you'd found it on his body. I thought it would all come out—all the scandal—and everyone would know—now, when it need never be known—I couldn't bear it—I couldn't *bear* the children to know."

Her voice broke, and she put her hands over her eyes. Then, quickly recovering herself, she said harshly:

"So I thought I'd forestall you. I thought I'd come and tell you myself about my love-affair. It was all over—my mother will tell you it was all over. I was not going to leave Charles—and I hoped perhaps you wouldn't need to publish the letter—if you knew it had nothing to do with the murder—if you knew it was Freddy. So I made up my mind—and I told you about the telephone."

She stopped, at the end of her tether, and light broke on Simon. When he had been trying to trace a letter to Charles, a letter which might give the clue to the fatal meeting at Fosse Wood, his efforts had been taken in a wrong sense. Anne and her lover had thought he was on the track of their correspondence! Well, he must try to find out why Wadham should have shot Charles. If he had really been on the track of Anne's intrigue, and if he meant to make use of his information, clearly he could only do so while Charles was alive. His information, or alternatively his hold on Anne and Sylvester, were only valuable as long as Courtley was there, either to pay for whatever Wadham could obtain in the way of evidence, or as a threat to hold over Anne and her lover.

Anne had fallen silent and was gazing at Simon in miserable anticipation.

"What motive do you think Mr. Wadham could have in killing your husband?" he asked Anne bluntly, for he wanted to know what interpretation she would put forward herself. She did not hesitate.

"I think if you look into Mr. Wadham's affairs you may find an answer," she said. "I am sure something was wrong. I believe he was trying to get my letter to use as a bargaining weapon with Charles. They may have failed to come to terms, or they may just have quarrelled over it all. Charles was a very violent man, you know. In any case, that's for you to find out, not for me!"

Sturt saw that he would get no further information and indeed he was anxious to use what he had already got.

"Well, Mrs. Courtley," he said, "we must act on this new idea, and for the present I imagine you'll realize you must not see or communicate with Mr. Sylvester."

Anne nodded acquiescence and Simon and the sergeant hurried away. Sending Groves to superintend a thorough search of Wadham's bedroom and study, the inspector himself decided to tackle Sylvester, and began at once.

As he came down the staircase after leaving Anne's room, Pamela came out of the drawing-room. She had evidently been waiting to see him. She looked pale and constrained.

"What's the matter, Inspector?" she said anxiously. "No one will tell me. Doctor Williams just says Mummy has had a bad shock."

Simon stepped into the room with her. He felt very uncomfortable. He realized that this girl might know nothing of her mother's affairs, he believed she was much less sophisticated than she looked, and she might never dream that her own mother was engaged in a love-affair in secret. In any case, what Anne had told him was confidential.

"I'm sorry, Miss Courtley," he said gently, "this is all terribly worrying and distressing for you. But I'm afraid I can't tell you very much." He paused for a moment, and then went on, seeing the girl's increasing agitation and distress: "You see, this affair is very complicated. We've had to go into your father's private business, and something has come to light which has been a great shock to your mother—nothing against your father," he added hastily, for the girl had turned deadly pale. He realized then how deeply she felt the dragging into light of all the family troubles. She had laughed and joked and tried to pass it all off, but he understood now how her pride was hurt by the revelation to the whole world of her father's disposition. She clearly could not bear the idea that there was anything worse to be told of him. Simon thought with distress how dreadfully she would take it to heart if she was to hear ill spoken of her mother! He had seen for himself the day before what a shock it had been to her even to doubt the part her mother had played in advising her to conceal her love for Barclay.

So, unexpectedly moved by the look in her blue eyes, the tragic fear which made her lips tremble, he decided to do what he could to give her a little comfort.

"I must trust you, Miss Courtley, to be very discreet and to keep what I say absolutely to yourself. Can I?"

She looked at him with a sudden warmth and glow of friendliness. "Yes, of course you can! I promise I'll keep whatever you say absolutely to myself."

"Well, your mother's upset over something that's come out about Mr. Wadham. Something serious, and which may involve her having to give some very important evidence against him."

The relief that shone in her eyes was unmistakable. "Freddy! Oh, is that all? Why, I've always known he wasn't to be trusted! Oh, I am glad you've told me."

It was so clear that she had dreaded something far worse, that Simon was half amused, half puzzled to know what it could have been she suspected.

She was acute enough to realize that herself. She grew scarlet with confusion, and said quickly: "It's just that I felt so awful when I saw them helping Mummy upstairs, and she seemed so fearfully upset and ill. I thought something quite ghastly must have occurred!" Then, as if determined to give no opportunity of letting slip anything else which might give Simon more ideas, she said hurriedly: "Well, I'll just go and tell Granny you say we needn't worry, Mum's all right! She's in a fearful state too!"

And with a smile which she meant to be cheerful and gay, she ran out of the room.

Simon stood for a moment very thoughtful. Certainly she was charming, certainly there was something very appealing about her, but was she as straightforward and sincere as she seemed? With a sigh, he decided he must not think along those lines, he must stick to his prosaic task of acquiring information.

As he roused himself from his momentary abstraction and moved towards the door, he was halted in his steps by the fact that from the door itself came a faint sound. Someone was standing outside and fiddling with the knob—or so his first thought ran, for the handle was moving in a faint uncertain way. Then, while he stood still the latch clicked, and Mrs. Mitcham came slowly into the room. When his eyes fell upon her face, Sturt was conscious of a pang of astonishment, for he had never expected to see that calm serene countenance so ravaged and worn by emotion. Mrs. Mitcham seemed to have changed in the past twenty-four hours, from a handsome woman to an old and exhausted creature. Misery and fear—yes, Sturt was definite that it was fear—stared at him out of her eyes. Well, was it fear for herself or for her daughter? He stepped towards her, and, as she looked silently at him, could not prevent a note of concern entering his voice, so ill and exhausted did she look.

"Why, Mrs. Mitcham, do sit down," he said quickly, "you don't look at all the thing."

Silently she sank into the chair he pushed forward. Then, clearly rallying her forces with a great effort, she faced him.

"Inspector," she began, and even her voice seemed to have lost its force and to have the wavering faintness of an old woman's voice, "please tell me what is wrong. What has my daughter been saying to you?"

At once Sturt was conscious of relief. So it was for Anne she felt this overwhelming anxiety!

"Mrs. Mitcham," he replied, "you know I can't tell you anything of what has passed between Mrs. Courtley and myself as an official. You must ask your daughter yourself anything you want to know!"

The look of misery was accentuated as she replied, "That's no good, she won't let any of us see her. But I must know, I *must* know, why she came to the police station and what has upset her so dreadfully and made her so ill." There was a note of entreaty in her voice which induced Sturt to think and answer quickly. "Well this much I can tell you. Mrs. Courtley felt herself obliged to give us some very disagreeable information about Mr. Wadham."

He had expected her to show the same relief that Pamela had experienced, but to his surprise the look of fear was intensified as she muttered to herself, "Wadham! Freddy Wadham! Oh! No!"

Sturt, taken aback, sat down himself and faced her.

"Mrs. Mitcham," he said firmly, "do realize this elementary fact. The truth always helps the innocent, it can't hurt them. If you know something, and I perceive you do, I beg of you to tell me, in the interests of your family."

He bent his gaze on hers, and again a faint shock of surprise went through him. That gleam in her faded grey eyes was a gleam of defiance, of anger, of a fierceness he had not believed her capable of entertaining. She looked at him steadily, then rallied her forces, withdrew into herself, shut him out from whatever knowledge she was guarding. A deep silence filled the room, until at length she answered, slowly and carefully weighing her words. "No, Inspector, I have nothing to say to you. My daughter's affairs are her own business. I can tell you nothing about them!"

Something tempted Sturt to say, "Yes, that may be so, but have you nothing of your own affairs to tell me?"

He was not quite quick enough to see the look that flashed across her face as she swiftly turned her head aside. He could and did see her fingers tighten on the arms of her chair, but when she looked towards him again her expression had hardened into complete aloofness.

"*My* affairs? They have nothing to do with this dreadful business."

"You can't tell me anything? Anything that bears in any way on the matter?"

"How can I? I was away at the sea all that afternoon, as I believe you know." She spoke coldly, but Sturt made one more effort.

"And the night before?"

"The night before! What has that to do with it?"

"That's for me to say, Mrs. Mitcham; I ask you simply do you know of anything unusual that occurred the night before the murder?"

"No! Nothing! I was tired, and went to my room early. I went to bed and to sleep."

Simon hesitated. He had really no belief that this woman, whose character he recognized as innately upright, was a murderess, yet he felt he must clarify the situation. Her love for her daughter and for her granddaughters, did provide the possibility of motive. He must make sure there had been no opportunity, and he believed she was concealing something bearing on the matter.

"You must forgive me," he resumed after a brief pause, "but there are points I must clear up. Can you tell me if anyone knows you were in your room on that evening between the hours of ten and midnight?"

She looked at him with a strange questioning gaze, then answered slowly. "I think not. No one came to my room after I went up."

"And will you answer another question? Were you aware that your daughter was contemplating leaving her husband?"

"No," she replied firmly, "I did not—on the contrary I knew she was making great efforts to live on better terms with him. He and I went into the matter in a long talk yesterday morning—" She broke off, seeing surprise in Sturt's face.

"But," said Simon, "when did you speak to Mr. Courtley of this? I have checked all his movements during the whole of yesterday, and I have no record of any time spent with you."

Mrs. Mitcham had flushed faintly, but the colour died away leaving her cheeks whiter than before, as she answered:

"I saw Charles early, before breakfast. We were both in the garden, and we spoke about my daughter. We planned she should come on a visit to me."

"And you were satisfied as to her relations with her husband?"

"Yes," in a firm decided tone, "I was hopeful matters were going better, indeed I was confident they were. Charles and I had a perfectly satisfactory talk."

Sturt saw he would get nothing from her in that direction. He decided to say no more, but he resolved to make further inquiries as to her movements during the late afternoon. He rose and moved to open the door for her, saying, "Then I won't detain you any longer." Yet, as the words left his lips, he noted and registered in his mind that with his acceptance of her statement had come such relaxation of tension that she was trembling in every limb. He stood with his hand on the door gazing intently, but beneath his look she seemed to stiffen, to revive, to call up all the force of her character. She rose and went past him with a firm step, and with a composed resolution which he recognized as immovable.

Uncomfortable, and now almost suspicious, Sturt saw her cross the hall and disappear upstairs. Was the daughter, after all, a reflection of her mother? Had he to deal with *two* determined, strong-willed women, both bent on deceiving him? With the utmost dissatisfaction he turned to ring the bell and once more asked to see the parlourmaid. Nelly appeared, clearly vexed and flustered at the prospect of cross-examination.

"Nelly," began Sturt, "at what time did the party who had been out to bathe arrive back from the beach?"

She thought for a moment, then replied: "Miss Prudence and Mr. Dick came in at about six o'clock, I think, sir. I saw them drive up about then."

"And Miss Pamela?"

"I believe she was dropped in the village, sir; she came in later."
The girl spoke with obvious uneasiness.

"And Mrs. Mitcham?"

"Well, sir, I don't really know about her. She wasn't in the car
when Mr. Dick drove up and I thought she and Miss Pamela must
have been walking up together; but they didn't, at least, I don't
think they did."

"What makes you think they were not together?"

"Miss Pamela came in by herself, when I was laying the table,
about a quarter to seven, and she'd a box of cigarettes she'd been
buying in the village, in her hand. She brought them in to me for
the side-table, to hand round with the coffee. I'd seen Miss Pamela
come running down the drive. Mrs. Mitcham wasn't with her, and
I don't know where she'd been."

"Would anyone else know when Mrs. Mitcham came in?"

Nelly paused, and then as if deciding she must be frank, spoke.

"No, sir, but I can tell you myself she wasn't in before a quarter-
past seven. The housemaid who looks after her had her day off, and
I popped up to her room at the quarter-past to see if she needed any
help over her dressing, but she wasn't in her room, and hadn't begun
to dress for dinner—her dress was laid out on the bed. I had to go
down about my own work, and I was quite surprised to see her come
into the dining-room with the others later, in her grey dress and all.
I thought how quick she'd been, though, of course, dinner was a
bit late that evening, Mrs. Courtley having waited for the master."

She was silent, remembering how the party had waited for the
man who was at that moment already lying dead.

"Did Mrs. Mitcham seem at all agitated or upset that evening?"
Sturt went on.

"No, sir—not *upset* exactly, she did look fagged out and tired,
and I know Mrs. Courtley made that an excuse for not waiting later

for dinner. And she looked grey and drawn all dinner, but it had been a hot day and I expect she found the beach hot and tiring."

Nelly was clearly puzzled and worried about these questions, but she showed no perception that anything could be suspected of Mrs. Mitcham herself.

"Do you know anything about Mrs. Mitcham's home and parents?" Simon queried. "I want to trace some relations."

Nelly looked amazed, but possibly thinking that deaths always involved wills and relations, added promptly:

"I know she came from Ireland, sir. I've often heard her speak of her old home to Miss Pamela and Miss Prudence, telling them she was brought up in the country and loved it, and loved animals and all that."

"Irish," reflected Sturt, "and country-bred. That probably, indeed certainly, means she was brought up in a shooting house and knows all about shooting."

He thanked the girl and sent her away. He rather ruefully decided that he must keep his eyes open. Mrs. Mitcham clearly knew all about the difficulties of her daughter's married life. She equally clearly was a woman of resolution and one who could keep her own counsel. She had been absent and unaccompanied by any of the family at the time when Charles was meeting his death at Fosse Wood.

Sturt's whole instinct made him revolt against the idea of any woman having fired that destructive shot or planned that deliberate murder. He decided that he must make another visit to the agent.

Sylvester was to be found, he was told, in the estate office. This was a small, rather attractive little house, not very much more than a glorified cottage. The office proper consisted of one big room in the front. Over it, Sylvester had a bedroom and sitting-room. He was looked after by an elderly woman, who occupied the back regions, and who both cooked and did the housework and answered the telephone if the agent were out.

At this particular moment Peter was busy in the office, and Simon tackled him at once.

"Mr. Sylvester, I've just had an important statement made to me by Mrs. Courtley. She has told me of her relations with you, and I wish to trace the letter which I understand she wrote to you three days ago."

Sylvester looked utterly astounded. Clearly he had not expected anything of the sort. He laid down his pen and turned to the inspector.

"I quite see that my private correspondence with Mrs. Courtley may, in the circumstances, be of interest to you, Inspector, but I'm sure you'll realize that I was hardly likely to keep such letters by me," he said aggressively. "I have destroyed all the letters I have had from her."

Sturt met the challenge at once. "I know that you made a habit of keeping at least one letter by you, Mr. Sylvester," he began, "and I also know Mr. Wadham was aware of that." This shot in the dark took effect, as Sylvester's face showed. "Now it is important for me to know whether that letter is in your possession or Mr. Wadham's. If you have it, I hope you will produce it."

Sylvester thought over this. Then rising from his chair he went over to the fire-place, and taking a spill from a case on the mantelshelf, bent down and lit it at the small fire which was smoking and puffing on the hearth. Lighting his pipe from the spill, he came back slowly to face the inspector.

"You are asking a very difficult thing," he said. "Even supposing me to have the letter you mention, I don't produce my private letters from a woman, unless it will help her. Mrs. Courtley is not accused of murdering her husband, and therefore there is no need for me to consider that aspect. And why do you think Wadham may have the letter?"

"Because he is being accused of trying to get hold of it for his own purposes," said Simon, making up his mind to be explicit. "Mrs. Courtley has told me he was spying on you both, and that must have been either with the object of making his market on such information with Mr. Courtley—or with you." He paused, then went on: "Actually, it would be of great assistance to me if you would be frank in this matter, Mr. Sylvester. Will you tell me straight out whether Mr. Wadham had in any way approached you with a view to his knowing of your liaison with Mrs. Courtley, and of the profit he might extract from his information?"

Sylvester grew red. "There would be no profit to be made out of me, Inspector," he said bitterly. "I offer no market for anyone. I haven't a bean in the world, and Wadham knew that."

"Possibly," returned Sturt, "but if you'll forgive my saying so, Mrs. Courtley might have been able to produce funds, and its seems to me Mr. Wadham might have preferred to try that line, rather than take his goods to Mr. Courtley."

"Why?" came curtly from Sylvester who puffing hard at his pipe was clearly beginning to show his agitation.

"Well," said Sturt, who had thought out this line on his way to the office, "if Mr. Wadham could produce a letter which would enable Mr. Courtley to apply for a divorce, he might, of course, get some 'consideration' in return. But Mr. Courtley would not, in those circumstances, be very likely to keep him on in his employment, it would be too awkward. And, if you'll allow me to say so, Mr. Courtley was possibly a more difficult person with whom to make an advantageous deal, than yourself. Mr. Wadham probably realized that. What I want you to tell me is whether you have any indication that this was so."

He looked hard at Sylvester, who remained deep in thought. In an effort to clinch the matter, Sturt added sharply: "You must realize, Mr. Sylvester, this has a very direct bearing on the murder. If Mr. Wadham meant to negotiate with you, it will help to clear him of suspicion which has been directed to him."

There was no doubt that at these words Sylvester felt some shock. He shot a quick glance at the inspector, and the gloom of his expression seemed to intensify. He still said nothing and Simon went on:

"You must see clearly that if Mr. Wadham has, or had, that letter—if he were not negotiating with you, then he must be suspected of negotiating with Mr. Courtley—and that lays him open to grave suspicion."

"Why?" inquired Sylvester grimly. "Surely if he meant to bargain with Courtley that implies he would have an interest in his life, not in his death?"

"It would cast suspicion on him for this reason," said Simon, determined now to put his cards on the table. "If he attempted to bargain with Mr. Courtley, he was dealing with a violent and therefore in one sense a dangerous man. We must try to find out on whose side Mr. Wadham meant to act, for we now know he was aware that Mr. Courtley was going to Fosse Wood yesterday afternoon. That, of course, implies there was a prearranged meeting. We know Mr. Courtley met his death at that appointment. What I must ask you now is, had Wadham a letter which would have given him cause to quarrel with Mr. Courtley?"

"I can tell you nothing, Inspector. I had, it is true, received a letter from Mrs. Courtley—but it contained nothing of importance. It was merely a note asking me to come down and see her. Neither Wadham nor anyone else would have found it of any interest or importance whatever."

He looked defiantly at Simon, who merely replied: "In view of that reply, Mr. Sylvester, I must take it that you are unwilling to help me. Does that imply that you will refuse to let me look through your papers, and must I get a search-warrant?"

"Oh! You can look through my papers as much as you like. I tell you, you'll find nothing of interest as regards the murder! In fact, as I'm sure you'll leave everything as you find it, I'll leave you to it, Inspector." And with that Sylvester got up from his desk. "You'd rather I went out, I dare say?" he went on. "I've plenty to do if you'd like me to be off."

Simon emphatically did prefer to have the place to himself, and said so. "But I'm afraid I must ask you to satisfy us you've not any papers on you," he added.

Sylvester raised no objection, and sending him into another room with the officer who had remained in the hall, and directing him to search Sylvester carefully Simon himself sat down at the desk and prepared to scrutinize its contents.

Chapter XVII

AN ARREST

B ut neither the search of Sylvester's person, nor the most detailed inspection of office, and bedroom, produced any result. No letter was to be found.

There remained the search of Wadham's office. Sergeant Groves had been detailed for that task, while Simon interviewed Sylvester. Returning to the police station, Sturt was now met by a radiant and jubilant figure.

"Got him! Inspector," Groves began, as soon as he was inside the door. "What a fool! Just like all these people, go and forget one minute what they've done another."

"What have you found?" said Simon sharply, realizing that Groves, an experienced man, would not be so confident without due cause.

"The rest of that wadding paper!" replied the sergeant triumphantly—and he went over to the desk.

There, on a tray, was laid out the stained little scraps of paper which had been found in the wounds on Charles's body. Protected by pieces of glass, they were neatly arrayed, and there by itself was the one little fragment with the three letters still decipherable 'OUY.' Beside it, Groves now put another cleaner scrap of paper, apparently cut from some magazine. On it appeared a signature E. DE JOUY. As far as could be judged, the size of the lettering, and the style and type were identical. The two bent over the table.

"This is from an article in a magazine. I found a pile of them in Wadham's study. I cut this from another number. It's one of a series of articles written on some of this Chinese stuff there's been such a rage about since that exhibition."

Sturt nodded. He had himself visited the exhibition of Chinese art, he had even bought one or two little handbooks, for the subject had both interested him and shown him his own ignorance. He had tried to acquire a little knowledge and he perfectly remembered the name of the well-known expert.

"Yes," he said at once. "Clearly you're right. The piece of wadding is from one of de Jouy's articles. What else?" For he knew that identification alone was not enough to account for Groves's excitement.

"Here you are!" retorted Groves, and produced a copy of the magazine from his case and spread it open on the table. "Here's last month's number—also in Wadham's room—and the very page torn out with the end of one of the fellow's articles. It's proof he used that page to stuff that cartridge." He flipped through the pages of the magazine and sure enough, the concluding paragraph of de Jouy's article was missing.

"What a fool!" the sergeant went on exultantly, "think of leaving this here!"

"Well, I don't know," said Simon thoughtfully. "In the first place he could never have foreseen that scrap of paper would survive. Remember that shot was fired practically touching Courtley's body. No one would dream that any fragment of the wadding would survive, or be legible, much less identifiable. That's a pure piece of luck for us. And this magazine," flipping the pages over, "is one he'd hesitate to destroy. It's expensive you know, and only taken in by connoisseurs. Mr. Wadham must have been interested in the subject. He's clearly taken it in for some time, if as you say there were other issues there."

"Yes," said Groves. "That is so. There's a whole series, arranged in order and going back for a couple of years."

"So you see, he'd not dare destroy the entire copy, that would be so obvious, and he must have hoped that no one would notice the missing page. Probably once he'd looked through the magazine Mr. Courtley wouldn't want to read it again, though he'd want it kept."

"But why choose such a piece of paper?" puzzled Groves.

"Oh, there are various answers one can give to that," replied Sturt. "For one thing, he wouldn't use note-paper, that would be identifiable. When we went through Mr. Courtley's papers and desk I noticed what good quality paper he used throughout and a paper of a distinctive blue shade too. Wadham's first idea would be to avoid any paper that could be identified with the household. Something from a magazine would clearly be better. And I think I can tell you why he used this. He'd want a good stiff paper for wadding. Ordinary newspaper wouldn't be so good. Anyway, we needn't worry ourselves as to *why* he used it. The fact is, he did, and that's good enough for us."

For he saw clearly the overwhelming importance of this discovery. Wadham was now definitely linked with the crime by a fact—not solely by Anne's statement. Was there yet sufficient evidence to prove him actually the murderer?

The sergeant's voice broke in on his reflections. "I've not done yet, sir, we found something else." He bent again over his dispatch case. "Here's an old-fashioned bullet mould. We found this put away on the top of a cupboard in Mr. Wadham's office. They're things you do still find about, you know."

Sturt nodded. Himself brought up in an old-fashioned sporting home, he knew that such implements were still occasionally used by keepers, or by men who for one reason or another wanted to make their own shot.

"This would account for those large outsize pellets, you know," urged Groves, proud of his discovery, "and I can tell you this, the mould is old—wouldn't have been used for donkey's years you'd have thought—and stood up there right on the top shelf—but it hadn't a speck of dust on it!"

"Nor a sign of finger-prints, I'll bet," smiled Sturt.

"No, it's been wiped clean," agreed Groves.

"Well, that cuts two ways," said Sturt cheerfully. "Good for you, Sergeant, anyway. We'll just test the magazine and see what prints we get off that."

Sending the sergeant off Simon began to pace up and down the little office, considering where the case now stood.

He had here proof that the cartridge had been filled with wadding that came from Freddy's room. He could also prove from Anne's new evidence as to the telephone call that Freddy knew of Charles's projected visit to Fosse Wood at the vital time. He could prove that Freddy could shoot and that he had access to a gun. He could prove that in his office was a mould which could have made the bullets and which had been recently touched.

Could it now be shown that he was himself present at Fosse Wood when the murder was done? And could any motive be found?

He remembered Anne's hints. Courtley had, she said, some hold over Freddy. She had implied that Freddy's difficulties had in some way put him under the power of his employer. These hints must be investigated. He must try to find out how much Courtley had known.

Armed with his authority, Sturt now called at the bank and asked to see Wadham's account, and at once fresh evidence came to hand. Two days before the murder, he had paid in a sum of three hundred pounds in notes. The notes were traced and proved to have been part of a sum paid out to Charles Courtley, who had come in himself and cashed a very large cheque.

The inspector sent for Freddy. He began by telling him at once that this payment had been reported and asked for an explanation. "For you understand, Mr. Wadham, your pass-book makes it clear that this was an unexpected payment, over and above your usual monthly salary."

Freddy had grown very pale. He looked at Simon with frightened eyes. His whole face seemed in a moment to have become worn and haggard. For a brief space he hesitated. Then began stumblingly: "I can't tell you, Inspector. This was a confidential matter. Mr. Courtley paid me this for a special piece of work. But it was confidential. It's private business. I can't tell you."

His frantic reiterations carried no conviction. "Have you any proof?" queried Sturt coldly.

"No, of course not! I tell you it was confidential! It was to be utterly private!"

"That's unfortunate, Mr. Wadham. You see, these notes were paid to Mr. Courtley. You are required to bring some proof that he handed them to you."

Sweat burst out on Wadham's face. He realized his dilemma, and Sturt pursued relentlessly.

"I must be frank with you. Your bank account tells its own tale. You were clearly in desperate need of money. My other investigations have shown you were being hard pressed by your creditors. I must warn you, this is a very serious matter."

Wadham twisted his hands together, his gaze wandered round the room. Then he swallowed hard, and collecting his strength said, as calmly as he could: "It's no good, Inspector. I *can't* explain."

"Very well," said Sturt; he paused—then: "You leave me no alternative. I must detain you pending further inquiries."

Wadham sank down on his chair. He seemed to collapse upon himself. He buried his face in his hands and groaned aloud. Such emotion betrayed him. Both he and Sturt realized that. Mere peculation or at worst theft could not produce such despair. The face he lifted to confront Simon was ghastly. Fear and horror were stamped on it beyond concealment. Sturt felt a throb of excitement and satisfaction—he was right! Wadham was guilty. No other cause could produce this effect.

Yet, when Wadham had stumbled from the room, his head hanging, his face pale and sweat-dabbled, to the manifest astonishment of Groves, Sturt remained behind, worried and thoughtful.

For though he had a good deal of evidence, and though he was convinced that here he had the murderer, still he realized his case was terribly weak at one point. Freddy still had his alibi. He could still claim that at the vital moment he was far away, at the 'Broken Bough.' Well, that alibi must be broken.

To that object he devoted all his energies during the next week, and eventually, after endless consultations, the weighing of pros and cons by all in authority, it was decided to charge Wadham with the murder of Charles Courtley.

Chapter XVIII

TRIAL AND ERROR

T he entire neighbourhood was gratified and thrilled to hear of the arrest of Freddy Wadham for the murder of his employer. Nor did that gratification, based on the natural human love of knowing people who are in the public eye, suffer any abatement when the trial came on.

The death of a rich man is always more exciting than that of a poor person. For there is generally a good range of motive, and with any luck a good element of scandal. The Courtley case was highly productive of the latter.

Another interesting point was that most people who knew the Courtleys slightly, and no one knew them really well, had thought their marriage did not appear to be a very harmonious affair, but few had suspected its entire breakdown. The trial dragged into the light of day all Charles's peculiarities; his bad temper, his bullying, and his failure to keep his wife's affection. The scenes which so constantly devastated the household, the departure of Anne from her home, her relations with Sylvester, all came out.

Everyone had known and respected the Sylvesters, most people had wondered how Peter could bear to take a job under the man who had bought his property, and had wondered still more when they had made the acquaintance of Charles.

Still, it had been Sylvester's own affair, and after the first surprise, people had accepted the situation. Being of a solitary disposition on the one hand, and on the other being in no sense an eligible bachelor, for his father's death had shown the collapse of the family fortunes, he had had few friends and the loneliness of Carron Cross, together with his poverty, had prevented him from having much society. No one amongst the gentry had apparently suspected his intrigue with Anne. If the villagers knew, they had only talked amongst themselves. Now, however, it all came out, though there was still some pleasurable uncertainty and speculation as to the exact nature of the relations between the two. Simon had after all kept his own counsel as to Anne's confession. All that the public knew was that letters had passed which would perhaps have enabled Charles Courtley to sue for divorce (though whether with justification or not was not known), and which in any case would have created much trouble.

When the trial came on, therefore, the public anticipated the pleasure of a 'love-interest' combined with the normal excitement of a murder. They flocked to the court, expecting a full-blooded drama. That indeed they were to receive, but not along the lines that they anticipated.

Interest, of course, was felt when Freddy entered the dock, and those who had known him before felt a pang of surprise and sympathy when they saw the change which a few weeks had wrought in him. Indeed some felt that he stood confessed of guilt, his appearance was so ghastly. He stood there, his head at first bent, his face a horrid yellow pasty colour, his cheeks sunken in. When he tried to straighten his shoulders and look round the court, he achieved nothing but a hasty furtive glance. His hands obviously trembled as he tried to stiffen his hold on the barrier before him. Everyone looking at him realized that to the normal juryman here was clearly a man with some dreadful guilt upon him. He seemed self-condemned.

Then came the dramatic moment when Anne was called. She stepped into the witness-box calmly and steadily. But that pose was not maintained for long. As the trial proceeded, amazement grew, for she abandoned her attitude of restraint, and she surprised both police and public by the violent animosity she showed towards Freddy. She asserted that the relations between herself and Sylvester were not 'guilty' in the technical sense of that term. Of course she had been unhappy with her husband. She did not deny that, but declared firmly it was his harshness towards the children which provided the real cause of the estrangement. She stuck to it that she had at first only contemplated a judicial separation, and this her mother confirmed. She could show that having left her husband she had gone to her mother, not away with Sylvester. She had given in to her mother's entreaties and had gone back to Charles, determined to make one further effort in order to run no risk of separation from her children. She declared that Sylvester had always been a friend, but nothing more than a friend, and she asserted that the whole idea of anything more than this was an invention on the part of Wadham.

He, she said vehemently, was the true villain of the piece. He had not been a satisfactory secretary, and her husband had been thinking of dismissing him. Faced with the loss of his job, Freddy had tried to make some profit for himself. He had told Charles, she asserted, that he, Wadham, could provide him with evidence that Anne was carrying on an intrigue with Sylvester. Charles, furious at this, had secretly plotted with Wadham, resolving to divorce Anne and retain for himself the custody of the children.

Wadham had been the go-between, acting as a spy for Charles, negotiating on his behalf for Anne's letters, and at the same time trying to keep in with Anne, and pretending to Sylvester that he was acting in their interests, not in that of his employer. It was on what she swore Wadham had told him of her husband's plots against her that the tale of Charles's vindictiveness depended.

The whole court thrilled when Anne boldly made her statement. Nor did cross-examination shake her. She declared her positive belief that Wadham had tried to 'frame' a case against her and Sylvester. She swore that the letter, sent by her to Sylvester and delivered on the very day of the murder, simply referred to a present she had thought of making her husband as part of her policy of reconciliation, for his birthday. She had intended giving him some special book on the planting of commercial timber, in which Charles had begun to interest himself, and had written to Sylvester as an expert to get one for her.

Excitement grew when, losing her cold self-assured manner, the fruit of years of repression of her feelings when dealing with Charles, she said vehemently, "I didn't love my husband, but I never wished him any harm. That man," and she nodded across the court at Wadham, standing in the dock, "*did* wish him harm. I know he went to meet him at Fosse Wood, I know he could have got up close to Charles without being suspected by him, and I am sure he shot him dead!"

In vain did counsel try to check such unsupported statements; the effect Anne wished was produced. Everyone realized that in one respect Anne had hit the right nail on the head. Freddy alone, amongst the men who might have fired the shot, was on sufficiently good terms with Charles to have been able to come up near enough to him.

She failed, however, in so far as she overreached herself by the violent prejudice she showed. Public opinion, including that of the jury, was shocked by a woman showing such animus towards an accused man. She could not really hope to figure as the outraged wife, and her vehemence was put down to spite.

"Probably wanted him to make love to her, and is getting back on him because he wouldn't," was the general criticism.

The case against Freddy rested largely, of course, on her evidence as to the telephone call. She swore what she had already told Sturt, that she had distinctly heard, and recognized, his voice answering the telephone. The words were, "I'll be at the timber-cutting, at Fosse Wood cross-ways, at 5.30."

The importance of that part of her evidence was fully recognized. As she repeated clearly and distinctly those words, everyone turned their eye on Freddy. If Anne were telling the truth—and being on oath and facing severe cross-examination made it more probable that she was—then Freddy's complicity in the murder was definite. It remained to weigh the evidence in favour of his being the actual person to fire the shot.

Next the facts as to the curious wadding of the cartridge were proved. The pellets, it was shown, were of a larger size than went with the usual cartridge. They had been inserted no doubt with the express intention of inflicting such wounds as would be fatal. An ordinary dose of shot, at such close range, would no doubt have done the trick, but these being pellets made death certain.

The scrap of paper with the letters OUY was produced, and the magazine with the missing page, found in Wadham's study, together with the other copies with the articles signed 'DE JOUY.' The existence of the bullet mould in his room and its recent use were proved too.

One further support to the case of the prosecution was found in the statement of Freddy's affairs. He was shown to be hopelessly in debt, hard pressed by his creditors, and with no means of extricating himself from his difficulties. Anne stated that she knew her husband would never advance or lend money to any employee.

The payment of three hundred pounds by Charles to Freddy's account was sworn to, and the prosecution drew the deduction that this money had been stolen by Wadham. Here they declared was the motive for the crime. Faced with exposure and ruin, he had tried to save himself by the murder of his employer.

The general opinion at the close of the case for the prosecution was that Freddy's chances were poor. There was a consensus of opinion that he had been engaged in some dirty work and the probabilities appeared to be that he was in truth the murderer. But the case against him was not overwhelming, and this added zest to the hearing of the defence.

That defence was simple. Freddy went into the box and gave evidence himself. He entirely denied the truth of Anne's story. He had been out of the house on the fatal day by three o'clock. He had never answered the telephone. He had, it was true, tried to get into touch with Sylvester, over the letter which had passed between him and Anne, but that was because he was really friendly with him and wanted to warn him of Charles's animosity. He swore that he had never negotiated on Charles's behalf, that throughout he had done his best to help Sylvester to avert scandal.

So far it was his word against Anne's—and no one really believed either of them.

Everything for him turned on his alibi. The defence called Peter Sylvester and Barclay to swear that they had been with him at the 'Broken Bough.' But here, to the general stupefaction, the defence was not altogether successful. The two men agreed that they had met Wadham in the late afternoon, but neither would swear to the hour. They had themselves been together at the time and had been there for some unspecified period, before Wadham had joined them. A sensation was created when they each swore that Wadham had left before they did, but as to the time, they declared they had not noticed at all, being taken up with the accident to Barclay's hand. They could not, or at least would not, give any more precise statement. It was, therefore, possible for the prosecution to allege that he had only been with them for a short time—perhaps for half an hour at about five o'clock. This gave him just sufficient time to be back at Fosse Wood by five forty-five.

The maid and old Walter gave evidence slightly more in his favour. They agreed that Wadham had gone off by himself, on foot, when the two others had departed in the car, but the girl thought the time was close on six. Nearer than that she would not go. Actually she proved a bad witness, frightened and confused. When counsel pressed her she became more muddled and ended by bursting into tears. The general impression was that her evidence was worthless, owing to its vagueness.

Old Walter was no better. He had apparently been stricken with deafness. He misunderstood every question put to him, he muttered his replies and refused to speak up when exhorted in fierce bawls to do so. But he was rather more certain of his ground than Mary. He 'believed Mr. Wadham went off just a few minutes—like before Mr. Peter.' And he was quite positive, as Mary had been, that Sylvester and Barclay had been at the inn till 'right close on six.'

When the jury retired, the tension increased. Everyone felt it was touch and go. Most people believed Freddy to be guilty, but they also thought there was more in it than met the eye. Few believed in Anne's truthfulness, and everything hinged on that.

The jury shared those doubts, and framed their verdict accordingly. Freddy's guilt really depended on that telephone call, which if truly reported could scarcely have an innocent explanation. But that in turn hung on Anne's unsupported word, and the general effect of her attitude was to throw doubts on her. Anyone so prejudiced, so determined to fix the guilt of the murder on Freddy, could not command the unqualified confidence necessary to bring in a verdict of guilty. Freddy was in consequence acquitted.

With this acquittal, Charles's murder seemed to pass into the range of unsolved mysteries.

Chapter XIX

THE MONUMENT IN THE WOOD

A year had passed, and once again late summer came round and the countryside round Carron lay hot and still in the sunshine. Chance—or Fate—sent Simon Sturt to visit some friends who lived on the other side of the country. Finding himself there, in the same season, and in the same hot breathless weather, in the neighbourhood of the famous crime, he found that he could not resist an impulse to revisit the actual scene. He had come down, tired and overworked, from London. His nerves had been strained by a long and difficult piece of work. As he stood late at night by his window, before turning in to bed, his eyes ranged over the vast quiet expanse of countryside lying silent beneath the moon. Away in the distance a dark belt of woodland stood sombrely against the sky. Gazing at it, half stupefied by fatigue, something in his brain stirred, and the name 'Fosse Wood' swam up from his inner consciousness, and with that all his earlier dissatisfaction and unease over the Carron murder rose up in full flood.

He had never got to the bottom of that mystery. He was still sure Wadham had been involved, was still convinced in spite of all the evidence to the contrary that Anne had been playing a double part in the affair. He had never understood why she had tried so desperately to incriminate Wadham, unless it had been to divert suspicion from herself or from some other man. He believed firmly there had been a tacit or even a definitely arranged conspiracy to defeat justice.

He had so often pondered the whole business and he had come to the conclusion that the country people had combined to shelter the murderer. He had an instinct that the people at the 'Broken Bough' inn had known more than they had ever told. Mary Game and old Walter he would swear had concealed something.

As he reflected, his mind, wandering back over the past, made itself up. Next day he would go back to the place and see whether anything had cropped up in the interval. He hoped too that perhaps, with the passage of time, and coming fresh to the scene again, something he had previously missed, something obscured then, might stand out now. Some little detail which had escaped notice might just possibly strike him afresh.

Acting on this decision, he determined to collect such information as he could from his hosts. They would probably be able to tell him some of the local gossip, for both sides of the country met and mixed at the one large country town.

His inquiries next morning at breakfast as to whether they knew at all what had happened to the Courtleys, at once aroused their interest. Yes, of course, everyone had been so thrilled over the famous case, and everyone had been curious to see what would happen once the trial was over.

Wadham had disappeared. He'd probably changed his name, and certainly had left that part of the world. Apparently in a sort of revulsion after the trial, people had been quite sorry for him, thinking he had been made the scape-goat. The general opinion had been that possibly he was not guilty, but that *if* he had the pluck to kill his bullying employer, he deserved to get away with it!

Simon could not subscribe to this view. He knew what the public did not know—that Wadham had been a bad lot, and that he deserved no sympathy at all, whether guilty or innocent of the murder.

He was more concerned, however, with the actual Courtley family. Indeed, he would not admit even to himself how often he had found his thoughts turning to Pamela. Somehow, he was haunted still by her face. He could not forget her pathetic effort to 'keep her end up,' he could still remember with a pang how frightened and stricken down she had been once her pose was abandoned. He never quite liked to think of that scene between her and her mother.

So it was not quite casually that he asked next for her.

"Pamela? Oh, I believe she took it all much more to heart than one would have expected," answered his hostess. "She always looked so hard, and as if she didn't care a bit about anything. Why, all the time of the trial she was there you know, all made up and dressed in the most conspicuous way, and laughing and joking with that young Dick what's-his-name, so that everyone thought her a perfect disgrace. But after it was all over she broke down completely, she was quite ill in bed for four or five weeks, over there at Carron, and I'm told she's a different creature now—most subdued and doesn't go anywhere. Just mopes about by herself."

"Isn't she with her mother then?" asked Simon, who was not really surprised, he found, at this account. He had known Pamela was only assuming all that bright hardness as a cover for something very different.

"No," answered Mrs. Hardwicke, "she quarrelled with her mother, I believe. Anyway, I heard some talk that she wouldn't have her mother near her when she was ill, and they've been apart ever since. I don't know that I'm surprised, either. After all, even if one takes a charitable view and believes there was nothing wrong in that affair with Sylvester, still, there was a lot of horrid gossip and lots of girls would resent their mother getting herself talked about like that—not to mention the exhibition she made of herself in the witness-box!"

Simon perceived that his hostess did not like Anne Courtley, and so almost smiled as he asked: "And Mrs. Courtley? Has she, too, done anything surprisingly out of character?"

"She! No, indeed not! She's behaved just as one would have expected! Carried it all off as bold as brass! One would have thought she'd have sold Carron and gone away and left us all to forget her and all about the whole affair. Not at all! She's kept on the place and I believe means to come back here soon. She's abroad now, enjoying herself in all the gay places in the South of France."

"Alone?" queried Simon.

"No. Her mother's with her, I believe. Poor old thing, *she's* changed if you like! Utterly broken up by the whole affair, we all felt so sorry for her. She got to look so old and so ill. We were all quite glad when Mrs. Courtley took her off abroad. I'll tell you one queer little tale I heard. Some of the people here happened to be in the same hotel with her at Monte Carlo, where she went directly after the trial. They'd got some local papers with them and one had an illustration of Charles Courtley. They'd left this on a table in the lounge by chance and were horrified to see Anne Courtley go deliberately across and pick it up. And then she took it across to her mother and showed it to her and said: 'Good heavens! Isn't it like him?' and *laughed*. Her mother tried to hush her up, but our friends said they felt simply disgusted. Even if she didn't feel any grief, she needn't be so heartless and brazen about it all!"

Simon agreed. Anne had been released by Charles's death from an unhappy life, but she might have been expected to show more dignity and self-restraint in concealing her feelings.

Even that, however, was not the end of her queer behaviour. In the first place, most people had expected she would marry, certainly at the end of six months' mourning.

"For of course, she didn't mourn at all, either in her heart or in her clothes!" remarked Mrs. Hardwicke sarcastically. "And really, after the gossip over Peter Sylvester, the best thing she could have done would have been to marry him."

"Well, I don't know," put in her husband. "After all, she'd always denied they'd been anything more than good friends" (a snort of contempt from his wife made Simon smile here), "and if we were to believe her, she'd never been in love with him, so why should she marry him?"

"Because she's not likely to do any better," retorted Mrs. Hardwicke. "Most decent men would fight shy of marrying her after all this scandal, and that trial. Peter Sylvester *is* a decent man, and think how nice it would be if he got back his old home and that property and all! Her husband had left her everything he had, you know."

"What's become of Sylvester?" asked Simon, deeply interested in it all.

"Oh, she's kept him on to manage the estate, and he's there, just as he always was."

"And Barclay? I gather from what you say he and Miss Courtley's engagement has never come off?"

"Oh! hadn't you heard?" Mrs. Hardwicke's face clouded. "He was killed—killed in a motor accident about three months after the murder."

"Killed!" Sturt felt quite shocked. That splendid vital man dead! What a waste of a fine human being!

"Yes," broke in the Colonel, "smashed himself up on his motor-bike. But even before then he and Pamela had broken things off. I don't know if that was why she's taken things to heart so. May have had a tiff with him, and then, of course, fretted when he was killed and she couldn't make it up."

His wife looked as if she did not altogether agree with these remarks, but Simon felt she did not want to discuss Barclay and Pamela, so he tried to divert the conversation to another point.

"They haven't cut down Fosse Wood? I thought I recognized it from afar last night as I looked out of my window."

"No, indeed not! Sylvester stopped that as soon as he could— but I tell you what, that's one of the most peculiar things about the whole affair. She's put up a monument in the wood, one of the most extraordinary things you ever saw!"

"A monument!" said Simon, quite taken aback.

"A monument," repeated Mrs. Hardwicke, delighted at the effect she had produced. "A huge great monument. It's—what do you call a tomb when there's no body inside?" turning to her husband.

"A cenotaph, my dear," replied Colonel Hardwicke, smiling at his wife's description.

"Of course—a cenotaph," she repeated with great satisfaction. "It's a sort of memorial to her husband. Not a tombstone, of course, he's not buried there. She had him cremated and buried at the crematorium, I believe. So there's no grave—couldn't be in that place, anyway, it's not consecrated, and it's a public footpath and all that—but there's this monument, a great tall thing too!"

Simon could hardly believe this tale, but both assured him it was true. The ground was hers, and she could do as she liked and so she had erected this memorial, a tall pointed obelisk, with an inscription.

Everyone had been horrified at the idea, but no one apparently had been able to persuade her to change her mind. She had even superintended the putting up of the monument herself. It had been a nine days' wonder, and crowds of people had gone to visit it. But now the interest had died away and the local people even had stopped going there. Indeed, it had actually made people avoid the spot—saying it was 'haunted' and all that. More might have transpired, but some visitors coming in cut short the conversation, and the subject lapsed.

Sturt was deeply intrigued. What an extraordinary thing for any woman to do! His resolve to go across to Carron was strengthened. He must see this monument for himself, and find out if he could why she had come to do such a strange act.

So early in the afternoon he set out on his expedition, determined to approach the whole scene in a detached manner as an outsider, no longer as one concerned professionally. He hoped vaguely that in this way his brain might be found fresher and more free to perceive what he might have missed before.

He walked quickly through the sunlit wood, where bright shafts of sunlight struck down through the oaks and beeches. Presently he came to the path which had been familiar to him. He quickened his footsteps as he reached the little cross-roads where the rides intersected. Ahead of him something white gleamed. He came out on to that now notorious path. There, from the side, rose a tall, slender obelisk, made of white stone. Startling and incongruous it reared up from the short turf. Behind it lay the little clearing, its bracken sunlit, its patches of heather losing their bright colour now that summer was gone. Nothing, to Simon's eyes, could have been stranger than this solitary column, so alien to the woodland scene, so horrifying in its perpetuation of a dark episode. At the square base a panel had been let in with some lines cut upon it. Simon stared at it.

IN MEMORY OF CHARLES COURTLEY,
WHO LOST HIS LIFE NEAR THIS SPOT

—and the date.

Utterly puzzled he read the brief inscription. What did it mean? Not grief, that was certain—no 'loved memory,' no 'beloved husband' here; only a bald crude statement of a fact. Definitely a disagreeable memorial! Before his mind's eye rose a picture of Anne, cool, composed, assured. Her clear grey eyes, her strong vital sweep of hair, her square chin. This memorial was the deliberate act of a resolute woman. She had acted with intention, in putting it where it stood. As he stared at it, Simon felt all his old feelings revive. She *must* have had a hand in that murder. Surely this monument was in reality one raised in triumph? She had attained what she wanted, Charles had died, and no one had been brought to justice. And to mark that achievement she had built this column, engraved this stone. Far-fetched? With a gesture between a shrug and a shiver Simon turned away. He went on down the woodland paths, his mind uneasy, his whole being in revolt against what he felt to be a wicked memorial to a wicked deed.

Chapter XX

THE SECOND DEATH

It was growing late by now, so he decided to make for the little inn which he remembered stood not more than a mile or so away. He would, he felt, like to know old Walter's reactions to this monument, not to mention those of the enigmatic Mary. He was still slightly resentful of the way those two had combined to baffle him.

So he made his way through the silent coolness thrown by the shade of the great trees, until at length he came out on the open space where the sign of the 'Broken Bough' still stood on the edge of the green sward, and facing it the little inn seemed to be sleeping placidly. He was determined to see Mary Game again, and find out what he could from her, hoping she would be more ready to open out, now the trial was a thing of the past.

There was no sign of anyone about, so pushing open the inn door, he went into the little passage and knocked on the 'private' door.

A strange girl came out to him. Sturt looked at her, momentarily taken aback. He had been so full of former days, that he had confidently expected to be met by Mary herself! "I beg your pardon," he said, quite disconcerted, "I came to see Miss Mary Game. Is she in?"

The girl looked at him, startled in her turn. "Mary Game? Why, she's not here! She's dead!"

"Dead?" Sturt felt a shock at the words.

"Yes. She died over three months ago."

"How did that come about?"

"She died in her sleep. But if you knew her, perhaps you'd like to talk to Mrs. Gwyn? I wasn't here myself, of course, but she can tell you all about it. I'll call her."

Still feeling startled, Sturt stood waiting while the girl went through to the back premises. He had been so intent, picturing to himself Mary's anticipated reluctance to discuss the monument and the murder that he found it quite difficult to grasp this startling piece of news.

His thoughts were interrupted by the entrance of Mrs. Gwyn, none too pleased to see him. She took him through to her own sanctum, and rather shortly inquired what he wanted to know about Mary.

"Why," said Simon, rallying himself, "I was staying down here again, and thought as I was walking in the forest, I'd have a look at that monument that's been put up. So, passing by, I just came in to have a word with you all. I'm horrified to hear of Mary's death. A young girl like that, one doesn't expect to hear she's dead. What was the matter with her?"

"The doctor didn't really know," replied Mrs. Gwyn, rather slowly. "We found her dead in her bed one morning. Quite peaceful. She'd died in her sleep. Of course there had to be an inquest, but the doctors couldn't find anything wrong."

"Extraordinary!" exclaimed Sturt. "You mean they couldn't find any illness?"

"No, none; and no foul play either," this very severely, as a reminder she had not forgotten Sturt's profession. "She'd just died, as they thought from heart failure. Anyhow, there wasn't any poison or anything of *that* sort."

"Hadn't she been ill, or anything?" queried Simon, for he longed to get all the details of this sudden death.

Mrs. Gwyn shook her head. "No, she'd been as usual. Had her day off, the very afternoon before, and went off as well as anything, as far as *I* could see."

"Where did she go?"

"Now, it's no good you questioning *me*, Inspector. We had it all out at the inquest, and I can tell you the doctors and the police, they went thoroughly into everything. She'd just gone out as usual, came in at her usual time, and went up to bed.

"I was away myself for the day, but Mr. Gwyn, he said she went off as far as he knew at her ordinary time. We don't know when she came in. She'd the key to the side door, and no one saw her or heard her. But she'd come back and taken off her outdoor things…" Here, Mrs. Gwyn paused again. By now she had relented in her attitude to the inspector, and having warmed to her tale, decided to let loose ideas which had perhaps been thoroughly suppressed till this moment.

"But, now, that was the only little odd thing. She'd just lain down on the outside of the bed in her frock and shoes. The doctors thought she must have felt queer, and laid down till she felt better… and then her heart failed and she'd died before she'd ever got properly to bed. Anyhow, that's how we found her. Quite peaceful and still, and they said she'd been dead for hours."

Both were silent. Simon realized it was too late now to find out anything very definite. If an autopsy had been held, and no trace of anything found, the possibilities were there was nothing to find. Yet there was the coincidence, a strange unexpected death of a person connected with a murder. He looked at Mrs. Gwyn.

"And were you quite satisfied that the truth was discovered, Mrs. Gwyn?"

The woman looked at him, and a spark of indignation came into her shrewd grey eyes.

"Well, no, I'll tell you *my* idea, Inspector. I've never felt alto-gether happy about it. I'd known Mary very well, and been very fond of her. It never seemed to me natural or possible she, a strong, healthy young girl, should have died like that. And I worried in my mind because I knew there was something up. She'd been different, uneasy, something bothering her. That was what troubled me. Ever since that trial she'd had something on her mind. And I've gone over it and over it, and I can't but think she'd kept something back. She wasn't happy in herself, and she got depressed—and she'd no reason for that that I know of."

"No trouble with a young man?" queried Simon. "No love-affair to make her unhappy, I mean?"

Mrs. Gwyn shook her head thoughtfully. "Well, there again, I'll tell you what I've never told to anyone else, for I was *fond* of Mary, and when she was dead I didn't want any talk. She'd got her own young man, George Hearn, and they were engaged, and going to be married in a year or two. A nice settled steady affair, and no trouble of any sort *there*—" this emphatically. "But I'd an idea she was seeing someone else. Don't get me wrong, she wasn't having a love-affair behind George's back. That I'm certain of. But she'd slipped out two or three times, asked me for time off, when it wasn't her regular day. Made excuses, of course, something she wanted to buy over at Marple, and couldn't wait for. And I'd my own ideas. I tell you, Inspector, I'm not so easily taken in, and I'd the opinion Mary used to meet someone. But why or what for, that I can't tell you, or even guess."

Simon sighed. There it was. Something strange, something hidden. This shrewd woman with her knowledge of the people she lived amongst was not likely to be fanciful, not likely to be mistaken. If she had suspected something wrong, well, almost certainly something wrong there had been. But, how could anything come to light now?

"You didn't tell the doctors or the coroner this?"

"No, I did *not*. What had I got to say? Just a few ideas of my own that Mary wasn't altogether happy? That'd only have started gossip and talk, and I saw no reason to let that come about. I didn't want people talking and thinking nastiness about Mary, when I was sure there was nothing of that sort about her. She was dead, poor girl, and no good would come to her, and George was as upset as anyone could be, poor fellow. I didn't want to add to his trouble. No. If there'd been anything to be gained, or anything for me to tell, that'd have been different. But, as I told you, the doctors said there wasn't anything suspicious, or anything they could find about her death. So I've just held my tongue—and perhaps I'd have done well not to say even this to you, Inspector."

"You needn't worry, Mrs. Gwyn. I know how to treat confidences. It's safe enough with me. But it all goes to confirm what is my own view. We never got to the bottom of what went on here that day, and of course I still can't help hoping something may come out, even now.

"What about old Walter?" he went on, determined to leave nothing unsaid while he was about it. "He was a clever old fellow. What did he say to Mary's death?"

A peculiar look crossed Mrs. Gwyn's face.

"Well, Inspector, I shan't tell you any fancies, only facts. Old Walter, he took on terrible over Mary's death. Fretted himself ill, as you might say—and went to her funeral and caught cold, a bitter day it was, in February, and pouring cats and dogs. No day at all for an old man like him to be out, much less hanging about a graveyard. But go he would, nothing and no one could keep him back, and he caught cold, as I said, and it turned to pneumonia and he was dead within the week."

Simon was aghast. Both those witnesses dead! What extraordinary ill luck. The very two from whom, despite past experience, he had still hoped to obtain some information. Well—if dead they could not tell him what living they would not.

He hesitated, then resolved to risk her reaction to another aspect.

"Well, Mrs. Gwyn, that is sad news. What a lot of changes you've had. I expect you want to forget the whole thing. I don't suppose you like that Memorial in the forest, it must remind you of it all too much. I wonder what people round here think of it?"

Chapter XXI

MRS. GWYN'S REVELATIONS

Mrs. Gwyn looked at him, half disapprovingly. She was silent for a moment and then unable to resist giving vent to her true feelings, broke out.

"That monument! Yes, I should think you *have* heard of it. It's the talk of the neighbourhood! A regular scandal! How Mrs. Courtley could do such a thing I don't know, I'm sure. The fuss there's been about it! But of course no one could stop it, she'd a right to put up anything she chose on her own property, and to her own husband!" She paused, and Sturt, quite willing now to egg her on to further gossip, took up the line she had opened.

"Well, yes, it certainly is an extraordinary affair. After all, she didn't care for her husband, as she wasn't ashamed to say in court. I should have thought she'd have been glad enough to leave people to forget it all."

Mrs. Gwyn shook her head briefly. "She's an odd woman, and they say she's so bitter she can't let it alone. She put that up out of spite."

"Spite?" queried Simon. "Why, what's that to do with it?"

"Well," said Mrs. Gwyn, determined now to speak out all that clearly seethed in her mind. "She was furious you know that the story had to come out at all—and more furious still that Mr. Wadham got off!" She paused, obviously realizing that the acquittal was no more likely to have pleased the police, as the unsuccessful prosecutors.

But reckless now of his feelings she hastened on. "Yes, she'd never reckoned all her affairs would have to come out in court, you may be sure of that. Carrying on with Mr. Sylvester! Ashamed she may well have been."

"But," interrupted Simon, determined to goad by opposition, "you can't blame her so very much for that, Mrs. Gwyn. After all, in these days we hear too many of these stories to be surprised. She'd a disagreeable, bad-tempered husband who neglected her, and with a handsome man like Mr. Sylvester about, one could almost bet what would happen. And you know we have to be charitable! She said there wasn't any truth in the tale!"

Mrs. Gwyn looked at him for a moment, then decisively pulled up a chair, sat down, and leaned towards the inspector, resolved on a supreme effort.

"Mr. Sylvester—well, of course, I don't know that I'd altogether blame her—though with those two young girls of her own at home she ought to have thought more of them. Still! let's say we can see what drove her to Mr. Peter—but what sticks in my throat is the way she's gone on since. I'd not think too much of her affair with Mr. Peter if she'd stuck to him and married him after a decent time. We'd all have been glad to see him back in the old place. But he was only one of *two*! and she'd seemingly decided to give up Mr. Peter and yet didn't marry the other!"

Triumphantly she gazed at Simon's face, where indeed surprise showed.

"Two! What do you mean, Mrs. Gwyn? There wasn't another man in the case? You're not talking of Wadham, are you?" For a wild thought had shot through his mind that perhaps after all there had been something between her and Wadham—and her animosity at the trial had been the traditional 'fury of a woman scorned.'

"No!" replied Mrs. Gwyn firmly. "Not *Mr. Wadham*—he wasn't her type. She fancied a different sort of man. It was Mr. Barclay she was after!"

Simon looked at her in utter astonishment. "Mr. Barclay! But he was her daughter's admirer? He was supposed to be engaged to Miss Pamela?"

"No," replied the woman, "you may have thought so, plenty of people did—but it was Mrs. Courtley he was after. The girl was only a blind."

Mrs. Courtley and Barclay! Simon could not believe her. "But surely, Mrs. Gwyn," he began, "that can't have been so! I know people talked about her and Mr. Sylvester, my own friends over at Headley knew all the rumours about that. But there was never a word about her and Mr. Barclay!"

Mrs. Gwyn looked at him pityingly. "The gentry mayn't have known, but some of the local people hereabouts knew! Why, sir, I'll tell you now what I've told no one else. I knew well enough about her and Mr. Sylvester—that we all knew—and I knew too she used to come over and meet him in the woods. What I didn't know at the time was, that the last few months it was Mr. Hugh Barclay she was meeting not Mr. Peter. It was *Mary* who told me that!"

She paused, and perhaps the misgivings she had always secretly felt, welled up and found relief in pouring it all out to the sympathetic, handsome inspector, whose charm had now quite won her.

"Yes, Mary told it all to me when that trial was over. She kept it to herself till then but she'd seen them together, and once or twice she took notes Mrs. Courtley brought and asked her to deliver to Mr. Barclay. Mary was terribly upset about it, that's why she poured it all out to me. It seems she hadn't thought anything much of it at first. She knew, as we all did for that matter, about Mr. Barclay courting Miss Pamela, and how Mr. Courtley had forbidden it. And

she, Mary I mean, had just believed Mrs. Courtley was helping in
her daughter's love-affair. We all thought, you know, sir, that Mrs.
Courtley was still taken up with Mr. Peter. Then, I'm not sure why,
nor what it was, but something made Mary suspect that wasn't so.
She wouldn't tell me what it was, she was that upset."

"Why," queried Simon, "what should upset her over that?"

"Oh! well," returned Mrs. Gwyn rather reluctantly. "Mary had
been a bit sweet on Mr. Barclay herself. You know how girls get these
fancies, sir, especially for men above them in station. Mr. Barclay
used to come here a great deal last summer, doing his painting of
the trees and all that, and always took notice of Mary. He was such
a fine attractive man, you know, and George, Mary's young man,
seemed to her a bit dull at times, I think. Anyway, I don't mind
telling you now, between ourselves, I'd been getting a bit worried
over Mary. I knew she'd do nothing wrong, and I trusted Mr.
Hugh, but I thought she was getting her mind full of Mr. Hugh,
always talking about him and admiring him. I felt she was getting
discontented over George and going the best way to work to spoil
her chances for a good steady husband. And she upset me too, upset
me a great deal, by the way she took on when she began to suspect
he was after Mrs. Courtley."

"Why should she mind that so much more than believing he was
engaged to Miss Pamela?" inquired the inspector.

"Well, that's what I asked her myself, and what she said was
that she didn't believe he'd ever marry Miss Pamela, she thought
Mr. Courtley would see to that—and somehow she said she never
had believed Mr. Hugh really meant anything serious there. So she
hadn't minded that. It was only after the murder she changed so
much, got so worried and miserable. She saw then, as we all did, that
Mrs. Courtley didn't propose to marry Mr. Peter—and Mary began
to put things together in her own mind, I think, over Mrs. Courtley

and Mr. Hugh. It all seemed to come on her like a thunderclap one day, and she began to make herself right down miserable over it. She was always fretting and looking downhearted, no matter how much I told her to put it all out of her head it was no concern of hers."

Simon mused for a moment, then asked:

"How did Mary come to take the notes you speak of?"

"Why, I was at Carron in the old days, sir, in service and I used to go over and help, at one time, and I've done the same for Mrs. Courtley, if they'd the house full. But since this place has come on so—with the teas and all that," and she gave a proud glance at the 'tea-garden,' "I've given up that sort of odd job. So I used to let Mary go—it was a bit of a change for her and she liked to go to Carron and see the smart dresses and all that. Mrs. Courtley and Miss Pamela were always very kind to her—used to give her dresses and what-not often enough. And, of course, like everyone else, she knew what Mr. Courtley was like, and the awful way he used to go on. Often and often she'd come back and tell me how sorry she was for them two—having such temper to bear with. So it was quite easy and natural for Mrs. Courtley to ask her to take notes."

"And easy too," thought Simon, "if Mary knew as much as that, for her to be a danger after that trial." And he wondered savagely if Mary's friendliness had betrayed her in another way, if this tale were true.

"Mary began to get restless after the trial. She told me then she believed Mrs. Courtley and Mr. Hugh were meeting each other. She as good as hinted to me she'd been on the look-out and had caught them together. She said she reckoned now they'd been meeting before, during the summer, and just throwing dust in people's eyes with Miss Pamela! Spoke quite bitterly she did, and I could see then how she'd been perhaps thinking all the times Mr. Hugh came over here he'd been noticing *her*, Mary, herself, and it vexed her to see how silly she'd been!

"I told her she'd better not say such things! Such talk wouldn't do any good to Mr. Hugh if it got about! And she'd no real means to know what he and Mrs. Courtley were up to. That gave her a turn, I can tell you! Why (warming with her recollections) I can see her now, poor girl, the start she gave, and the look she gave me! Flushed up, she did, and said, 'Oh! Mrs. Gwyn,' she said, 'that'd be the last thing I'd want to do! Hurt Mr. Hugh, no, never!' And there I agreed with her," Mrs. Gwyn went on heartily; "no one in this part of the world would have said a word to hurt Mr. Hugh. No one would have given him away. There's not much hidden from a village, you know. Others besides Mary may have had their suspicions, but I never heard a soul say a thing. Everyone hated Mr. Courtley, and I don't know that many would have minded if his wife were making a fool of him. But I reckon no one would have told on Mr. Hugh. Everyone loved him round here. He'd been brought up here by his mother, and a nice lady she was, and daughter of Mr. Sylvester of Carron, of course. We'd all known her and Mr. Hugh all our lives. You can take it from me, sir, people knew how to hold their tongues over all this. I only tell you now because Mr. Barclay's dead, and it can't harm him now, poor fellow."

She ceased, and Simon sat marvelling. So this hidden story had been there all the time, concealed by the peasantry for that ancient reason, loyalty to the local stock, dislike of the 'foreigner.' No wonder old Walter and Mary Game had held their tongues! No wonder they had insisted so firmly on Sylvester's and Barclay's alibi. They had the backing of the countryside behind them!

Like a flash he remembered how he had asked them whether Barclay were meeting Pamela at the inn. They had assured him, of course, that he was not, but they had never let him suspect who it was he had really been meeting that summer.

His brain went back to the murder. Anne and Barclay! What difference did this make to his theories? He began to think feverishly.

Mrs. Gwyn broke the silence that had fallen between them.

"You see, Inspector, that's one of the things that troubled me since I've known this. Mrs. Courtley, she'd tired of Mr. Peter and she'd taken up with Mr. Barclay. Well, perhaps that was their affair. Mr. Peter didn't mind, to all appearance. It didn't make any difference to anyone else. What they chose to do, that they did and while he was alive no one minded about Mr. Courtley's feelings! He got what he deserved—all round. And you knew, Inspector, that murder didn't specially trouble us either. A hard, cruel, wicked man! He made everyone around him miserable, and the world was the better without him. It didn't worry me, I can tell you, that no one was brought to justice over it. *Whoever* did it was a better man than Mr. Courtley, I reckon. So why add a decent man's death to a bad one's? But since then—well, I tell you, things haven't been going nicely around here. Mary's death, that was one bad thing. Mr. Barclay's, that was another misfortune— and I tell you we don't like this monument reminding us all and rubbing it all in."

Again Simon looked at her resolutely. "Now, tell me, Mrs. Gwyn. I heard Mr. Barclay had been killed in an accident. You don't yourself think there was anything wrong about that?"

"No, I don't. Just a plain common motoring accident that was. Happened at Marple cross-roads. Mr. Barclay was going along on his motor-bike, and a lorry came up the hill and crossed the road and smashed right into him. One of the brick-works lorries it was and often enough we've been told there'd be a smash at that crossing. These lorry drivers tearing along to keep to their times, they can't always be careful. No, it wasn't the accident, it was the way Mrs. Courtley took it. She'd gone abroad for a bit, you know—wanted to let gossip settle down, I expect. But we all thought when time had gone by, she'd come back and marry one or other of them two perhaps. Then, this accident came, not three months after the murder. I'm told she carried on simply terribly when she heard the news. Came hurrying back from France—came by air, indeed!—and went through all his things. Mr. Sylvester, being his cousin, he had charge of everything, and she got his leave, I suppose."

"That seems a little odd?" inquired Simon, deeply interested in these side-lights.

"Odd!" snorted Mrs. Gwyn. "Not a bit! You may be sure there were things she didn't want other people to see—wanted to make sure there were no letters or anything—and thought she'd see to it herself, no doubt."

Sturt nodded. Yes, that was self-evident. Such a story must be hidden, such secrets carefully guarded.

"And, of course, nothing came out?" he asked, almost perfunctorily.

Mrs. Gwyn paused dramatically. "Well, nothing as you might say came out. But there was one thing that people talked about—oh! just a little thing," she added, hastily afraid of raising the inspector's hopes—"but there it was! Mrs. Courtley, she insisted on seeing the body, and she went into the room where they'd lain him out, by herself. Well now, after she'd gone, they found she'd put a ring on his hand—a plain gold ring, like a wedding-ring—and put it on his wedding finger. The undertakers, they noticed it, and asked if he was to be buried in it—they have to ask when people are buried wearing rings or such-like, as of course you know—and Mr. Sylvester, he looked surprised at first, so they say, and then said oh! yes—to let it be."

She paused dramatically, and Sturt, deeply interested, asked, "How on earth do you come to know that, Mrs. Gwyn? You didn't——" he paused, uncertain how to express himself—"you didn't by any chance help to lay out the body?"

"Oh, no, sir," replied Mrs. Gwyn, too full of her story to take any offence at the suggestion. "No, indeed not, but Mary——" she broke off, as Sturt's surprise showed in his face, then went on—"Mary's aunt, she does the laying-out in the villages round about here, for Mr. Smith the undertaker, and it was she told us. Came in here she did, for a cup of tea on her way home, and she was so full of it she blurted it all out in front of Mary and me."

"And how did Mary take that piece of gossip?" asked Sturt, as lightly as he could, for he had no wish to arouse in Mrs. Gwyn the thoughts stirring in his own mind.

"Well, sir," returned the woman with a shade of discomfort, "she never said a thing for a moment, just stood and stared at her aunt, quite white in the face, and then burst out laughing—quite hysterical sort of laughing it was, and kept on laughing and saying, 'Gave him a funeral ring, instead of a wedding-ring.' And her aunt was quite taken aback and sorry she'd said anything, I reckon. So I told Mary not to carry on like that, and made her aunt feel she'd better be getting on, and after she'd gone I spoke to Mary and told her not to show spite to Mrs. Courtley. So she pulled herself together, and we didn't speak of it again, and though she went on looking peaked and wretched, I thought she'd get over it all if we didn't talk of it. I wasn't going to say anything to anyone else either, mind you," she went on, fixing the inspector with a firm, relentless gaze. "I wasn't going to say a word of all this gossip, and I never have, and the more so when the poor girl died as she did. I wasn't going to have any spiteful talk, but I'll tell you now, sir, it was partly the way Mary looked and spoke that evening that's made me think she'd been more romantic, as they say, over Mr. Hugh than I'd guessed." Then, as if anxious to leave an aspect of the topic which troubled her, she reverted to the woman of whom they had been originally speaking.

"But, as to Mrs. Courtley, sir, well, what was one to think? Putting a wedding-ring on his wedding finger! That must have meant something.

"It's a thing most women wouldn't do—flaring it all out, as you may say, when, Mr. Barclay being dead and gone, she might as well have kept it dark. And it was after that she turned so bitter, they say, and went off and gave orders for that monument. And that's why people don't like it. Gives you a nasty taste, as you might say."

Simon realized what this odd little story implied. If suspicion was true, if Courtley had been murdered to set his wife free to marry Barclay, then here was the bitter irony of the situation: Barclay's death, if it were the death of the man Anne had loved and meant to marry, made the murder quite pointless. Being the kind of woman she was, this must have been the supreme frustration of her life—and all her bitterness had poured itself out in that horrible monument. It stood there now as a bitter commentary on a useless deed.

Chapter XXII

DRUGS

S turt walked away from the inn full of disturbance. First of all, somehow he did not believe in Mary's 'natural death.' He remembered her so well—a perfectly sound, sturdy, healthy-looking country girl. It would have been odd enough in any case to be told she had died of 'heart failure.' Coupled with Mrs. Gwyn's other revelations, he was quite sure there was more behind it. Obviously Mary had been mixed up in some queer business. Probably too it had been connected with the murder trial. It could not be coincidence that the change in her, noticed by her employer, tallied with the close of that trial. Mary must have known something, as indeed Sturt had suspected. Knowing something, had she committed suicide, for fear some guilt on her part would be traced? Or had she known too much for someone's safety, and had she been 'removed'?

The first step, clearly, was to see the doctor who had conducted the autopsy. From his previous experience at Carron, Sturt knew that this was probably Dr. Williams of Marple, and to his house accordingly he now betook himself. Dr. Williams was at home, and able to see the inspector, though he showed his surprise when his visitor was ushered in.

"Well, Inspector, it's a long time since you and I met. How are you, and what are you doing in these parts?"

"Just holidaying really this time, Doctor," smiled Simon. "I'm staying with friends near here for a bit of a rest after a tough job. But," he hesitated, then decided to be frank, "it's turning out rather a busman's holiday." He paused, and the doctor, realizing that this preliminary meant business, offered his guest a cigarette, and himself lit his pipe.

Simon, glad to settle himself comfortably, proceeded to explain.

"It's like this. I've been walking in the forest and I went in to the 'Broken Bough' inn, meaning really to have a talk with that girl, Mary. Well, as you of course know, I found she was not there—that she'd died, and died suddenly. Now, Doctor, I want you to tell me all you can about that death, for to tell you the truth, I don't quite like the sound of it."

The doctor's face had clouded and darkened. For a moment he drew at his pipe, then turning to Simon he said: "Well now, it's no good, Inspector. I grant you that girl's death was unexpected—and in some ways inexplicable. I couldn't find any disease. I couldn't account for the heart failure. But I'm bound to tell you I also found no trace of foul play. We took a lot of trouble over her—tested for poisons and for drugs. We couldn't find anything. And it's not necessary for me to say there were no marks of violence—no sign of suffocation or drowning, or any of the things people die from in novels and doctors fail to detect!"

He spoke with some bitterness, and Sturt guessed that there had been a good deal of talk and possibly of criticism over this death.

"Well, of course, I take your word for it. But somehow, you know, I don't like it. I've always thought that girl could tell more than she knew—she and old Walter."

"I've no opinion as to that," responded Williams shortly. "I can only tell you I was called in to the girl—far too late, of course, even if anything could ever have been done."

His words struck a chord in Simon's mind. "Far too late? Do you mean you think you might have done anything if you'd been called in when she was first taken ill?"

If the doctor suspected him of laying a trap (Simon remembered perfectly well that Mrs. Gwyn had told him the girl had never shown signs of illness), he disguised his feelings. He answered briskly: "No, I don't mean that. She never was ill. Went out one day perfectly well—and was found dead the next. No, what I meant was that there was too long an interval between the probable time of death and the autopsy for us to be absolutely certain there could have been no question of certain drugs."

Sturt stared at him. "What do you mean?"

"Why, this. She probably died quite early on the Thursday night. I believe she usually came in at ten-thirty p.m., and we roughly fixed the time of her death as eleven-thirty p.m. That's to say within an hour of her return. Remember, she'd laid down on the bed in her clothes—that showed she'd felt 'queer' as they say—as soon as she'd got upstairs. She'd not even taken off her frock.

"Now her body wasn't discovered till about eight the next day, when Mrs. Gwyn went up to her room to see why she wasn't down. They sent over for me, but most unluckily I'd already gone out. Gone to a confinement case ten miles the other side of Marple. My patient was in a bad way and wasn't on the telephone, so I was there till late afternoon and no means of getting at me. I wasn't back home, after doing a few calls, till quite eight o'clock on the Friday night. Meanwhile, Mrs. Gwyn got hold of old Murchison, he's retired, you know, but lives in Marple, and he went off as it was an emergency. Of course, he told them the poor girl was dead, and nothing to be done and that they'd better wait for me, as I was her regular medical attendant.

"Well, all that meant we didn't get the autopsy done till late on Saturday. Now that was all right for certain obvious tests—arsenic, and so on—but, Inspector, that's too late for some of the narcotics. If the girl had taken an overdose of some of the barbiturics there'd have been no trace at all after roughly twenty-four hours—and we'd gone longer than that."

Sturt felt violent annoyance. So he might be right—there could have been 'unnatural' death here after all, and no means of tracing it! The Courtley case was running true to its record of unsatisfactoriness!

"Well, of course, that's not what one likes to hear, Doctor. Possibilities, but no proof! Still, I stick to my point. There may have been something wrong about the death."

The doctor shrugged as he knocked out his pipe. "May have been! Well—possibly. But I can tell you this. Mary Game was a perfectly respectable girl—and she'd a perfectly respectable, steady young man. She'd no need to commit suicide—and I know her whole family history, there's no suicide or insanity or anything of the sort there. And as for anything else—why, who on earth would want to get rid of a harmless girl like that? No, Inspector, these sudden unexplained deaths are occasionally met with. They're a worry to *my* profession, but I don't think this one need cause any anxiety to *yours*."

With that, he rose to dismiss his rather unwelcome guest, and Simon, realizing there was nothing more to be gleaned here, rose too and took his departure.

But he felt that, groping in the dark, he had perhaps touched something blindly and unwittingly. Mary Game *could* have been poisoned, and perhaps where medicine had failed to find a trace, detection could accomplish more. He decided he would try to find how and with whom Mary had spent her last day.

Naturally he was hampered by the lapse of time, but to counterbalance that there might be the fact that with the excitement over Mary's death, people would have had the events of those days more deeply impressed upon their minds.

Such was Simon's hope, and the next afternoon he went off to interview his old friend Sergeant Groves, with the feeling that he might perhaps succeed in gleaning some useful information.

As he swung down the well-remembered street of Marple towards the police station, he noticed a very smart vermilion sports car drawn up outside the post office, and just as he came abreast of it a girl came out of the building quickly, and dashing across the pavement almost collided with him.

"Damn you, why can't you look where you're going?" she snapped, evidently acting on the principle that attack is the best form of defence. Simon could scarcely help smiling at her impudence, for she was the one who had rushed across without looking. But as he raised his hat, prepared to apologize, the smile which had lit up his face faded. The girl was Pamela Courtley, but she had so altered as to give Simon a distinct shock. She had recognized him in the same moment and stood staring at him. Her make-up could not disguise her hollow cheeks, her brilliant lipstick only accentuated the drawn lines round her mouth. And nothing could disguise the look in her eyes. Even before recognition had dawned, Simon's trained observation had noticed the haggard, miserable look of her whole face, her dreary, anxious expression. Now, as she stood looking at him there was no mistaking the fear which leaped into her face. Compassion was the first feeling Sturt felt. This poor girl! She had lost all that gaiety, that defiant brightness and spirit which had characterized her before. She was now a wan, haggard wraith of what she had been.

All this swept through him in a flash, and before he had even replaced his hat on his head he had collected himself.

"Why, Miss Courtley," he said, "how are you? I didn't expect to see you here, I thought you were abroad."

"No," she replied curtly, eyeing him with a hard, angry gaze.

"I'm here all right—but not expecting to see *you*. What are you doing down here?"

"Just staying with some friends, over at Headley; having a bit of a holiday."

She still looked suspiciously at him, but clearly was at a slight loss how to cross-examine him further. Then, deciding apparently that there was no need to disguise the hostility she felt, she went on: "Oh! I shouldn't have thought this would be a popular neighbourhood with you! I always imagined detectives, unlike criminals, wouldn't want to revisit the scene of a crime!"

The taunting bitterness which crept into her voice stung Simon's pride. He felt himself flushing as he replied as coolly as he could: "This is really my own part of the world, you know, Miss Courtley. I was born and brought up in the other half of the country, and East Anglians always enjoy getting back to the district when they can." He wanted to prevent her suspecting his renewed interest in the Carron murder.

Apparently the line he had taken was successful. Her face relaxed from its look of miserable rigidity, and her voice was perceptibly more friendly as she answered: "Oh, of course, I forgot that. I suppose, after all, really you're more at home down here than we are." She hesitated and made towards her car. Simon stepped across to open the door for her. It was not politeness which impelled him to ask, "And how is Mrs. Courtley? Is she at home now?" Then he realized he had better have held his tongue.

At once the girl's face darkened, and a sullen twist came to her lips. She answered shortly, "Mummy's abroad. She doesn't care to come back here now." She turned her face away, as if ashamed to let him see her.

Simon inwardly wondered that the girl did not share her mother's natural aversion to the place, but as he prepared to say good-bye,

Pamela, who had got into the car but had not started it up, and who was sitting biting her lip and staring down the road, turned in the driver's seat, and leaning over the door, blurted out:

"I suppose you've heard about the monument she put up in Fosse Wood?"

"Yes," answered Simon uncomfortably. "Yes, the people I'm with were speaking of it."

A blaze of colour flared into the girl's thin cheeks. "Of course! And I suppose you'll be going over to see such a curiosity?" And then, evidently realizing from his expression that he had already done so, she went on with intense bitterness: "Oh, I see you *have* been. Well! Quite suitable for you to go. It must have helped you to remember what a fool you made of yourself!"

Simon hardly knew what to answer, and before he could collect himself she gave a loud blare on her horn to warn a car in front of her, and without waiting even to say any sort of good-bye started her car impetuously, and dashed off full tilt down the street.

Simon stood involuntarily staring after the fast disappearing car, and then, shaking off the disagreeable impression left by this short encounter, went on towards the police station. Yet so marked was the change in the girl, so vivid the sense of utter unhappiness and desperation she had imprinted on his mind, that for the time being his thoughts took a different direction, and when he found himself greeting the sergeant his first impulse was to inquire after this living girl, leaving for the moment his investigation concerning the dead one.

So when preliminaries were over, and the sergeant rather expectantly paused, as if to let him say to what this visit was due, he began.

"I've just met Miss Courtley. Is she living at Carron Cross just now?"

The sergeant looked at him thoughtfully and his face grew graver. "Yes, Inspector; that's to say she's down here a good deal. The house is partly shut up. Mrs. Courtley doesn't come, but Miss Pamela comes off and on pretty regularly." He paused, but as Simon only waited for further particulars, went on rather slowly.

"That family's all broken up, you know. Mrs. Courtley—she's mostly abroad nowadays. Miss Prudence was sent off to school, and she doesn't come here at all. Miss Pamela isn't with her mother, she just dashes about, from all I hear, and doesn't stay anywhere long."

Simon put two and two together. "Do you mean Miss Courtley has quarrelled with her mother?" he asked bluntly. The sergeant looked more uncomfortable than ever. "Well, I don't quite like to say that. But what I mean is, they go different ways. They don't seem to see much of each other at all."

Simon drew out his cigarette case, and as he tapped his cigarette on the back of his hand, asked pointedly, "How widespread has the gossip been, Sergeant?"

Groves flushed, and looking at Simon, "What gossip do you mean, sir?"

"Well," said Simon deliberately, "I mean the talk about Mrs. Courtley and Mr. Barclay."

The sergeant looked for a moment in astonishment. Clearly he had not imagined such local detail would be known to Sturt. Then, quite relieved that he had not to be the first to repeat the rumours, he said more cheerfully:

"You know well enough, sir, there's always a lot of gossip in a country place. People all talk, and generally a bit spitefully. There *was* a good deal said when Mr. Barclay was killed in that accident, and I expect that's something to do with Mrs. Courtley keeping away. People didn't like what she did, there's no getting away from it."

"And did her daughter like it?"

"No," said Groves firmly. "I'm sure she didn't. And most people felt sorry for her. She's a nice young lady, Inspector, and I reckon she was really keen on Mr. Barclay. I believe myself it all came as a real shock to her, her mother making that fuss. Of course, who's to know what she really thought? But I go by the change in her."

"Yes," interjected Simon, "she's terribly altered. I saw that for myself."

The compassionate Groves nodded his head. "No young girl ought to look like that, Inspector. Regular burnt up with misery, I call it myself. And that's all since Mr. Barclay's death. She didn't look like that over the murder—nor even," he added reflectively, "after the trial. So either she believed there wasn't anything between her mother and Mr. Sylvester, or perhaps that didn't bother her—seeing she knew well enough what Mrs. Courtley had put up with from her husband. No. She kept her spirits and her looks through all that. It was after Mr. Barclay's death she changed so—and it's been since then she's parted company with her mother."

Simon felt a pang of sympathy for the girl. If she had loved Barclay, and loved her mother, she must indeed have suffered horribly if she had been brought to believe that those two had been deceiving her and all the world. And he realized that in addition she must have had to face the fact that she herself had just been used by Barclay as a convenient means of hiding his real feelings. On this point he tested Groves.

"What do you think, Sergeant? Or rather, what's the general opinion? Was Mr. Barclay never engaged to Miss Courtley; was that not genuine?"

Groves shook his head doubtfully. "Can't say, sir. When Mr. Courtley was alive, it was all supposed to be going on behind his back—Miss Pamela and Mr. Barclay, I mean. But after the murder, when we supposed that would all come right, nothing came of it—no open engagement, I mean, and then Mr. Barclay was killed and then it was all the talk about him and Mrs. Courtley came out."

Both men were silent. It seemed a sordid, horrible affair. The daughter being used as a stalking horse to cover an intrigue between the man who was supposed to love her, and who apparently had only loved her mother. Enough indeed to account for the change in the girl.

Shaking off the oppression the idea brought, Simon came to the original business which had brought him to see Groves.

"Well, Sergeant, I didn't really come here to ask you about Miss Courtley. I came in to see if you could tell me anything about poor Mary Game."

The sergeant looked as if this were no better than to jump from the frying-pan into the fire.

"What did you want to know, sir? You'll have heard, of course, there was nothing wrong about her death?"

Simon smiled at the defensive tone. "Well, I've seen Doctor Williams, and heard the medical side. But what I want you to tell me is what was known about her movements on the day of her death. I suppose you went into all that?"

"We did, sir, and I'll get you the file."

Disappearing into the inner office, Groves soon came back with a little lump of papers, which he deposited on the desk before him, and then, flipping rapidly through them: "Here you are. Details as far as we could trace of movements of deceased on Thursday, the 10th February.

"She dressed, and went off for her day out, leaving as far as could be ascertained at three p.m. Called in at her young man's home to leave word she was going to Marple and wouldn't be going out with him. Said she'd a tooth to be attended to unexpectedly. Went to Marple and did some shopping. Called in at the dentist's and had the tooth stopped. Went in to Doctor Williams on her way home. Thought to have done some more errands, but she wasn't noticed anywhere after that. Seen walking towards the 'Broken Bough' about nine p.m. That was all we could get."

"What did she go in to Doctor Williams for?" inquired Simon, who of course recollected the doctor had merely told him Mary was a patient of his, but had not mentioned her having seen him that day.

"She'd been under the doctor for a scalded foot, a few weeks earlier, and went in to pay him. We checked up on that. No, sir," as though sensing a query in Sturt's manner, "what we couldn't account for was the gap after she saw Doctor Williams at seven p.m. and the time she was seen crossing the bridge on the road to the forest at nine. But we couldn't account for it, try as we might, and we just had to leave it."

Simon meditated a moment or two. Mary had been a local girl, well known, well liked.

"Hadn't her friends anything to say? Had anyone thought she wasn't well? Hadn't she said anything to anyone that day?"

Groves shook his head. "No, sir. She'd been in and out of various shops. We traced all that through the parcels we found in her room. She'd talked to the shop people over the counter, and all that, and they all said she was just as usual. Hadn't passed any remarks to anyone. She'd had a cup of tea in the café, and then gone off carrying her parcels, along the London road. No one up in that direction remembered seeing her, but of course we didn't really trouble a great deal, once we knew there wasn't anything out of the way in the cause of death."

The sergeant was beginning to grow restive. Clearly he felt a great deal of trouble had been taken, and the fact established that the girl's death, though unexpected, had nothing peculiar about it, much less anything criminal. He rather resented these doubts being raised by an outsider long after the affair had been closed.

"Well," said Simon, getting up, for he saw there was nothing further to be gained from the police records, "of course, I'm probably just worrying over nothing. I'll confess, Sergeant, I didn't like to hear of the girl dying in this rather odd way. But it all seems to have been gone into pretty thoroughly, and I suppose that's all there is to it." He had not said a word as to the information he had gleaned from Dr. Williams. That he kept to himself. It was all very indefinite. But with that at the back of his mind he quietly resolved to stick to his private resolution. He would go back to the 'Broken Bough' and make one more effort to see if Mrs. Gwyn could not produce anything further. She might, if she exerted her memory, be able to tell him some little detail which, even if unimportant in her eyes, might give him a clue.

Chapter XXIII

THE ACCIDENT

So to the little inn he returned. Mrs. Gwyn welcomed him with reserve. His friendliness and charm of manner had so far softened her as to make her prepared to welcome him as an individual. But equally, his official capacity gave him a tinge of something unwelcome. If he came as an ordinary customer, he was welcome. If he came 'to pry,' as she mentally put it, she wasn't altogether glad to see him.

All this Simon deduced from the manner in which she met him as he entered the inn. "Out for a walk, sir?" in rather a severe tone, was her greeting, fixing her shrewd eyes upon him.

Simon decided he had better accept this impersonal attitude. "Yes, Mrs. Gwyn, I've come in search of tea this time, if you can give it me."

The woman's expression relaxed at once. "Yes, certainly, sir. Will you come this way. I'll bring you your tea into the parlour. The girl's off just now."

She opened the door of the front room, where teas were served. This, owing to the revival in road travel due to hiking and touring activities, had now been filled up with 'peasant weave' curtains and table cloths, and adorned by a shelf running round the walls laden with battalions of pottery rabbits in all colours, yellow and green horses, and other small objects now recognized as indispensable to any 'tea-room.'

Simon sat down rather ruefully. He was aware that whereas before he had been accepted as an official doing his duty, his present activities were earning only resentment. The countryside had endured its brief notoriety and now it only wanted to keep out of further trouble. The reappearance of the inspector was not to be welcomed if it was to be the prelude to further unpleasantness.

Simon, however, was nothing if not dogged. He had hated the failure in the Courtley case brought about by the trial and by Wadham's acquittal. All the smouldering dissatisfaction he had felt had been fanned into fresh life by the little incidents of this visit.

As he sat drinking his tea and looking out at the beautiful woods, he could not forget that obelisk, standing in that little clearing, not so very far from where he now was. His mind wandered over the reconstruction of the extraordinary drama which had played itself out in this place, and which that sinister cenotaph commemorated. He realized now how much inner history had been hidden from him at the time. The country people, true to their traditions, had known how to keep silent—poor Mary, perhaps, to the cost of her own life.

Mrs. Gwyn came into the room at this moment to inquire if he had all he wanted. He answered her almost absently, and as she turned away to rearrange some crockery in a corner cupboard, his gaze followed her dreamily. She was so competent, so businesslike, she looked such an ordinary everyday sort of woman. Yet she had known for some time of the passionate story linking the names of Anne and Barclay, had known and never breathed so much as a hint. He wondered how much more she might guess or suspect.

Even as these thoughts drifted through his mind, a violent interruption came from outside. Loud cries and shouts, the clattering of a horse's hooves dashing along the road, a woman's shrieks.

He rushed to the door, Mrs. Gwyn close behind him, and as they dashed out they were just in time to see a dramatic little scene.

A fair-haired girl, in scarlet sweater and buff jodhpurs, had just been flung violently from her horse and lay sprawled, luckily for her, on a great heap of bracken, cut and piled ready for stacking near the yard gate. Two men were hanging on to the bridle of the plunging and rearing horse which they were trying to hold and soothe. Mrs. Gwyn and Simon hurried across to the girl who lay still and crumpled. Sturt turned her over anxiously. There was no sign of injury, no blood—that was perhaps to the good. He felt her pulse—to his relief it was beating.

"She's all right, I think," he said; "just fainted, I hope. She can't have got concussion falling on this soft heap—and I don't see any other blow anywhere."

Mrs. Gwyn flew off indoors to fetch water, and by this time the horse having been quieted and standing with its head bent, trembling and exhausted, one of the men came across.

"It's that young Evelyn Woodard from over at Marple," he said to the inspector, "one of the girls in the hairdresser's there. Learning to ride she's been, and not too good at it yet. The horse must have taken fright and run away. She couldn't stick on when he came round that corner there so fast."

Mrs. Gwyn came hurrying back with a great bowl of cold water, which she began sprinkling on the girl's face. She clutched some smelling salts too, and Sturt held them to the girl's nose. Quite soon, to the relief of both, her eyelids quivered—she opened her eyes and looked vaguely round. Her gaze came to rest on the horse, standing trembling and sweating, held by one of the men, and she gave an involuntary little cry as recollection came flooding upon her. Then she spoke, with a gush of words set loose by her emotion.

"Oh dear, the horse shied! Shied at that awful monument! Oh dear, oh dear! I was so frightened! I've not been so frightened since I saw Mr. Courtley killed!"

In the still air her voice, shrill with hysteria, rang out quite loud and clear. Sturt could hardly believe his ears. He glanced at Mrs. Gwyn and then round at the two men and saw similar stupefaction on their faces.

"What? *What* did you say?" he said insistently, determined to seize this opportunity. "When you *saw Mr. Courtley killed?*"

"Yes, yes!" sobbed the girl, now quite frantic with shock and reaction. "I did! I did! I saw him killed on that very spot! And to-night—to-night—why it was just the same! The sun, and the place, and the time! And the horse saw it too, I tell you! The horse saw it too and shied!"

She began to sob violently, and Sturt saw that she must be taken indoors and calmed before anything coherent could be hoped for. But he was clear that here was light on that past crime, and he grimly resolved to have the truth out of Miss Evelyn Woodard.

The girl was carried indoors and taken up to Mrs. Gwyn's room. A doctor was sent for, as she was clearly suffering from shock and might have other injuries. Sturt decided to wait on and not leave the inn. When the doctor came, he was glad that he had done so, for he said at once that Evelyn had been much more severely hurt than had been apparent. Her spine had been jarred and the back of her head, and above all she was suffering to a marked degree from shock; indeed, the doctor was at first puzzled by the fearful state of agitation and excitement in which he found her. But after listening to the stream of incoherent sentences with which she greeted him at first, he made up his mind and sent down word that he wished to speak to the inspector.

As Sturt mounted the stairs, Dr. Williams came out of the bedroom to meet him, and beckoned him into a little room at the side.

"Inspector, I've asked you to come up, because this girl is saying things which seem to me important."

Sturt nodded. "She took me aback by something she said outside with regard to the murder of Mr. Courtley," he said briefly.

The doctor's anxious expression lightened. "Ah, so you know? Well, that is it. She is talking about that murder, saying things which if true are clearly vital. She's asking for you and says she wishes to confess to you. In her own interests I think she should be allowed to see you. This excitement is very bad for her, and unless we can check it it may have very serious results. But if these statements of hers are to be taken as evidence, do you want any witness present?"

"No," replied Sturt, "I can take her statement in your presence. You can certify she's not delirious, I suppose?"

"Why, certainly, she's not delirious. She's absolutely sane and sensible—only terribly overwrought. Anxious to get something off her mind really, and from the medical point of view she ought to get it off and have a chance to settle down."

Sturt nodded agreement. He realized that he had stumbled on something which if true would be more than likely to oppress any girl's conscience. He only had time to wonder what details he was going to hear before the doctor had ushered him into the room where the girl lay.

She had been tossing about in the great bed, but at the sight of the inspector accompanying the doctor, she tried to jerk herself upright. Mrs. Gwyn, who sat beside her, hurriedly put her arm round her and propped her up, while the doctor stuffed some more pillows at her back. Tossing her fair tumbled hair out of her eyes, she stared anxiously at Sturt, scarlet patches in her cheeks, and the trembling fingers with which she pulled and twisted at the sheet showed her state of nervous tension.

"Why, Miss Woodard," began Sturt, anxious to calm her as far as possible, "don't look so miserable and upset. I only want to help you, by hearing whatever it is you want to say. Don't be frightened, do please trust to me to help you to do what's right."

His firm gentle tones reassured the girl. She looked hard at the clever sensitive face, and seemed to gather up her own strength. With a great effort she clasped her shaking hands together, fixed her eyes on them and said, in a low voice which she could not keep quite steady:

"I'm not really afraid of what I've done. I never meant any wrong. I never wanted to do what was wrong. But…" She paused, and struggled with herself. None of those listening interrupted her, and she went on, speaking at first with a great effort.

"I was frightened. Terrified. I've been so afraid I've tried not to think of it. I've tried to forget. I've *wanted* to forget. I've wanted not to have to tell. But to-night… when I found where I'd come on my ride… when I saw that awful, awful spot… it all came back to me… and now I know I can't rest, I can't keep it in… I can't go on like this any longer." Her voice choked and she stopped. Mrs. Gwyn would have given her a drink, but she pushed the glass impatiently aside. Clearly now that she had resolved to pour out her story, she wanted to get it over as soon as might be.

"I'll tell you what happened. I'll tell you all I saw. Only, don't let those men get at me—and don't let them get at John!" She turned an agonized look on the inspector and he spoke at once.

"I'll see that *no one* gets at you, Miss Woodard, nor at your friend (for he guessed 'John' to have been someone in whom she was interested and whom she wished to safeguard). If you're afraid of any sort of interference, you can be quite at rest. The police will protect you."

Again she seemed to draw reassurance from his firmness, and from the recognition that here by her side were the forces of law and order. With a faint sigh of relaxation, she closed her eyes for a moment, gathering herself together for the supreme revelation.

"This is what I saw. This is what I must tell you," she began in a low voice. "John and I were going to the Fair, the St. Giles's Fair, at Marple, the day that Mr. Courtley was killed. We started off, across the common, and it was very hot, and we got very hot. So we thought we'd have a bit of a rest, before going on to the Fair. John said the woods were so cool, we'd just stop till the sun wasn't so fierce and we found a place in the bracken—near where that awful monument is"—and as she spoke she shuddered all over—"and we sat there and talked. And then it was so hot I lay down and went to sleep, and John just dozed for a bit, he said. And then—" her voice rose a tone—"and then I woke up all of a sudden and I heard men talking near us and John signed to me to be quiet, so I kept still, and so did he. The men's voices sounded sort of queer... I can't describe it... but they were talking ever so close to us and very quickly, and we peeped through the stems of the bracken—it was so high it was right over our heads. And we saw three men standing quite near us, on the pathway. They were standing close to each other, and one of them had a gun."

Again she had to pause, her voice had grown so thick and hoarse. Sturt felt his heart beating violently. *Three men!* Was she going to tell the names? Could she, had she known them, have recognized them? He gave a swift glance at the other two listeners, and saw reflected in both faces the same incredulous horror, and the same fascinated anticipation. The girl's voice resumed:

"I couldn't see at first who they were. Then they began to separate. And I could see the man on the other side of the path quite distinctly—it was Mr. Wadham, Mr. Courtley's secretary. And then I saw the other two as they moved back along the path—it was Mr. Sylvester and Mr. Barclay... John still pushed me down to keep still and I couldn't see what they were doing, but they were each stooping down, one on each side of the path, stooping down in the heather and bracken, I mean, and they seemed to lie down flat. And we thought it so queer, we just looked at each other and kept still... you could somehow tell they were all up to something, and we both, I suppose, felt that they'd not like to know we were there in the bracken watching them.

"And then Mr. Courtley came." Her voice settled to a hard mechanical recital, as if by its monotony she tried to keep at bay the terror with which the recollection she was evoking overwhelmed her. "He came along the path, swishing at the bracken with a stick. And Mr. Wadham, he was standing waiting for him and he called out to him, 'I'm here,' or something like that, and Mr. Courtley seemed to step out a bit quicker when he saw him, hurrying up a bit, and then... then he stumbled over something... and Mr. Wadham, he gave a sort of shout and Mr. Barclay and Mr. Sylvester, they stood up where they were and came running near to the path. And Mr. Sylvester, he bent down and snatched at Mr. Courtley's foot so as he couldn't get up, and Mr. Barclay, he raised his gun and shot right through Mr. Courtley... And John and I, we just pressed our faces down to the ground and prayed and prayed the bracken would hide us and they not see us."

She stopped, and raised eyes filled with a burning light to Sturt's face. He tried swiftly to obliterate from his expression the horror which this recital had raised in his mind. There was a dead silence.

Sturt broke it. His voice at first seemed harsh and loud after the girl's broken, monotonous tone.

"When those two men stooped, have you any idea what they were doing?"

"Yes. We talked about that afterwards. I couldn't look any more after the shot. I felt as if I were going to die. I just lay still and kept my face to the earth. But John looked, and he told me first he saw something white fly through the air to the ground and then Mr. Sylvester wound up a piece of cord, and that the cord had been stretched from him to Mr. Barclay across the path, and that Mr. Courtley had stumbled over it, he thought."

Sturt understood. The three men had combined together. Wadham had been the decoy. Courtley had come to meet him, and seeing him standing in the wood had come readily on. The other two had tripped Courtley with the cord and as he lay prostrate, the one had held his foot and so prevented him from rising, while the third had fired the shot—fired between the legs of the fallen man, and as the body had sagged forward, the convulsion of death had torn off the shoe in the hand holding the victim's foot. He understood it all!

But how incredible, how utterly incredible that this girl and her John should have been there, been within a stone's throw and seen it all, and never have breathed a word. Why had they kept silence and shielded the three murderers?

The girl seemed to understand what was passing in his mind. She looked directly at him, her face twisted now with feverish anxiety.

"I suppose you're wondering why we didn't tell? Why we didn't come forward to the police? Oh, I know we ought to have done! I *know* we ought. But we were both so frightened. We'd seen them do it"—she began to sob—"and we were afraid of what they'd do to us! We didn't dare to do anything then—they'd the gun, and we'd nothing. We *couldn't* do anything then."

Sturt tried to soothe her. "No. You couldn't perhaps do anything at the moment. But why did you not tell later?"

"There were three of them to swear against us two, and of course we hoped you'd find out," she sobbed; "we waited a bit and you arrested Mr. Wadham, and we kept hoping you'd arrest the other two. And I didn't want to be mixed up in it, and nor did John, it was so awful, so *awful…* And then there was the trial—and we were sure you must have come on the truth, and that you'd catch them all three. We kept on hoping and then the trial went the wrong way at the last, all unexpectedly, and Mr. Wadham was acquitted, and we just didn't know what to do. People said he couldn't be tried again, no matter what came out, and John said… John said…" but here her tears became so beyond her control that she could not say another word.

The doctor broke in. "Inspector, she's done enough. She can't go on any more. You'd better leave her alone. Surely she's told you enough?"

Simon hesitated for a moment. He would need 'John's' name and address. But the girl was weeping so convulsively, was clearly so broken down, that he saw he would get nothing more for the time being. Had he not got enough for the present? He decided that he had, and closing the notebook in which he had been taking down her words, he went quickly out of the room.

He waited downstairs for what seemed a long time. At length the doctor appeared, his face pale and grave. He drew a deep breath as he sat down by Sturt. "Well, Inspector, what an awful business. I suppose you think this is the truth she's telling?"

Sturt nodded. "I do. No one would make up such a story. It's amazing, of course. But it could quite well have happened as she described. If she and her young man were asleep in the bracken they'd be motionless and there'd be no sign of them. And those three men wouldn't suspect there was anyone there. I remember a big clump of bracken, away to the side—it was too out of range for the gun to have been fired from there, and of course no one dreamt of spectators. I don't suppose those three thought of that either. They'd be too intent on what they were going to do. Her account is perfectly in keeping with all the known facts. We never understood how that shot was fired between the legs, but it's quite clear now. As they tripped him up with the string across the path, he'd fall without any struggle. And if they stood on the grass verge, they could seize him and shoot without themselves stepping on the path. Yes, it's all clear. And I've no doubt about that detail of Sylvester holding his foot, and finding himself left with the shoe in his hand, just throwing it away. That was the 'white thing' that the young man saw fly through the air."

The doctor nodded agreement. He too could visualize the scene. The stumbling bald account given by the girl upstairs had held the stamp of truth. Neither of the men doubted that what they had just heard was an eyewitness's account of the murder of Charles Courtley.

Before he left, Simon went quietly upstairs and beckoning Mrs. Gwyn out of the room, he impressed on her, with all the force and weight of his official position, the absolute necessity of keeping silence as to what she had heard. He must go and take steps; meanwhile she must remain with the girl, and see that no one else came near her.

Then, briefly explaining to the doctor that he must at once return to Marple, he set out through the wood.

Chapter XXIV

AT BAY

S turt felt quite exhausted. So much had happened that afternoon—the surprise of the accident, and of its strange results,
had been like a storm. He had hardly got his breath again. Turning
the girl's story over in his mind, he accepted it as true. He concluded
that 'John' could easily be found, and induced to corroborate the
tale. If that were so, then he had two witnesses, as required by the
law, to the facts of the murder. So far, so good. Yet, the position
was not really all that could be desired. Wadham was now revealed
as one of the murdering group, but he had already been tried, and
acquitted, for the murder of Courtley. According to the law, he could
not be tried again for the same offence. Barclay—who apparently
had actually fired the shot—was dead. Only Sylvester remained of
the trio, as one who could be brought to justice. And motive? That
was still obscure. And Anne? Surely, in view of all he had heard,
of her liaison with Barclay, her bitterness at his death, her behaviour since, she must have been an accessory? Sturt shook his head
frowningly. He saw that though a great light had been shed on the
mystery, it was not yet completely solved.

He reached Marple, and went to the police station directly.
Groves was out, and Simon sat down in the little office to wait for his
return. He reflected on the bearing which his new information had
on the death of poor Mary Game. He saw that, granted the truth of
Evelyn's account of the crime, which he for one did not doubt, then

the famous meeting of the three men, Wadham, Barclay, Sylvester, at the 'Broken Bough' that summer's day a year before, had clearly been the rendezvous appointed before the murder. They must all have gone straight from the inn to the fatal clearing in the Fosse Wood.

Now Mary had sworn that two of them at least had been at the inn talking late over their tea, beyond the time when the murder had been committed. Obviously she had lied, as Simon had always suspected. But, if she had lied, she had done it in the interests of these men and they had always known it. Their lives had depended on her silence, or at least they must have believed so, being ignorant of those actual eye-witnesses hidden in the bracken. And too, she had known of Barclay's secret liaison with Anne. She must have suspected a great deal. It was more than possible, in view of this certainty of their guilt, that one or other of those three had determined to make safety certain. They must have realized how all depended on the girl! Mary's death would silence the only person who could jeopardize them, for Wadham and Sylvester were themselves involved. There must lie the cause of her mysterious death.

Then he thought more seriously of Anne. Given the fact of her connection with Barclay, surely she had known beforehand of the plot? He thought of that letter sent on the fatal day which he had never traced; he was sure now it had given some vital news to the conspirators or in some way given the signal for the execution of what was planned.

Just as his meditations brought him to this point, he was conscious of noise and movement in the room beyond the inner office where he sat. The door opened and Groves came in, full of surprise and uneasiness to know the inspector was awaiting him.

The first thing Sturt wished to be done was to get hold of 'John.' Simon had not wished to upset poor Evelyn Woodard further, and fully realized that had he pressed for the young man's name and address he ran the risk of alarming her. He guessed that he would not have much trouble in discovering her friend's identity.

So, without telling Groves of all the new developments, he merely said that he wanted to trace a young man, engaged to Evelyn Woodard, Christian name 'John.' Groves knew the girl's family and her home and within an hour he reported that the young man in question was a clerk at the local electricity works, and living in a village two miles away. Sturt gave orders that he was to be summoned to the station as soon as possible, and accordingly the sergeant, rather mystified, departed on his motor-cycle combination to fetch him.

Simon waited for them at the police station. He began to look ahead and consider what plans he must make. As yet he had not sufficient grounds for an arrest, but he must have everything in train. He sat at the desk, jotting down the headings of his proposals. Someone came into the outer office, and he heard the voice of the constable on duty, talking to a woman. Presently a knock came at his door. The young policeman's face appeared, rather puzzled. "Miss Courtley, sir, wants to know if she can have a word with you."

Simon wished he could refuse. He did not want to see the girl. At the back of his mind was what he recognized as an almost vindictive determination to drag into the light whatever part Anne had played. He was so sure she had supplied the motive for the whole crime. And now here was her daughter, the last person he wanted to see. Still, he felt he could hardly refuse, so curtly bade the man show her in.

The girl stepped into the room, where the gathering dusk had come down unobserved by Simon as he sat absorbed. Rising to his feet, he switched on the electric light, and as the hard bright glare struck full on Pamela's face, hardened as he was by his experience of human nature in misfortune, Simon could hardly repress a movement. She looked ghastly. Her make-up only brought into relief the grey pallor that underlay her skin. Simon guessed at once that for long this girl had known the truth, had known that her father had been murdered by the man she loved, but who had not loved her, who had only deceived her cruelly in order to hide his love for her own mother. Filled with compassion for her, and with sudden rage against those who had dealt with her so cruelly, Simon did not speak, he hardly knew how to greet her.

She did not, however, leave him much opportunity. Standing straight in front of the desk she fixed him with her feverishly bright eyes.

"I've come back," she said, "because I saw you come in here this morning. I saw you turn in here after I'd gone up the street. So I knew it wasn't true what you said." The bitter inflexion of her voice stung Simon a little. "I knew you weren't here on holiday after all, as you said. You're here on business. I want to know what business?"

For a moment Simon was silent. Then he drew forward a chair for the girl, and motioned to her to be seated. "I see I must tell you a good deal, Miss Courtley," he began gently. "I'm very sorry you have worried yourself about this, but as you have, I must be frank with you."

She gave him a little contemptuous smile, but said nothing.

He resumed, feeling his way cautiously. "I was here on holiday, and I went through Fosse Wood out of mere curiosity, I'm afraid— not in connection with any official affairs at all. But, being at the 'Broken Bough,' I heard of Mary Game's death—and that did lead me to official investigation."

As he spoke, the girl's pallor increased. She almost gasped—her skin seemed to turn green: she swayed forward in her chair. Alarmed lest she was going to faint, Simon hurriedly poured her out some water from the carafe found in every government office, and hurrying round the desk, held it to her lips. After a few minutes she sat up, and brushed her hand across her forehead, wet with perspiration.

"That's all right, I'm better now," she said. "Go on with what you were saying."

Sturt hesitated, not certain whether she were really fit for talk.

"Go on! Go on!" she reiterated impatiently. "I must get this over. Tell me about Mary. Tell me!"

Shocked at her appearance and realizing that the greatest kindness was to end her suspense, Simon made up his mind.

"Miss Courtley," he said, as gently as he could, "I've nothing definite to go on. I can only tell you that I have grounds for believing that Mary Game died from the effects of a drug, administered to her in order to prevent her ever telling us the truth."

"I knew it! I knew it!" broke from the girl, in a tone of anguish. "I was *sure* it was something of the sort. But the doctors said there was nothing, they said there *wasn't* any trace of poison or drugs?" Her eyes, wild with anxiety, stared into his. Simon shook his head.

"They were too late, I think. There are drugs, narcotics, which leave no trace after twenty-four hours. I suspect she had a dose of something of that sort."

"What drugs—tell me." Her hoarse voice rang out loud in the bare little room.

"What are called barbituric—such things for example as dial, or medinal, or luminal—taken in sufficient quantities."

"But you can't get them in big quantities," she gasped. "I know you can't. You can only get them through a doctor, and a few at a time."

Simon looked at her piercingly. So she was familiar with these drugs? An ominous silence fell between them. Slowly she dragged herself to her feet. Now she avoided his eyes.

"You only suspect," she said. "You don't know. I expect you're wrong. You were before. You just see horrible things everywhere. It's what you're paid for, I suppose."

Simon made no reply. In silence he opened the door for her, and she went out and went away.

After she had gone, he went back to his seat conscious that his heart was beating rather fast. He had something fresh to think of now. Certainly this girl knew how Mary had died—knew, that is to say, that someone had been able to silence her by the very drugs Simon had mentioned. Very well. That meant that possibly Pamela herself had done so. She had loved Barclay, had loved him very deeply. Barclay's actions had been known to Mary, it was conceivable that Pamela had tried to obliterate all knowledge of his share in the crime. Conceivable too that she had done so believing he loved her, and had found too late that had all been pretence. Simon felt horror at the thought. This Carron case was appalling. He began to think that murder for money, sordid as it might be, was less awful in its effects than murder instigated by passion.

He tried to get back to his official calm. He was here as the representative of law, impartial, a man paid to find out crime and bring wrong-doers to justice. Pity had no place here.

He was thankful to hear the chug-chug of the sergeant's motor-cycle coming down the street.

For the next half-hour he had no time to think of Pamela, and her pale miserable face vanished for a time from his mind's-eye. He had instead to struggle with an obstinate and badly frightened young man.

For John Stedman was very badly frightened. That was abundantly clear. Simon adopted his most official tone, for he saw that nothing but the might and justice of Scotland Yard could produce the needful impression.

"I have received information," he began, "which leads me to ask where you were on the afternoon of September fifth a year ago."

"That's a long time back, I don't remember what I was doing then. It's impossible I should," stuttered the young man, though it was obvious from his pallor and stammering hesitation that he knew perfectly well what events he was being asked to recall.

Simon hastened to refresh his memory. He told him that 'of course he would recollect' that the date in question was the local Fair day of that year. That the Fair was being held at Marple that afternoon; that he might remember he was going with the young lady to whom he was engaged, Miss Evelyn Woodard?

Stedman, forced to agree to this, grew more desperate, and more sullen. He admitted that he 'supposed' this was all true, but that he 'couldn't remember all that way back.' Nor could Simon's questions get anything further from him. He took refuge in that formula 'he could not remember,' and seeing that this baffled the inspector, grew bolder and clung to his obstinate iteration all the more.

Simon felt desperate. Unless he could drag out the truth, his whole case would collapse. He was bound to have two witnesses, and he was certain too that if Stedman stuck it out, the girl would go back on her word.

Rapidly he decided that he must come out into the open. Summoning all his official authority, he opened his notebook, and reading from it told the horrified young man that 'from information received' the police now knew that he had been in Fosse Wood on the afternoon in question; that he had been there at the vital time; and that he had actually been in the close vicinity of the spot where Charles Courtley had been murdered.

Clearly the miserable shaking John now thought that suspicion rested on him. He sat silent, his mouth hanging open, gazing helplessly at the inspector. Simon closed his book and speaking sharply said:

"Now, Mr. Stedman. What have you to say?"

Utterly speechless, John gazed at the inspector. Clearly he realized that something had come to light. Clearly, too, he was resolved to stick to his denials as long as he could. But Simon gave him little chance. Leaning forward across the desk he fixed his blue eyes on the shrinking brown ones opposite.

"I warn you," he said, "that this is an investigation into murder. Anyone possessing information, and not coming forward to assist the law, is guilty of being an accessory after the fact."

Still the man was silent, though the sweat poured down his face. Suddenly Simon realized that possibly this was not selfish cowardice. The girl had been a witness too and perhaps this silence was an attempt to shield her. He spoke at once.

"I should tell you, Mr. Stedman, that Miss Woodard has already made a statement to us, a voluntary statement," for he did not want it to be thought the girl was under arrest.

Instant relief showed itself in the man's voice. Tremblingly he wiped his face, and then said in a low voice.

"Well, if she's told you, there's nothing more to be done. I'll tell you my story too."

Simon felt a throb of unutterable relief. He had won! He drew a deep breath of thankfulness, and took up his pen to note down what was to come.

Haltingly, for he had been terribly frightened, the story came out. In every detail it corroborated the account already given by the girl. The brief conversation of the three men, their actions, the shot, the winding up of the piece of string, all were confirmed. Stedman had seen it all. He had seen, too, that Barclay's hand had been bandaged. That was one reason why he was so definite that it had been he who fired the shot. Every detail had been burnt in on his mind, and when he had gone in horror over all that he had seen, he had realized that Sylvester of course must of necessity have been the one to seize the victim's foot, just because Barclay's hand was hurt.

"I reckoned it out that he, Mr. Barclay, could let off the gun," he explained, "but he couldn't do more with that bad hand. He couldn't have held on to Mr. Courtley's foot," and he shuddered as the recollection of that horrible little scene came back. "Mr. Courtley he'd stumbled and fallen on his face and his legs shot up a bit in the air, and Mr. Sylvester he reached forward and held up his leg with both hands—and then Mr. Barclay he fired, and Mr. Sylvester he let the leg drop and flung something away into the bushes."

"And Mr. Wadham?" queried Simon grimly.

"Mr. Wadham, he stood a bit away, in the heather. He'd been there all along, you know, just standing there. 'Mr. Courtley' he called out as he came up just before he stumbled. I think, looking towards Mr. Wadham as he was, he hadn't his eyes on the path. Mr. Wadham never moved, he just stood where he was all the time."

"And after the shot?"

"They just all stood there quite still. Then Mr. Wadham he looked as if he were going to be sick, I could see how pale he was, and Mr. Barclay turned round and laughed at him, and they all went off into the woods."

A little silence fell. Stedman had grown steadier as his recital had gone on. Now he faced the inspector with more courage. "I know it was wrong of us to keep quiet, but I've told you it all now, Inspector, and if I've got to be punished for not coming forward before, well, I'll take it. Only Miss Woodard, she's not to blame. She'd have told if I'd have let her—but I wouldn't. I made her keep quiet, and I'll take the blame for it."

Sturt assured him he need not be afraid. He and Evelyn Woodard would be called as Crown witnesses, and by giving their evidence now, would be absolved from their action in concealing the truth.

The statement having been copied and signed, Stedman was dismissed with the strongest warning that he was to say nothing at all to anyone on the matter.

Once he had gone, escorted home by the sergeant, who was completely overcome by this unexpected development, Simon sat for a while motionless at his desk. He shaded his face with his hand. Truth was out. There could be no longer any doubt. Here he had his second witness. But justice could not be done on Barclay. He was dead, never having profited by his crime. Wadham too, he must escape the major penalty, he could not a second time be tried for his life. Only Sylvester could be charged with the murder—and perhaps Anne Courtley.

Chapter XXV

THE THIRD DEATH

O ne thing he decided, Sylvester must be arrested and at once.
Despite the warnings given to all concerned, Dr. Williams,
Mrs. Gwyn, and Stedman, Sturt was sure that something would
leak out. His presence in Marple, and at the police station, the accident to Evelyn Woodard, and the fact that her fiancé had been sent
for and questioned by the police, must be already known. Pamela
Courtley had grasped quickly enough the significance of Simon's
presence in the town. She had realized that he was on the trail, she
had understood that the murder case, which all had believed closed,
was to be re-opened. What she had guessed, Sylvester could guess
too. If he was involved in the second murder, or if he knew, as he
must inevitably know, that Mary Game's death was linked with that
of Charles Courtley, then the visits of the inspector to the 'Broken
Bough' must have alarmed him. He might decide to brazen things
out, but he must doubt whether the truth could be successfully
concealed a second time. It was more likely that he would try to
save himself by flight.

So it came about that within half an hour, Simon, who had
only waited for the return of the sergeant, set out for the estate
office, where once before he had interviewed Sylvester. He had
resolved to arrest him without waiting for a warrant, as he was
entitled to do in virtue of the fact that this was an accusation of
murder.

252 D. Erskine Muir

As they approached the little house, Simon saw that lights shone from it. Both upstairs and down the windows were lit up, and even as he walked towards the door he saw the shadow of someone inside coming down the staircase. Quickly he raised his hand and knocked. There was movement within, then silence. He knocked again, and louder. The sergeant, stepping back, looked up at the lighted windows above.

"He's gone upstairs again, sir. He's in the bathroom now."

The bathroom! Simon's thoughts made a leap. He spoke quickly. "Come on, Sergeant, we must break the door in."

Between the two, the door was almost instantly smashed. They rushed headlong across the little hall, up the stairs, and just as they reached the head, the door opposite to them opened. Sylvester came out. He looked at them in apparent astonishment. "What's this? What on earth are you up to? What do you want breaking in like this?"

"We want *you*, Mr. Sylvester," responded Simon promptly, and stepping forward he laid his hand on Sylvester's shoulder. "I charge you with being concerned in the murder of Mr. Charles Courtley."

Sylvester stood stock still. Then turned his head to gaze into Simon's dark blue eyes, on a level with his own, now blazing with a queer light.

"Your second shot, Inspector?" he sneered. "Well, let's hope I have Wadham's luck."

Simon felt rage surge up. True it was, Wadham *had* been lucky. Still—something could be done to level up even that score! Meanwhile, at least here was one murderer caught. He motioned to the sergeant, who produced handcuffs.

"Aren't you going to let me pack?"

Simon shook his head. "If you'll tell the Sergeant what you'll want, he'll get it for you," he said briefly. He did not mean to trust this man an inch.

Sylvester turned towards the other room. "Well, come on, Groves. Let's see what sort of a hand you are at packing," he gibed. The two went into the bedroom. Moved by some impulse, Simon stepped forward into the room out of which Sylvester had come. As Groves had said, it was the bathroom. Over the fitted basin was a small cupboard. Its door was open, and showed rows of medicine bottles and toilet preparations. Simon's heart sank as he saw that. He stepped swiftly across, and noticed at once a tooth glass, stood down on the basin by the taps. He picked it up, it was marked with wet white sediment. Something had been drunk there recently, drunk surely after the first knock at the door had come. Sylvester, from upstairs, had seen the police approaching and their knock had been the signal to him that all was up.

Simon went quickly out of the bathroom, and entered the bedroom where Groves was hurriedly putting things from the drawers into a suitcase, while Sylvester directed him. At Simon's entrance both men turned. Apparently his face told its own tale. Sylvester broke into a yell of laughter.

"Yes, Inspector! I've diddled you too! No one's going to hang for Charles Courtley's murder!"

Poor Sergeant Groves stared aghast as peal on peal of mocking laughter filled the room—then stepped quickly forward as the raucous sound ceased suddenly, to catch Sylvester as he fell. In a moment the room was in turmoil. The wretched man writhed and bent in violent convulsions. Neither Simon nor Groves could hold him, until at last with one fearful twist of his body he lay still.

Simon stood up, and wiped the sweat from his brow. "Go as fast as you can for the doctor," he directed, "though I'm afraid it's no good now."

Groves clattered down the staircase and went running down the street. Simon stood and looked at the contorted body on the floor. Suddenly he started. Sylvester had moved. Simon bent down quickly—yes, Peter's eyes were opening again.

He was not dead. He revived, but only to go into a fresh paroxysm of pain. Simon's fears were justified. He had kept strychnine in his cupboard, and as the police broke in, had swallowed a fatal dose.

Though Dr. Williams was fetched, he could not counteract the effects of the poison. He could only try to mitigate the agonizing attacks of pain as they came on. Sylvester was a strong man, and he did not die quickly. Simon sat beside a dreadful death-bed, hoping to get a little more light on dark places.

He succeeded. Sylvester knew that he was dying—and meant to die defiantly. He admitted the whole truth now.

He, Barclay, and Wadham had planned the murder. He did not say much as to their motives. "What *you* want to know is *how* we did it—not why." But he said that he and Barclay had been the initiators of the scheme. They had both hated Charles. Sylvester had been wrought up to a final pitch of fury by the threatened destruction of his beloved Fosse Wood.

He denied that Anne had been privy to their scheme. He avowed cynically that he would never have wanted to marry her. "I'd seen enough of her," he gasped. As to Barclay's wishes, he declared he "didn't know. I didn't worry about all that—I just wanted to rid the world of a pestilent fellow—I knew his wife wouldn't miss him—and I didn't care."

Wadham had come in later. He had been sent to Sylvester to get Anne's letters, by Charles himself.

Soon the cousins had discovered they were dealing with a rogue and one who hated Courtley just as bitterly as they. That he had been in Courtley's power they knew, though they had not known why, and only guessed it had been from some very shady action in his past. He had quite soon agreed to play a double part. He had arranged to decoy Charles to Fosse Wood, and had done so by raising doubts in Charles's mind as to the timber contract. On the Tuesday morning, while working with Charles, he had declared the timber merchant was taking trees from outside the contracted space. He had told Charles he could show him this. Charles had been furious at the idea of anyone cheating him, and had suspected Sylvester was at the bottom of it. Wadham had arranged the rendezvous, and had duly notified Sylvester. Anne's version of the events had been right. He had slipped out first to find Barclay at the oast-house, had failed, had left a note bidding him ring up, and gone back. Charles, wishing to deal with Sylvester, had gone himself down to the office, and while he was away, Barclay had rung up.

They had all three met near the 'Broken Bough.' There Barclay, firing an experimental shot, to see how the home-made pellets worked, had hurt his hand, for the first cartridge had been badly made. Luckily, he could still use it, and they had gone on with their plans. They had hurriedly altered the charge in the second cartridge, and in their haste had used a scrap of paper Wadham had with him.

This was the tale gasped out at intervals as that long, frightful day wore on.

In the intervals, Simon's thoughts travelled far. There were still things he passionately wanted to know. Nothing that Sylvester said could very much affect Wadham, he was safe from any second trial for murder, and that, of course, had helped to liberate Sylvester's tongue.

There were other people to be thought of though, and Simon determined to risk a further effort. He bent forward, when Sylvester in a moment's remission of pain lay still and silent.

"Mr. Sylvester. I want to clear a suspicion out of the way, I want to free an *innocent* person if I can," he stressed the word, for he realized in this way alone could he get the dying man to speak. "What about Mary Game?"

Sylvester shook his head feebly. "I know nothing at all about that," he whispered. Yet a darker shadow seemed to fall across his face, a slightly different expression bitter and hard passed over it.

Simon hesitated. This man had not shrunk from Courtley's death, but surely the murder of an innocent girl, who had helped to save his life, must have been different? "I'm sure she was murdered," he said distinctly, "and I believe I know who was responsible. Tell me this, did you or Mr. Barclay meet her that evening?"

But Sylvester only closed his lips more tightly. He would not answer. Dreading the oncoming of another attack, Simon hurriedly put his final question. "Tell me, that letter, Mrs. Courtley's letter, what became of it?"

With a jerk the closed eyes opened, and a gleam almost of sly triumph came into them. "That letter? I did you there, Inspector! I hope—I hope—hope you never find it." The words came with a rush, cut short by the ghastly spasms which nothing now could alleviate, and this time Sylvester never rallied again. He passed from one paroxysm to another, until unconsciousness and at length death, put an end to horrible sufferings.

Sick at heart by all he had witnessed, Simon went wearily back to the police station. It was very late now, and after giving orders for Wadham to be traced, he went across to his old rooms, where he had booked a bed, and snatched a little sleep.

Chapter XXVI

THE LAST STRUGGLE

The next morning a warrant was issued for Wadham's arrest. "If we can't have him for murder, at least we can get him a long sentence for perjury," remarked Sturt to the Chief Constable who had been sent for. "Now, sir, we've got to consider Mrs. Courtley."

The Chief Constable looked glum. He thoroughly disliked this revival of scandal and hated the fresh outburst of notoriety which was bound to overwhelm the district.

"I hate a case with a woman," he said briefly. Sturt secretly concurred in this, but at the same time he felt in duty bound to raise the question.

"Well, sir, I think we have to go into this, for the practical certainty is she was behind the whole affair. Sylvester had loved her, and though they'd tired of each other, apparently he remained fond of her and perfectly willing to be on good terms. He and his cousin were devoted to each other. To my mind, Sylvester had no adequate reason by himself to kill Mr. Courtley, he acted with Mr. Barclay, and the only motive *he* had was to rid Mrs. Courtley of her husband."

"Yes," sighed the Chief Constable, "that may well be so. These two men, of course, had their own personal feud with Courtley. They were the last of the old family here and they hated his methods with the place. I quite realize that wasn't enough to produce murder. Mrs. Courtley probably *did* prove the real incentive, but that doesn't mean she herself is implicated. They could have planned the whole affair without her knowing anything of it."

"They could, of course," replied Simon, "but I'm pretty sure she was in it all. Just think, sir, she'd bought that gun, the right sort of gun for the crime; she'd been meeting Mr. Barclay, the very night before the murder, in secret, for we can be sure now it was *she* who met *him* in the yard that night; she wrote a letter to Mr. Sylvester the next morning, after she'd been known to have had a quarrel with her husband, and the man acted that very afternoon. I'm confident if only we'd got hold of that letter, we could prove her complicity."

The Chief Constable shook his head. "Granted that's all probable, Inspector, we've no proof. Unless you got that letter, and unless it was extraordinarily incriminating, you've no real grounds for action."

With this Simon had perforce to agree, but it was decided that at least he should make one further effort to discover whether by any chance any letters survived in Sylvester's rooms. Groves was accordingly summoned, and told to search minutely for any papers. Simon meanwhile paid a visit to Dr. Williams's surgery.

"I want some information from you, Doctor," he began, when he found himself seated by the side of the big desk. He produced his notebook. "I want to ask if you prescribed any of the barbituric narcotics for Mrs. Courtley? At any time within the past two years?"

Dr. Williams looked across at the inspector with a searching glance.

"Yes," he answered briefly. "I did prescribe di-dial for her to take during the trial, and for some weeks afterwards."

"What dose?"

"Di-dial made up in five-grain doses."

"Is that a stronger preparation than usual?"

"Yes, but she had got into such a state of sleeplessness after the murder and during the trial that I found the ordinary dose produced no effect. I considered it better to give her the stronger prescription, rather than run the risk of having her take two of some weaker tablets. People are worse, less reliable I mean, over taking several weak tablets than one strong one."

"Then, how many of these di-dial could she get at a time?"

"Only ten, and the prescription could only be renewed three times."

"What would be a fatal dose?"

"Forty grains."

"So, having the prescription made up even once would give her a total of fifty grains?"

"Yes."

"And being renewed three times, she could get ten at a time and, if she saved her tablets, collect a fatal dose while still taking occasional tablets herself?"

The doctor looked uncomfortable, for he realized in what direction Sturt's questions pointed.

"Well, you know, Inspector, patients can always hoard their tablets on any prescription. One just can't prevent that. I told Mrs. Courtley never to keep these tablets by her bedside, and actually gave her daughter a hint, told her this prescription was a strong one, and asked her to see her mother never took more than one a night."

Sturt felt his heart jump. So Pamela knew her mother had this prescription.

Briefly thanking the doctor, he went on to the chemist and from him obtained details and dates of the supply of di-dial sent up to Mrs. Courtley. It was as Dr. Williams had said, three sets of tablets prescribed over a period of four months. The chemist had always retained the prescription, no supplies could be obtained elsewhere, but a total of thirty five-grain tablets had been delivered.

Simon on leaving the chemist went straight to Sylvester's rooms.

Groves met him with the news that so far nothing had been found. Sylvester's desk contained a mass of papers dealing with the estate management, all carefully docketed. Amongst the orderly files was one labelled 'Fosse Wood' and Sturt could not refrain from glancing through this. He wondered what Sylvester's feelings must have been each time he saw the label with that ominous name. But the file was only illuminating in so far as it showed that Sylvester had been right; Charles would not have gained financially by the felling of the trees, his sale of the timber had been largely spite.

Nor was a search of Sylvester's own papers any more productive. There was no sign or trace of any communication with Anne. Yet remembering those last dying words, 'Hope you never find it,' Simon felt sure that famous letter had been preserved.

Rising from the bureau, he confronted the sergeant, whose task had been to go through the bedroom. Groves shook his head. "There's nothing there, Inspector, nothing whatever, I'll take my oath."

Simon sighed, for he knew Groves was to be relied on. They prepared to leave. Going down to the little back room, sacred to Sylvester's housekeeper, he told her that he must seal up the rooms and no one must be allowed to go into them. As he turned away, his eye was caught by something on the mantelpiece. Crossing the room he laid his hand on a china swan filled with spills of bright blue paper. "What are these?" he asked sharply, for the peculiar shade of blue stirred a recollection in his mind.

"Why, spills, sir," the woman answered; "spills Mr. Sylvester made for me. I like spills to light my candles with, and Mr. Sylvester, he was one of those gentlemen who can fold paper to all sorts of figures and things. He used to amuse himself and often he'd make me up bundles of spills. That's just a handful of some old ones."

But even while she spoke the inspector's fingers were busy undoing the neat twists of paper. He had recognized the blue shade as the paper they used at Carron, and suddenly he could recall the very look of that colour in Sylvester's hand, the morning a year ago when they had been discussing the case, in the little office below. He could see in his mind's eye Sylvester lighting his pipe by one of those spills.

But as he spread the fragments out, bitter disappointment came over him. The scraps left were too few, and the words on them too scattered. 'Dear Peter… last n… can't… do… care…' and on one piece a line which made him realize with utter fury this might have been the evidence he sought, 'F… careful… time right.' He turned on the housekeeper like a flash. "How long have you had these? Are there any more?"

Bewildered, the woman answered: "Why, I've had them a long time, sir. Those few blue ones. They didn't burn well, the paper's too thick, I think, or it's the way they're folded. Mr. Sylvester tried a new pattern that time, I remember, and it didn't seem to work. That's how it comes that lot never got used. I tried a few of them and then left the rest. No, there won't be any more—and as to how long I've had them, I'm sure I can't say. A long time, I know, but I just haven't bothered to clear them away."

"When did he make them, can you remember that?"

The woman paused. "It was last summer, sir. It was one of those very hot days in that spell of fine weather we had last September. I know that, for Mr. Sylvester he made a joke of it. He brought me these in and said he'd tried a new experiment, but I'd not need to use them then, not having fires. He put them in that vase—why"—and she looked quite astonished—"it comes back to me as clear as anything. He ran out of the room in a hurry, with one of them still in his hand, for we'd both seen you coming in at the gate with the Sergeant here!"

Simon nodded his head. Sylvester had been ingenious. He guessed the police were coming about the murder, he must have dreaded lest Anne's note, written on that very conspicuous paper, should catch Sturt's eye—he had chosen this way to conceal the paper.

Simon realized there was nothing to be done now. Sylvester had literally 'played with fire.' Perhaps intentionally he had left these scraps. Perhaps he had always wanted to keep some hold over Anne and had chosen this strange way of preserving her letters. At the time he may have been determined that in case of necessity he would have her letter in existence. He had gambled on the chance that neither the housekeeper nor the police would look in her room. That seemed the only way of accounting for his action. As to whether the whole letter had once been in those spills, or only pieces which would not fully incriminate her by themselves, but only serve as corroboration of any statement he might make—that would never be known now.

Taking the pieces with him, for if useless as evidence, still they might serve a purpose he had in mind, Simon left the cottage and girded himself up for his next task, one that he greatly dreaded.

He went up to Carron Cross.

He went to Carron Cross and asked for Pamela. A frightened looking maid showed him into the drawing room, which he remembered from former days. But the room no longer had its well-kept charm. There were no flowers, no books, no sign of occupation. Simon waited uneasily. He had realized from the maid's manner that the news of Sylvester's catastrophe had spread. Pamela must know what had occurred.

When she came in, his heart sank. Wretched as she had looked the day before, now she was positively ghastly. She had made no attempt to 'do up' her face, and her skin seemed almost yellow, her eyes had deep black circles round them and her pinched, wan cheeks looked as if they had shrunk together. She seemed utterly exhausted.

Simon came to the point at once.

"Have you heard, Miss Courtley, what has happened to Mr. Sylvester?"

She nodded, without speaking, not even raising her eyes. Simon steeled himself to go on. He knew he was a tormentor, but he could not help himself.

"Then you know, Miss Courtley, that this means the re-opening of the inquiry into your father's death? Mr. Sylvester and Mr. Barclay and Mr. Wadham were guilty. We've proof of that, and Mr. Sylvester has confessed."

He paused, but the girl still did not speak. She had half turned away, and when he stopped she buried her face in her hands. A violent shudder went through her thin shoulders. Simon's voice relentlessly broke the silence.

"They were guilty. They shot your father. So that means—Mary Game's evidence was false. She lied, in order to give them an alibi."

The girl was crouching down in the corner of the sofa now, her face buried, her hands clasping her ears as if to shut out the ominous words.

Simon went on mercilessly: "You must listen to me, Miss Courtley. This is of the utmost importance. Mary Game died, and died of an overdose of dial. I must ask you some questions and you must answer them."

Slowly the girl raised her face and turned towards him. There was not a vestige of colour in her grey cheeks, or in her trembling lips. But there was a sort of resolution, a mustering of her forces, and now she sat up and spoke with a calmness which surprised Simon.

"What do you want to know? I'll tell you anything I can."

Simon looked at her closely, and then speaking slowly he said:

"There was dial in this house—and only in this house. No other person in this neighbourhood had bought any such drug. But your mother, Mrs. Courtley, had a prescription and it was made up several times. Did you know that?"

She nodded. "Yes. After Daddy's death, Mummy couldn't sleep. She got worn out. Doctor Williams gave her the prescription… and during the trial she had to use it a good deal." Her dull toneless voice stopped.

Simon went on relentlessly: "She had thirty tablets of this drug supplied to her. Where was it kept?"

The girl hesitated and Simon held his breath. This was the crisis. Would she say she did not know? The murder of Mary lay between Anne and this girl. One or other of them had given that drug to Mary with the intention certainly of hushing up the death of Charles, possibly of saving Barclay, the man whom both had loved. If the girl had not done it herself, then she knew that her mother was guilty. It seemed to the man an eternity before she spoke.

"Mummy kept it in the drawer beside her bed. She took a tablet every night. I used to go in and settle her down and give her a lemon drink after she'd taken the dial."

Simon dropped his notebook with a crash. He drew a deep breath, and leaning forward spoke with a feeling the girl could not mistake.

"Miss Courtley, will you swear to that? Will you swear that is the truth?"

Almost triumphantly she looked full at him and her voice was firm and clear. "Yes, I will swear to it. Each night Mummy took a tablet and I gave it to her. And I did that all the time till the pre-scription was finished and she had no more."

Simon got up. There was nothing more to be done. He knew the truth, he was certain Anne had been Mary's murderess, but he knew too that if Pamela stuck to her statement nothing could be proved against Anne. He was sure the girl was lying, he was sure Anne had deliberately got that drug, deliberately hoarded it, getting fresh supplies from the doctor, until she had accumulated a fatal dose. How she had given it, no one would know—perhaps incited the girl to talk to her over tea—perhaps offered her a drink—but he was absolutely certain that through that dial Mary had been murdered.

But if Pamela on oath would declare that day by day the drug had been duly used, and each tablet thus accounted for, then the law was helpless, and Anne was saved.

He knew what he thought, and the girl knew too. He could see that in the anguished anxiety with which she stood waiting. Well, after all, she was standing by her own mother, and standing by a mother who had robbed her of the man she had loved. Simon could feel only compassion and pitying sympathy for any human being caught in such a dreadful trap.

He turned towards the door.

"Then that settles it," he said. "You need not worry, I shan't trouble you again."

He went out, and as he closed the door, got a final glimpse of the girl, still standing there rigid, her hands clenched, but defiant and triumphant. Whatever battle she had fought, she had won.

Epilogue

So the Carron murder mystery was solved. Wadham was tried and convicted for perjury, and received a sentence of twenty years' imprisonment. He never served them, for his health broke down completely under the shock of the second trial and he died in prison within a few months.

Anne Courtley stayed abroad. There was nothing to implicate her in the new evidence, and Simon had been obliged to abandon all effort to connect her with the murder of Mary Game, positive though he was that she had been guilty. However much she might be suspected, nothing could ever be proved. It was barely possible that Sylvester and Barclay had acted without her connivance. Barely possible, too, that gossip had maligned her, and that she had never loved either of the cousins. Her mother stuck by her through thick and thin and asserted that she was a deeply wronged and deeply injured woman. She was rich, for Charles had left her very well provided for by a will made when he first married and never revoked. A year or two later she married a highly respected Swiss, and spent the rest of her life in calm domesticity on the banks of Lake Lucerne.

Pamela did not join her mother. She was of age, and went her own way. She first went to America, then settled in London—and there Simon sought her out. Apparently, she has got over any dislike which his connection with the terrible past might have caused, and he on his side continues to find her interesting and attractive.

After the two trials the Courtley family had become so notorious that people pityingly remarked they 'wondered those girls did not change their name.'

It looks as if Pamela soon would.